D0829550

AVALON

Also by Gina Miani

THE HAMMER OF GOD SERIES:
The Plague Warrior
Battle Swan
The Hammer

AVALON

A Novel

by Gina Miani

Copyright © 2012
Gina Miani Detwiler
All Rights Reserved
ISBN 978-1479376803
Cover design by Gina Miani

For information contact the author
mail@ginamiani.com
www.ginamiani.com
www.facebook.com/avalonanovel

*Some of the places mentioned in this story
are real, though they are used fictionally.
Any resemblance to actual persons is
coincidental.*

For Steve,
who first brought me to Avalon

"Grandpa, tell me about Avalon."

"Haven't I told that story a hundred times?"

"Tell me again."

"If you say so. Well, Avalon was a magic place, full of apple trees. It had two hills and two springs. One spring flowed milky white from a white-stoned grotto, the other flowed red as blood, so they were called the Red and White springs, because they represented the blood and sweat that poured from the wound of Christ. Avalon was surrounded by a misty sea, so that it seemed to be made of glass, which is how it got its other name, the Isle of Glass."

"And Arthur was born there."

"No. But Merlin took him there when he was a small baby, to protect him. He was raised there by the Dwellers. And years later, when he was dying and his kingdom was lost, he returned there."

"To die?"

"No one knows. Some believe he is still there. And that, one day, he will return."

ONE

April 2003

As soon as we crossed the first bridge into Avalon, my grandfather would tell us to roll down the windows and "smell the shore." We always did, my brother and I, though after the initial blast of wind we were never sure what we smelled, other than the looming miasma of the bay at low tide.

I do this now, for the first time in twenty-five years, open the window and take my first whiff of Avalon. It's only April, yet the sharp scent of decay already rises, comforting and yet vaguely disquieting, stirring the long-stilled jar of memory.

I glance over and see my daughter Caroline's nose wrinkle, her brows furrow.

"What are you doing?" she asks in that perpetually annoyed teenager voice she has adopted. She has not taken the earphones out of her ears.

"Smelling the shore," I say cheerfully. "It's something we always used to do when coming over the bridge."

"Smells like something died."

"It's the wetlands, this side of the bay. It's stronger when the humidity kicks in. You're lucky today—it's only April."

"Yeah, right."

It's been a long trip for both of us—nine hours in the car together, the longest we have spent in each other's company since she was little. She was her daddy's girl, but Daddy was not here anymore, and I was a poor substitute.

I cross the second bridge and head toward the traffic light on Ocean Avenue. I brace myself—so far, so good. Avalon looks surprisingly the same. It's only been twenty-five years, I think to myself. That's not long in Avalon time.

"So this is it?" Caroline says, rather unimpressed.

"It's a small town," I say. "There's Hoy's." I point out the 5 and 10, a staple of our childhood, but thoroughly uninteresting to Caroline. "And Uncle Bill's Pancake House."

"Looks old."

Yes, it is.

There are changes though, especially in the houses. What used to be rows of small, square, tidy A-Frames and Avalon-style "upside down" houses have become one mountainous McMansion after another, forming a chain like the Himalayas down Dune Drive.

"Houses are nice," Caroline says off-handedly, though I can see she is clearly enchanted. Multi-gabled monsters with numerous decks, porches, balconies and bays line the avenue. Expensive-looking condominiums with trendy shops occupy every corner.

"Ed McMahan used to have a house here," I tell Caroline, although I'm pretty sure she has no idea who Ed McMahan is. "Johnny Carson used to joke about it on the Tonight Show, saying things like, 'I hear they are going to put up a traffic light in Avalon. As soon as they decide what colors to make it.'" I laugh. Caroline rolls her eyes.

"How come the streets end at 6th?" she asks. "What happened to 1 through 5?" I notice she has picked up a map I had tossed on the floor.

"Some say those streets were wiped out in the storm of '62."

"Oh yeah, the storm you were born in, right?"

I am surprised Caroline remembers this, though it was a detail her father was fond of recalling. Mariah, he would say, was named for the wind, because she was born March 3, 1962, the date of the Great Storm that leveled most of the island. Then he would sing in his rich baritone voice,

Away out here they got a name
For rain and wind and fire
The rain is Tess, the fire Joe,
And they call the wind Mariah

"Right," I say. "I'm not certain, but I think there used to be a creek that ran through the island, but the developers filled it in to make more building lots, and the resulting tidal shift eroded the north end of the island where those streets were supposed to be."

I turn onto 6th Street, and suddenly the house is before me, jutting out almost to the sea wall.

"Tell me that's not your house," says Caroline, her voice tinged with horror.

"That's the house. The Pink Poodle."

It is indeed pink, at one time a shade darker than bubble gum, with bright purple accents. And it is a Victorian, with baroque gingerbread trim, steeply slanted roof and broad, pointed turret. Victorians were the norm on Cape May, the most genteel of Jersey shore towns, but they stood out like beached whales in Avalon. The Pink Poodle was one of the few houses that had survived the storm of '62, though there was no telling how many people had prayed that it wouldn't.

My father loved to tell the tale of that storm. My parents lived in Avalon full time with my grandparents. Grandpa had built the house— he was a builder by trade, one of the first to specialize in the upside-down style "Avalon" house that featured a second floor living area and first floor bedrooms. Yet he built a Victorian for himself, like the ones he had grown up with in the suburbs of Philadelphia. My father helped him, learning the trade as he went. In March of 1962 my mother lay in her bedroom in the throes of labor attended by my grandmother while the Great Storm besieged the house. The two men, armed only with hammers and boards and tarps, saved the house while my grandmother delivered the baby. The way my father told it, my arrival went almost unnoticed in the fierce battle of Man against Nor'easter. I would have liked to have seen that battle, to have seen the adult men in my life raise arms against that savage enemy, for I had never seen my father stand up to anyone in all the years I lived with him, least of all my mother.

The house is a mere shadow of its former self. The color has faded to an anemic pink, the paint mostly chipped away. The front steps are warped and broken in spots; the whole first floor porch seems to lean, Pisa-like, resembling one of those fun house attractions at the county fair. Most of the spokes in the gingerbread trim are missing. The hedges are weedy and overgrown.

I stare. It looks so abandoned. I have never seen it without colorful beach towels hanging over the railings or a myriad of bikes and beach toys in the pebble drive. It reminds me of a house you'd see in a scary movie, the one at the end of the street that no one ever goes in or comes out of, the house of Boo Radley.

I am shocked by how small it is too. In my childhood this house towered over all the others, its turret thrusting into the stratosphere with majesty and wonder. Now it seems dwarfed by the new builds around it, the beautiful giants with their clean white trim and sparkling half moon windows. Yet there is sits, unmoved and immovable, as if time itself stopped at its door.

The "For Rent" sign is leaning up against the rickety porch. I had called the realtor, Betsy, to take it off the rental market for the summer. She had been relieved.

"Truthfully, it was getting harder and harder to rent," she told me. "No one wants a house without air-conditioning anymore. Besides, it needs so much work. You really should think about selling."

She didn't say it, but I knew she meant that the house was an eyesore, and oceanfront property was worth a fortune—this house that cost my grandparents about $80,000 to build might fetch over $1,000,000 in the current market. People had scoffed at them at the time—my grandfather's own lawyer had told him not to buy land in Avalon: "It will never amount to anything." It was a land of swamps and mosquitoes, of fat, green-headed flies that plagued anyone who dared to venture to the beach, of treacherous riptides that would wash away your babies in a heartbeat. My grandfather, thankfully, was not interested in real estate. He wanted a home by the sea.

Still, I could not make the commitment to sell the house on the phone. Something tugged at me. I had to see it again, at least one more time.

"Maybe you can find me a contractor," I asked the increasingly annoyed Betsy. "So I can get an estimate for what repairs need to be done. Does the Avalon Building Company still do work around there?"

"Wasn't that your dad's company?"

"Yes, but he sold it a while ago, I don't even know who owns it now."

"I'll check," Betsy replied without much enthusiasm, "and let you know."

On an impulse I had asked Caroline to come with me. It was her spring break.

"Didn't you want to go to the beach for spring break anyway?"

"*To New Jersey?*" she retorted.

But for some reason she agreed. Perhaps she could not imagine staying in the Raleigh house by herself, without her father there.

Now she glares at me.

"You don't expect me to sleep in that haunted thing, do you?"

"It was beautiful in its day," I lie.

We lived there only four years after I was born. Then my brother came along and my parents moved back to Philadelphia. My father had taken over the Avalon Building Company, ABC INC, from my grandfather but felt that the "Seven Mile Island" was too small a market and wanted to expand the business to the city. My brother and I were sent to Avalon every summer to live with my grandparents; my parents came down some weekends, though those weekends became fewer and fewer as the summers passed. Business did not improve very much for the Avalon Building Company. Despite the larger market in Philadelphia, the profitable jobs always escaped my father, whose slow pace and laid back style did not sit well with the needs of the newly moneyed suburbanites. He wasn't good with money, as my mother learned when she started working for him. She took over the financial end, doing the billing and the bookkeeping. She took on the estimating as well, because my father usually underestimated jobs to attract more notable clients. My mother was a realist, a worrier, and an excellent businesswoman, and she saved my father from certain ruin.

My parents had hoped that my brother would take over the business, but he was lured away by the burgeoning world of computers, so in 1990 my father sold his business for a song and moved to Florida, where my mother had always wanted to live. But he refused to sell the Pink Poodle, despite my mother's objections; lost in the sand traps and alligator swamps of Florida, he still clung to his roots at the Jersey Shore.

I get out of the car finally, fumbling in my bag for the house key. Caroline has gone ahead of me, bounding up the stairs to the porch and staring out.

"Nice view anyway," she pronounces.

"Yes, it is." I join her on the front porch, which looks out over the inlet toward Atlantic City. Here there is no beach at all, the ocean held back only by the disordered pile of rocks that form the seawall along the north shore of the island.

"So where's the beach?" she asks.

I point to the East, to where the beach begins, just past the rock jetty that extends out several hundred feet into the ocean, built to prevent further erosion.

"So far," she says, annoyed. "I thought you said it was a beach front house."

"No, I believe I said it was an oceanfront house."

"Same thing!"

"Not necessarily." I smile, and she scowls.

"The beach here eroded a while ago," I say. "You have to take that path over the rock jetty to get to it. But we're close enough, don't you think?"

"Not as close as we were in Nags Head," she retorts, folding her arms. I cringe.

"I grew up here," I tell her, absurdly thinking this would soften her heart. "This was a magical place…I have so many wonderful memories…"

"Well I have wonderful memories of Nags Head," she says. "That's where *I* grew up."

She turns away from me. I study her—her tall, coltish body with Jack's beautiful lines, his dark, silky hair. I'm fairly tall and dark-haired as well, but there is little of me in Caroline. And she's right. As I was named for a storm, so she was named for the place she was conceived, North Carolina. That is her world, and I have yanked her from it and dragged her to an alien shore, a place where she has no connections at all.

"Well, it's only for a few days," I say. "I think you'll survive."

A wind comes up, dashing off the rocks of the seawall and dousing us with ocean spray. The sea is so close here. At high tide you feel as though you could step off this porch and walk right into it.

"Look at *that* house!"

Caroline is ogling the house next door—a gorgeous gabled spectacle in butter yellow with balconies and chimneys sprouting everywhere. There used to be a tiny cape cod on that lot. Even then my father had complained that it was getting too crowded on the oceanfront. "Damn developers," he would say. "They ruined the place." That might have been another reason why he finally left Avalon. My father had been at the mercy of developers, and somehow their fortunes had never spilled over into his.

I slide the key into the lock, stiff and rusty with salt spray, struggle a moment before finally turning it and opening the door. The smell of age and dust greets me. Though the house has been rented out every summer it still has that unlived-in smell, the odor of the unloved. The heavy beige curtains are drawn, making the large, ponderous front room feel like a musty basement. Caroline steps in behind me.

"What's that smell?"

"I think the house may have taken on water over the winter. I'll turn on the fans." I go to the thermostat on the wall and crack on the fan. This is probably the last house in Avalon without air conditioning. Betsy had begged me to have it installed.

"Global warming!" she had exclaimed. "It's SO hot down here in the summer! The renters want air conditioning!"

"Why don't they just open a window?" I would say. How could you possibly sit inside a house that faced the ocean with the windows closed? It was beyond me.

I walk through the main room, turning on lights, though only half of them actually come on. The room slowly brightens, revealing a worn, yet still serviceable Herculon sofa, the mismatched tweedy easy chairs, the various and sundry tables cast off from my relatives' winter homes, threadbare cotton throw rugs and even a shag rug in front of the fireplace.

Beyond the main room, in a wash of sunlight, is the smaller "den" in the cupola, my grandfather's domain. I could see him sitting in the faded green wingback chair, reading the newspaper and smoking his pipe, back before my grandmother found out that smoke was not good for children or drapes and cast him out onto the porch. It was there he played solitaire or challenged me to a game of gin rummy and much later watched the news on a small TV.

"Gloomy," Caroline says in summing up. But I am seeing people there, my grandmother in her rocking chair by the window, straining to do her needlepoint, the battalions of children bouncing bronze-limbed off the huge sofa into piles of floor pillows, mothers shrieking at them to take off their wet bathing suits and stop getting sand everywhere, grown-ups sitting about at cocktail hour with their wine glasses and lo balls, gathering around the perennial puzzle which we never seemed to finish, talking about the heat, or the rain, or the amount of seaweed in the ocean, or the new restaurant that just opened. I would sit on the shag rug with a deck of cards, listening to this conversation, as predictable and soothing as the ocean itself, and wish that we could always be this way: a big, soft, drowsy family sitting around a big, worn, broken-in room, talking in lazy circles, while out on the sun porch children squealed and my brother's dog Sandy barked happily.

The whole scene is there before me, I stand transfixed until my daughter nudges me.

"Earth to Mom."

"What?"

"Where'd you go?"

"I was just...remembering."

"Oh, here we go." She sighs. "Where's the kitchen?"

I follow her to the back of the house which opens to a large, eat-in kitchen with turn-of-the-seventies appliances in vintage gold, a horrendous orange and yellow floral wallpaper, a metal framed dinette set with vinyl backed chairs in several different shades of ugly. The checked linoleum-tiled floor is chipped and warped, and several tiles are completely missing.

"Gross," says Caroline.

I check to see that the refrigerator, at least, is working, then I go up the narrow back stairs from the kitchen that lead to the bedrooms. I open the door to the master bedroom, feeling as I do a strong presence in the room, the gravitational pull of memory. The room is filled with light, thanks to the bank of windows in the cupola. The bed is a queen-sized wrought-iron antique of delicate swirls and elaborate castings, the bed of a royal princess. The white paint is chipping. The bedspread has been replaced with a beachy, pastel comforter, so out of place in that frilly, Victorian room. The heavy, hard rock maple furniture is the same as I remembered, yet smaller somehow.

I walk across the white shag carpeting to the cupola, the most magical place in the house. The rattan chaise lounge is still there, splintered but sound, the floral chintz cushions faded from the sun so it is impossible to tell their color. The view is spectacular, the ocean curving around us, still unobstructed by the encroachment of the mammoth houses on either side.

"I used to play here a lot," I tell Caroline. "My friends and I would act out fairy tales and King Arthur."

"King Arthur?"

"My grandfather's favorite. I'm sorry you never knew him." Under the windows, running the circumference of the cupola is a narrow window seat built on top of low shelves. But the shelves are mostly empty. I frown at this, then test out the chaise gingerly, waiting to see if I will fall through. I don't.

"I played here a lot," I say.

"Yes, I get it," Caroline says. She has already crossed the hall to the other bedroom, my parents' room and later the guest room. It's dark, cavernous compared to the airy brightness of the master bedroom, with a double bed that takes up most of the space. Next to it is another, smaller bedroom, the domain of my brother, Mark. It still has the blue-painted wood-framed bunk beds, which Mark had covered with stickers of his favorite teams, the Eagles and the Phillies. Someone has tried, unsuccessfully, to scrape them off. Between the two rooms is a tiny bathroom with a narrow shower stall covered only by a wrap-around curtain, so that the water always spilled out, warping the linoleum floor.

"I hope you're going to replace this," Caroline says, wrinkling her nose.

"It definitely needs replacing," I say with a sigh.

At the end of the hall is a narrow staircase to the third floor, nothing more than an attic space under the tower roof. That was my room. Being the first grandchild I had claimed it for my own. It was locked to keep out renters, but I can see the sign is still tacked on the door: "Mariah's Tower. Keep Out. Especially if you are a boy or a grown-up."

"What's up there?" Caroline breaks into my reverie.

"My old room."

"I want to see it."

"No…not now." I turn away from her without further explanation, returning to my grandparent's room to gaze out at the beach. I remember the night Rachel and I lay there on our backs, watching the meteor shower and wishing on every falling star. Mine had been the first, and mine had come true. Rachel, I think, did not get her wish. Though I never did find out what it was.

"We need to unpack," I say quickly, heading down the stairs.

"What about lunch?" she asks, following me.

"I have a cooler in the car."

We unload the Range Rover then sit at the linoleum table and eat the sandwiches I brought. Caroline starts opening cabinets to see if there is anything interesting. She reports her findings: a dozen jigsaw puzzles, Monopoly, Scrabble, Backgammon, several checkers sets, many incomplete decks of cards, brochures of Wildwood and Cape May, tons of old paperbacks. "Who is Jacqueline Suzanne?" she asks, and I laugh. She opens a set of lower doors. "What is that?"

I look and smile. "It's an 8-Track player," I say. "For playing music."

"Sketchy," Caroline says, one of those weird exclamations teenagers make that I don't understand. She pokes around in the kitchen.

"You have two pots and three lids, which don't fit any of the pots," she announces. "What is this?" She holds up a tall aluminum pot.

"A percolator," I say.

"What's that?"

"Makes coffee."

"Seriously?"

She puts it down and opens the oven.

"Gross!" she says. "You're going to need a new oven."

I'm sure that is not the only thing. Whenever I would get a call from Betsy about something that needed to be fixed, Jack would glare at me and ask for the thousandth time "when was I going to sell the place?"

"It's my father's house," I would say.

"But he gave it to you."

"Just to look after, not to own."

"You know he would let you sell it if you wanted to."

"I know. I'll talk to him about it."

I never did talk to him. Jack had abandoned Avalon long before, had fallen in love with the Outer Banks and thought it a much sounder investment. It was where all his doctor friends owned homes. The golf courses were numerous, the summers were longer, everything was better there. My brother and most of my cousins had also decided to summer at the Outer Banks. Everyone had abandoned Avalon. The Jersey Shore had taken on a taint of shabbiness, of old-fashioned out-of-dateness that seemed too much connected to our childhoods, like those cracked old photos of long-dead people you see in postcards.

I, too, had abandoned Avalon. I wondered if the house resented my being there, after I had turned my back on it for so long. How I had thought so often that one good hurricane would take it away and I wouldn't have to make the decision for myself.

There is a knock at the door.

"Probably Betsy," I say to Caroline, sighing. "Here we go." I get up a little wearily and answer the door.

"Yes?" I say, and then I freeze, blinking.

It is not Betsy.

"Mariah?"

I am staring at a face that seems blasted from some unnamed memory, a face I thought I would never see again. Tanned, weathered, lean, beautiful still, though a beauty sorely tested by time. The blond hair is silvery, as is the beard that wasn't there before, but the eyes are still as blue as the sky.

"Trey?" I say softly.

"Hi Mariah," he says with an awkward smile. "It's been…awhile. Didn't Betsy tell you I was coming?"

"Betsy?" For a moment I am confused.

"She said you wanted a contractor."

"Oh…oh." I swallow. "But…you're a contractor? Here? In Avalon?"

"Yes. Long story. Can I come in?"

"Oh, yes." I am fumbling, opening the door wider. I put a hand to my hair, wondering what I look like.

"I'm sorry…you just surprised me. I thought you were…"

"Dead?" he asks.

"Well…it's been so long."

"I know." He moves into the house, taking it in. He's dressed in a torn T-shirt and jeans, work clothes. "Sorry to barge in. I guess you just got here."

I close the door and see Caroline standing in the doorway to the kitchen, staring suspiciously.

"Caroline, this is an old friend, Trey Bennett. My daughter, Caroline."

"Nice to meet you," Trey says. He looks at her, and I see something like surprise in his face. There is an awkward silence, which I try to fill.

"Trey and I were friends when we were kids. He was your dad's friend, too."

"Really? You knew my dad? Were you a lifeguard?" she asks, suddenly very interested.

"Yeah," Trey says. "Did Jack come with you?"

I let a moment pass. "No," I say. Then: "Jack died last year."

He stares at me, shocked. "God...I'm sorry. I had no idea..."

"How could you have?" I am coming back to myself, shutting off that teenage girl who is threatening to take over. "Come in, sit down. Do you want a coke?"

I walk to the kitchen and draw out a coke from the cooler. "It's not very cold, I'm afraid," I say, returning to the living room and handing it to him. We sit on opposite ends of the sofa.

"I'm going for a walk," Caroline says and goes out the front door.

Trey watches her go. "Pretty girl," he says. "Looks like you."

"She looks more like Jack, actually." I pull a pillow onto my lap and fiddle with it.

"I can't believe it," he says. "Jack. What happened?"

"Brain hemorrhage," I say matter-of-factly. I know instantly that I am going to talk too much, say too many unnecessary things. "He had an AVM, Arterio-Venus Malformation. It's like having a bomb waiting to go off in your head, a jumble of veins and arteries all knotted up. He had it all his life and never knew it. He went out to play golf, which he did every Saturday when he wasn't on call. He mentioned to me he had a headache, which at the time I thought was strange. He didn't get headaches, or at least he never told me about them if he did. But…it was only a headache, after all. A strange way for a cardio-thoracic surgeon to die."

Trey shakes his head. "I'm so sorry. I can't believe it. Jack."

"It's still hard for me to believe. They said he didn't suffer much, other than the headache. They kept him on life support for 5 days. Then he died."

"I wish I had known. I would have… come to the service."

"I tried to find you," I say. "The last address I could find was your parent's house in Vineland. It was like you disappeared off the face of the earth. Where did you go?"

"Afghanistan," he says simply.

I think for a minute he is joking.

"Afghanistan? Military?"

"At first." He doesn't elaborate. I get the impression he doesn't want to talk about that.

"So what are you doing here?" I ask.

"You really don't know?"

"Know what?"

"I bought the Avalon Building Company."

I can do nothing but stare at him stupidly. "You bought my father's business?"

"Yeah. It's been for sale for years. There wasn't much of a business left, so I got a good deal on it."

"Oh. My father didn't tell me."

16

"He may not know."

"When did this happen?"

"Couple months ago. When I got here I saw the house was still being rented, so I thought maybe you still owned it. Or someone in your family. I did a title search and found out your dad was listed as the owner. I was going to call him myself, but then I got the call from Betsy. Crazy coincidence, huh?"

"Yes," I say. "Crazy."

"You look good, Mariah. Your hair is different. It's straighter…"

"The invention of the flatiron was a turning point in my life," I say with a laugh. "And you…with a beard."

"Yeah. From my…past life. Sort of got used to it."

"Oh. Looks good on you."

We stare at each other. And then, for some reason that passes understanding, I start to cry.

Trey is quiet. He doesn't move to comfort me.

"I'm sorry," I say. "Some days it doesn't seem real. And some days it is too real. Coming here…has brought back a lot of memories."

"I can imagine. Betsy says you're thinking of selling."

I laugh a little. "That's what she hopes."

"I'm sure."

"She says it's pointless to try to fix it, that the new owners will just tear it down anyway. Somehow, Trey, I can't imagine that. As much as we could use the money…" I stop myself. "I mean, as much as we don't really use the house anymore…"

"Truthfully, Mare, I would hate to see this house go. It's old Avalon. There are hardly any of these left. The houses they're building now…well, anyway, I think you should consider saving the house. It's got a legacy. It needs to be preserved."

I sigh. "Well, I guess it wouldn't hurt to make a list and see what it would cost. Can you do that? It's still my father's house, of course. I'll have to talk to him. Maybe if the repairs aren't too awful…"

He grins at me. "Let's see what has to be done."

For the next hour he takes me on a tour of the Pink Poodle, helping me to make the list of all the repairs needed to get the house up to code. When Caroline returns she follows us around furtively. I know she is staring at Trey, trying to figure out what sort of "friendship" we may have had back then. I would be hard-pressed to explain it.

When I finally see the completed list, I stare at it in despair.

"That made me hungry," he says cheerfully. "How about some ice cream?"

"No…"

"Sure!" Caroline says. I glance at her, surprised.

"Avalon Freeze is open this week only, for spring break," he says. "I'll drive."

"But…it's sixty degrees out," I protest weakly.

"I've got an extra sweatshirt in the truck."

We ride to the ice cream stand in Trey's ancient pickup, tools scraping back and forth in the bed, all three of us squeezed in the front seat.

Avalon Freeze is indeed open, though there are few customers. I expect Caroline to order a low-fat frozen yogurt but instead she gets a large twist, same as Trey. The wind has picked up so we jump back into the truck to eat the ice cream. Caroline is suddenly very talkative, peppering Trey with questions about his lifeguard days with her father. He answers easily, telling the right stories, making her laugh. Every once in a while he brings me into a story, and I quickly deny everything.

After that we drive to the boardwalk at 21st. I stare at the 21st Street Pavilion, lost in memory. Trey shows Caroline the initials carved into one of the posts—MM + TB.

"You and mom?" she says in amazement.

"Before your father stole her away," Trey says laughing. Caroline looks at me.

"I did that when I was like, 11. I didn't know you knew about it," I say, embarrassed.

Trey gives me a secret smile. "This is the beginning of the boardwalk," he says to Caroline. "It ends at 31st Street with the fishing pier—used to be a movie house and dance hall there called the Avalon Pier."

"What about rides?" she asks.

"No rides here," Trey says. "There were plans for rides like Ocean City has, but the town council decided against it."

"They didn't want kids to have any fun," Caroline assumes.

"We had fun," Trey says, looking at me.

In truth, as a child I had sometimes felt cheated by this—we had nothing but the movies at Pier and a run-down arcade to entertain us, while kids at Ocean City and Wildwood were screaming on roller coasters. But now I am so grateful to those early town planners for their wisdom in keeping Avalon a quiet place, tucked away from the world.

We climb into the truck and head back to the house. The sun is beginning to set. I have to remind myself that it's only April. Caroline goes in, claiming she is freezing. Trey and I linger on the porch.

"I still can't believe you're really here," I say.

"Yeah—strange how life goes."

"What was it like…Afghanistan?"

"It was terrible. And beautiful." He pauses. I wait. "I never saw a place with so many problems, unsolvable problems. But the people were amazing to me, so full of faith, so strong, so independent, so fierce. I fell in love with them."

"With them? Or with one?"

He looks sideways at me. "There was one." His face changes, hardens.

I look at him. "What happened?"

"She was killed by a bomb in Kabul."

He says it as if it were something he had read out of a newspaper. He doesn't say more, but I play that scene in my mind like a war movie: the bomb, the girl falling in a spray of blood, Trey screaming, catching her in his arms, the blood staining his shirt as he tells her he loves her…

"I'm sorry," I say, because there is nothing else to say.

How different Trey's life has been from Jack's, I think. That is not a surprise. They were summer friends, it was only Avalon that brought them together. I had always known where Jack would go, what he would do. But Trey had been a mystery. I had searched for him so many times over the years, I had finally given up. Now he is back again, and I can't help but wonder why.

"You've changed, Mariah," he says suddenly.

"I'm older," I say with a laugh.

"No," he says seriously. "It's weird, seeing you as a mother of a teenager, as a…I don't know…"

"As one of those rich suburbanites you used to complain about," I finish for him. "Tight-assed, controlling, as if we ran the universe. Like Jack's mother."

"Yeah, maybe, but the one thing I've learned is that you *do* run the universe." He laughs. "I hope you'll consider saving it. The Pink Poodle, I mean."

"I don't know. I would be crazy to."

"This house suits you."

"Yeah! Old and falling apart, I get it."

"No—it's unique, it has character."

"It has dry rot."

"It has a soul."

I sigh, turning to face the seawall. "So…you really think you can fix it?"

"Sure Mare," he says, using the nickname he had given me long ago— *Mare*, for the sea.

TWO

The next morning Caroline comes into the kitchen looking bedraggled, as if she hardly slept.

"How old is that bed?" she asks. "It has like no padding left. I could feel every spring."

"I know," I say. "We'll get new mattresses, first thing."

"Great," she grouches. "Did you make coffee?"

"On the stove. I got up early and went to the market. Want a crumb bun?"

We feast on crumb buns from Kohler's, which Caroline admits are amazing, then she announces she is going for a run on the beach. I look out the window—the sky is gray, overcast, hinting rain. I cannot even see the ocean for the mist. Loud noises emanate from the beach—bucket loaders bringing in sand, getting ready for the season.

When Caroline is gone I start a slow examination of the house, all my favorite nooks and crannies, all the secret places I used to play in. Yet I still avoid my room in the tower.

From my grandparents room there is a half doorway into a closet space where Grandma stored her Christmas decorations. I remember hiding in there, dressing myself in tinsel and lights as if I were going to a ball. The memory makes me smile.

I examine the bookshelves in the "library" as my grandmother called the small sun porch off the kitchen. There is hardly any view anymore; the new-build next door makes it feel as though the house were butting up to the Berlin Wall. But the books are still there: the entire Tom Swift series, Robert Louis Stevenson, *A Wrinkle in Time*, *Don Quixote*. My grandfather had owned perhaps every version of the King Arthur tales, from Malory to Mark Twain. I had read them all. I remember sitting on the porch late at night while my grandfather smoked his pipe and told me the stories over and over. After he died I had gathered them up and put them in the cupola of the master bedroom, but somehow they had journeyed back to the sun porch. Who moved them, I wonder? I finger the worn covers now, doubting there could be many renters interested in the stories of ancient Avalon.

My reverie is interrupted by a cooing from the doorway. "Yoo-hoo, anybody home?" Betsy. I forgot she still has a key.

"I'm in here," I shout, putting the books back on the shelf. Before I can go to the door to greet her she is stepping down into the sunroom, all two hundred pounds of her with frothy red hair, wearing bug-eyed sunglasses despite the gray weather outside. She has a large portfolio draped over her shoulder and a Blackberry in her hand with one of those irritating bluetooth devices stuck in her ear.

"Mariah!" she shrills, hugging me, as if we were best friends. "So what do you think? A disaster, right?"

"Trey thinks it's salvageable," I say. On the phone Betsy had always been cloying; in person she is overbearing in the extreme.

"Trey? You mean the contractor?"

"Yes, he's an old friend."

"Really? What a coincidence. He was new in town, to tell you the truth I was surprised anyone answered the phone. Anyway, I'm sure the repairs are astronomical."

"He is going to give me an estimate, then we'll see."

"Oh…so you haven't decided then? About selling?"

"No."

"Oh well. I just thought…since you don't even come to Avalon anymore…"

"I'm coming this summer," I say, surprised at my own words.

Her penciled eyebrows rise. "Are you?"

"This place was special to my husband and me," I say. It is half true. "I think it will be good for me to spend some time here. And my daughter loves the house…" an outright lie and I think she knows it…"She's never spent a summer here, and so I think we need to do that, one time at least. Then, I'll make a decision."

Betsy is clearly not happy. "Well, sure, I understand," she says, forcing a smile. "Just remember, this house could fetch a million or more…oceanfront property is at a premium right now, but who knows how long the market can sustain it…"

"Yes, I know," I say. "Thanks for your help, really."

She sighs. "Well…it's your call. Perhaps I should give you the name of another contractor, get a second opinion." Someone that will tell me flatly the house is not worth saving.

"No thanks," I say.

She seems to have run out of tactics. "Well, Mariah, if you change your mind over the summer…" she pulls a business card from her folder "give me a call."

"Thanks." I let her show herself out.

As soon as she is gone I call Trey from the phone number he had scrawled for me on the corner of an envelope.

"I've decided to come back for the summer," I say.

"Oh…that's great." I think he sounds pleased.

This is a dumb idea, I know. I need to sell the house. I need to sell all the houses. Jack was a fine cardiac surgeon, but a lousy financial planner. I didn't realize how in debt he was until he was dead, and his accountant provided me with the truth. Jack had virtually no liquid assets. He was mortgaged up to his teeth for the houses. And he had sold his life insurance without telling me, to pay the overdue taxes.

I should sell. My father would split the sale with me, I was sure of it. But I couldn't do it, for some reason. The house is calling to me. I can feel it. The ghosts are still here—my grandfather is still here.

Well, Trey is still here too.

That is a poor reason, and I would pay for it, I knew. But coming to Avalon has made me a girl again, with a head full of dreams and a heart full of romance. I don't want a lifetime. I want only a summer. Something sweet to remember, to get me past my grief. It seems a small thing to ask.

I hear the door creak open again and think it might be Betsy returning for another attack. I step into the living room to see Caroline coming in the door, looking half-frozen.

"It's raining now. I think I got frostbite."

"Take a hot shower," I say.

"Are you kidding? The water is like *brown*. Can we please go to a hotel?"

She is moving heavily upstairs to change. I realize that telling her my plans will not be so easy.

I wait in the kitchen until she returns with her hair in a towel, wearing a sweatshirt and jeans.

"I saw your friend jogging on the beach," she says, sitting at the table in front of a bowl of Campbell's tomato soup I made for her, hoping to soften her up. "He's in good shape for an old guy."

"He's not that old," I say.

"Oh yeah, sorry. What's with you and him anyway? Some weird vibes going on there."

"Don't slurp," I say automatically, sitting opposite her. "We were friends. All of us. We were like a…gang."

"Huh?"

"A summer gang. We would hang out at the pier or the beach all summer. I don't know if kids do that anymore. The theatre and the dance hall are gone."

"Sounds really boring," she says, rolling her eyes. "How can anyone do that for a whole summer?"

"They were the best summers I remember," I say, working up to telling her my news. "Your father and I and Trey and Rachel…."

"Who's Rachel?"

"She was a…friend," I say.

"I never heard you talk about her. Do you keep in touch?"

"Rachel? Uh…no. Listen," I change the subject quickly, "I know you aren't going to like this idea, but I would really like to spend the summer here."

She stops slurping. "You're kidding, right? I thought you were going to sell this dump!"

"I know," I say, "but I can't just now. I know this is hard, but it would mean a lot to me…"

"I was going to get a job this summer," she says, slamming down the spoon.

"You can get a job here," I say. "There are probably a ton of job openings."

"Scooping ice cream," she says derisively.

"You're seventeen. What kind of job do you expect? Trial lawyer?" My tone is too harsh. I try to modulate. "Honestly, Caroline, what kind of job can you get in OB that you can't get here?"

"A job working at Simson's where all my friends will be," she says. Simson's is a favorite teen hangout, a burger joint with the best music on the beach.

"I should have told you this before," I say, "but I'm selling the OB house."

Her eyes flash on me, genuinely shocked. "Are you kidding? Are you trying to ruin my life?" she shrieks.

"I have to," I say. "We can't afford it. We can't even pay the taxes on it. It will sell quickly, probably before the summer. The market there is even hotter than here. I'm selling the Aspen condo too."

"When were you planning to tell me all this, Mom?" she says, her dark eyes, Jack's eyes, bearing down on me, her teenage fury unfurled.

"I'm sorry," I say. "Please try to understand…" She gets up from the table and storms out. I count to five and the door slams, right on cue.

"She'll get over it," Trey says. We are walking on the boardwalk. It's after three, the rain has stopped and the wind has calmed. The air seems warmer. The boardwalk is deserted, so different from the summer, where you spend all your time dodging bikes and rollerbladers. Ahead is what is left of the pier, a pizza place, an ice cream parlor. There is still an arcade though it is different from the old one, and there is a skateboard park where the Avalon Pier used to be. It closed the year after the summer I left Avalon.

"She will, eventually," I say. "In the meantime it will be very quiet around that house, except for the ghosts."

"Ghosts?"

"My grandfather is there."

"How do you know?"

"His books. They were moved."

"By the renters, probably."

"No. Renters don't read Chaucer. When he died I put all his books in the master bedroom cupola. But they are all in the sunroom now. I could understand one or two being moved but not all of them. He's there."

Trey looks at me, aware that I am dead serious. Then he laughs. "You always had a great imagination," he says.

The pizza place, named "Three Brothers Pizza," is open, so we stop in for a slice. As greasy and delicious as I remember.

"I can't believe this place is still here," I say. We are sitting at one of the plastic tables on cracked and filthy plastic chairs. I don't suppose the three brothers spend any time in the off-season cleaning their furniture.

"Have you run into anyone else? From the old days?" I ask. I can't believe I actually said the words "old days."

"Tanya Thompson," he says.

"Trailer-Trash Tanya?" I say incredulously.

"She's married to an orthodontist and has four kids…she turned out pretty normal," he says. "Still in the house on 32nd. She called me a couple weeks ago, to get an estimate on a new deck. Still hot to trot. I wasn't in the door two minutes before she had my shirt half off."

"Well, you always did have that effect on girls."

"Every guy had that effect on Tanya," he says. He pushes his hair back from his face, a gesture I remember. One strand falls back in his eyes. "So when will you come back?"

I sense a certain eagerness in his voice, wonder if I am imagining it. "After school is out in June. Can you start on the big stuff now, before we get back? Particularly the water issue. I need to promise Caroline clear water to get her to come back, at the very least."

"I can do that."

"Here's a check," I say, passing a piece of paper to him. "I hope this will get you started."

He glances at it, puts it in his pocket. I don't suppose he is any better a financial manager than Jack was, from the way he handles it.

"Should be fine," he says. "I promise you clean, hot water and windows that open and close on demand. I'll even get rid of the ghost if you like…"

"No," I say quickly. "Leave the ghost." I realize a second too late that he is teasing me. "But get rid of the mice. And the cockroaches."

"As you wish, Princess Mariah."

When we get back to the house I invite him in and show him the books in the sunroom. He looks them over. "Some of these are first editions," he says.

"I know what you're thinking," I say. "I could sell them on eBay…"

"eBay?" He looks puzzled. Then I remember that he's been in Afghanistan for the past twenty years. "Oh, right…Avalon…that was King Arthur's place, right? But it wasn't real, was it?"

"Maybe it was. Some say the Glastonbury monastery was the original site of Avalon. It's a high tor, and was likely surrounded by water in Arthur's time, making it an island. That was around the 5th century. The monks there claimed to have discovered a lead cross that bore the inscription 'Here lies buried the renowned King Arthur in the Isle of Avalon.' They also found bones buried there and a damaged skull—according to the legend, Arthur died from a blow to the head. There was also a smaller skeleton found which might have been Guinevere."

Trey is smiling at me. "I forgot that you were really into this."

"My grandfather's stories," I say, blushing. "I was the only one who would listen." I did more than listen. I lived those stories, and in some ways they are as real to me today as they were back then. I remember playing in my grandparents' cupola, acting out stories of Guinevere and Lancelot, using towels from my grandmother's bathroom so I could pretend I had long blond hair. I don't tell Trey that in my imagination he had always been Lancelot.

I rush to change the subject. "The roof in here leaks pretty badly," I say, pointing to the skylights in the sunroom. "Maybe those should be replaced."

"Your wish is my command."

We leave on Thursday, a day earlier than planned, but the weather has been lousy and Caroline's mood has worsened. Trey is there to see us off with a bag of bagels and water bottles for the road.

"Thank you," I say.

"Anything for you, Mare," he says, bowing like a courtier. Caroline rolls her eyes at us and plops into the passenger seat of the Range Rover. The Range Rover...another thing that will have to go. Caroline loves this car—she had planned on inheriting it once she got her permanent driver's license. More bad news I will have to break. But not on this trip.

"It was nice meeting you Caroline," Trey says, bending down to look in the window. Despite her anger she smiles. She likes him. He is hard not to like. "Have a good trip," he says to me.

"Thanks, Trey. For everything."

"Sure, Mare."

Impulsively I throw my arms around him and hug him. He is surprised at first, but I feel his arms around me, holding me tightly, for longer than I expected.

"Will you be okay?" he asks when we finally part.

"Sure. As long as I survive this trip home."

"Drive safe. See you soon."

I smile. "Yes, soon."

As I drive away I look over and see my daughter staring at me. I know this look, I know what she is thinking. I look away quickly, because I know she is probably right.

THREE

May 2003

"I can't believe you are really doing this," Clare says, flouncing on the couch. She is supposed to be helping me pack, but she has done little of that. Instead, she drinks tea and wanders around the house, fingering items on shelves as if she is thinking of taking possession herself.

She has been my best friend, my only friend, at the Outer Banks. Clare and her husband Sam have been our summer neighbors for years; our children have grown up together. They live in Raleigh in the winter, like we do, but we rarely see them there.

Now it will be ending. The house is sold. The new owners are taking most of the furniture. I am packing up dishes, books, a few knickknacks to take to Avalon. There isn't much that will make the move. I rented a small U-Haul trailer and vowed that anything beyond that was not coming with me.

"You could have rented," she says. There is a crack of thunder overhead, one of those typical spring thunderstorms on the Banks. I am glad of it. Had the beach looked beautiful and serene it would be much harder to leave; as it is, with the rain coming down in sheets and the howling wind, I don't mind so much.

I pause to look around the house, so clean and modern, an architectural statement rather than a home, with its wall of windows facing the ocean, its cedar beams, cathedral ceiling, stainless steel kitchen. So different from the Pink Poodle.

"What are the new owners like?" Clare asks, and I sense the real concern about my leaving.

"I don't know. Husband and wife, both lawyers, two kids. I think they are from Pennsylvania."

"More Yankees. Used to be the South was for southerners."

"Clare, have you forgotten? Jack and I were Yankees too."

"But you two have been here forever —that's different. We can handle a few Yankees in our midst from time to time, but this invasion is worse than the war!" By the "war" she means the War of Northern Aggression, which the South will continue to fight until, perhaps, it wins.

"Can you just put those books on that shelf into a box?" I am thinking it might be a good idea to get her to actually help me. She goes to the bookcase listlessly and thumbs through the paperbacks.

"I still don't understand why you don't just sell *that* house and stay here. Your life is here, Mariah. Your friends are here. Caroline's friends are here. You know, you are compounding her grief by taking her away from her home at this time…"

"It's only for the summer," I say, feeling a little testy. "Anyway, I believe the current psychological thinking is that it's better to get away from the scene of your grief, start fresh. It's easier to cope with your personal tragedy when you create distance, geographically, anyway."

"Good God, when did you start reading those books? I thought you hated all that psychology nonsense."

"I do," I say, hoping she can tell that I am just irritated by her nagging.

"Oh, Mariah, honey, this is all just an insane reaction to what's happened. I'm afraid you are going to regret it. To sell Jack's house..." she stops short.

I know it already. This is Jack's house. Once it is gone, I can never come back here again. Like Cortez I am burning my ships, so I won't be tempted to return.

"You should come visit me," I say without much conviction. I know she will refuse, but I hold my breath on the off chance she might take me up on it.

"The Jersey Shore? Well, thanks...but we have company coming almost every weekend this summer. I'll have to see if there is a time..."

"Sure," I say. "I'm flexible."

She is satisfied that she has declined my offer so gracefully. If there is one thing that southern women pride themselves on, it is grace under fire.

"Sam wants to buy another boat," she says, deliberately changing the subject. "Can you imagine why one man would need so many boats?" She is off, chattering in her slow drawl, so hypnotic to listen to. I am lost in her voice for a while. I look outside the rain-streaked windows and realize how suddenly, irrevocably, my life has changed. As if the last twenty years, the prime of my life, had been swallowed up by one giant whale of a brain hemorrhage. How did it happen? Without Jack I no longer belonged here. I was an exile, but from where? Did I belong anywhere? My heart returns, as it always does, to Avalon, to the place of my birth.

FOUR

June 1978

Summer, finally.

It was my first night back in Avalon. For me, at sixteen, this was the most wonderful night of the year, when the dark, dreary winter was forgotten, and summer felt like it would go on forever.

My best friend Miranda and I had ridden our bikes to the Pier. It was a beautiful evening; the sky was clear, and the air was sweet and warm. I felt like dancing, like running down to the beach and spinning until I fell over. I was so happy to be back.

"There's a new lifeguard," Miranda said, grabbing my arm. "You gotta see him. He's gorgeous!"

"Wait!" I stopped to pull my hair into a ponytail. Like all 16-year-old girls, I hated my hair. It was dark and thick and wavy and impossible to control. I pulled it as tight as I could to make it look smooth. Miranda hauled me over the boardwalk and into the dance hall, on the second floor of the Pier, over the movie theatre.

The band was playing, and kids were dancing. Most of my friends were already there, Tanya, and Emily and Sarah. We screamed and hugged each other in reunion. I saw Trey, already tanned, his mop of blond hair curling around his face, one stray lock falling into his bright blue eyes. Those eyes still startled me, even after all the years of seeing them. He was nineteen, old enough to go to the Rock Room at the Princeton where they served alcohol. But he had chosen to come to the Pier instead. I was glad. I walked over to him.

"Hey Trey," I said.

I could never imagine Trey anywhere but on this beach. I wondered what he would look like in the real world, in a schoolroom or on a city street; the vision seemed impossible. Trey was a boy born for the shore. His family lived in Vineland. From an early age he would come into town with his dad and hang out on the beach while his dad worked. I had first met him when I was 10 and he 13. His older sister Rita worked at Sullivan's Department Store, and I would see him when I went there in the afternoons. He was usually alone, like I was, the children of working parents who hung around the boardwalk most of the summer. We never talked to each other, though I was pretty friendly with Rita, who was nice to me and usually gave me a piece of rock candy or a Coke when the "old man" wasn't looking.

One day I saw him playing Skeeball, and as fate would have it, he ran out of money. I happened to have a few extra quarters in my pocket, so I parked next to him and started playing as well. Then I pretended to notice that he was out of money so I offered him a quarter. I thought he might turn me down, not daring to take money from a girl, but he did take it and he said "thanks" in a really friendly way and started playing again. Pretty soon it was obvious that we were watching each other's scores, and the game turned subtly into a competition. So I ended up beating him five games to three. I told him he had to buy me a coke, but since he'd already established that he was out of money, I told him he could give it to me the next day. Which, amazingly, he did.

We played almost every afternoon that whole summer, and he beat me as often as I beat him, and while we played we talked about our families, discovered that our dads knew each other, both being in the building trade, and that Trey's dad was very fond of my grandfather who had built the Pink Poodle. He came over for dinner once, and Grandpa taught him to play chess. Sometimes he came over on rainy days and we played Monopoly until all hours. And even though I was only 10, I knew I was in love.

We saw a lot of each other that summer and the next, playing Skeeball or bodysurfing in the ocean or riding bikes up and down the boardwalk, scaring the old ladies. But as Trey became a teenager he started hanging out with other boys, the lifeguards and the rich summer kids. He grew tall in those years, his scrawny frame filling out from working in his father's ready-mix business and swimming, which he did competitively. We were still friends, but it wasn't the same.

"Hey Mare," he said, grinning down at me. "Played much Skeeball lately?" It was the way he always greeted me, as if assuring me that he would never forget his first real friend in Avalon.

"Every day," I lied. "What about you?"

"Same. How was your winter?"

"Awful," I said, meaning it. "Are you on 30th Street again this year?"

"Yeah," he said, shrugging. "Same as always."

Only the best guards were assigned that beach.

"You promised me surfing lessons this year, remember?"

Before he could answer Miranda grabbed my arm. "There!" she pointed excitedly. "That's him. The new guy. Look!"

I turned, and that's when I first laid eyes on Jack Pendergrast.

I just stared for a long time.

"Isn't he adorable?" Miranda cooed beside me.

Adorable? Pretty, definitely, with fine-boned features, aristocratic. Delicate even. His hair was dark, like mine, but cut much shorter than the current style, so he had an air of sophistication about him, as if he were more mature and seasoned than the rest of us. His body was long, clean-lined, regal; his eyes were dark, full of mischief. But his smile was everything; when he smiled he made everyone around him feel as though they were in on a wonderful secret. I stood still, transfixed, feeling a pull of something strange and unfamiliar, a wanting I had ever known before.

Miranda rattled on. "His father is a famous plastic surgeon or something. From North Jersey! They bought the Grain Elevator on Dune."

"You're kidding," I said.

The "Grain Elevator" was a house, a sort of avant-garde house with vertical gray siding and long, narrow casement windows. It had a tall square-sided protrusion, probably a funky staircase that had given birth to its name. It had been for sale for years. Most people thought it was the ugliest house in Avalon.

"I hear he's totally redoing it," Miranda said, "and adding a pool!" No one had pools in Avalon.

"How do you know all this?" I asked.

"Trey told me!"

I turned to Trey, who shrugged. "My father is doing the concrete." Trey's father worked on most of the renovations in Avalon; consequently Trey always knew the dirt on every new resident. "He made the beach patrol too. First time. Even Morey was impressed."

"Really?"

Then I noticed standing beside him a girl of pale, luminescent beauty, small and slim and blond, with light brown eyes, almost golden in the firelight. She had an air of something otherworldly, transcendent, as if she were some strange apparition, not flesh and blood. She looked cool and still while everyone else was hot and sweaty and full of motion. I had an impulse to touch her, to see if she would disintegrate, like a reflection in a pool.

"Who's that?" I asked Miranda.

"Girlfriend," Miranda said with heavy disappointment. "Isn't she a pill?"

"Definitely," I said. The band started playing my favorite song, Yvonne Elliman's "If I Can't Have You."

"Let's dance!" Miranda pulled me onto the dance floor. We started to dance, mouthing the words to each other and dancing like we always did, kind of crazy and silly. I pulled the band from my hair and let it fly free, so that I looked more like Yvonne, to whom I was often compared. Other girls joined in, and we all danced. When the song was over we fell onto the floor, laughing. I rolled over to get up and ran into something solid. A sandaled foot.

I looked up and saw Jack Pendergrast standing over me, looking down. He was smiling his amazing, unbearable smile. I felt my stomach seize, wondered at that moment how horrible my hair must be, how ridiculous I looked rolling around on his feet like that.

"Nice dancing," he said. He put out his hand to help me up. I grabbed it, jumping up and stepping away, pushing hair out of my face.

"Oh, well, I'm sorry…sometimes I get carried away." I could feel the blush slither from my face all the way to my toes. "You must be new here," I said, very lamely.

"I'm Jack," he said genially.

"I'm Mariah, and this my friend Miranda."

"Hey," said Miranda, sounding suddenly demure, which was not like her.

"Nice to meet you. This is Rachel." He turned to the girl with the large eyes. She smiled at me so beautifully I started not to hate her as much.

"Hi," she said in a sweet, soft voice, so friendly I could not help but smile back.

"This is your first time in Avalon?" I asked them both.

"Not mine," Jack said. "I was here last year." That surprised me. How did we all miss him? "Just for a week—my folks were checking it out. We usually go to Long Beach Island, but my mother thought it was getting a little crowded or something, so she went looking for a new beach."

"Most LBI'ers think Avalon is kind of…boring," I said.

"There are fewer New Yorkers," he said with another dazzling smile. "Rachel likes to dance too."

"No, Jack…not here…."

"Go on."

"Yes, come on!" said Miranda, grabbing my arm. The band started a Bee Gees song. Impulsively, I took Rachel's arm and dragged her in as well. To my surprise, she didn't resist. She had a funny, rather angular way of dancing, almost cubist. She was trying hard to have fun. She started laughing, a staged laughter, making a show of enjoying herself, and I found myself laughing with her in the very same way. In the back of my mind a plan began to form: *make friends with this girl, take her under your wing*. This was the way to stay in the dizzying orbit of Jack Pendergrast.

The next morning I went down to the 30th street beach to see Jack on his first day on the patrol. Rachel was there, all alone, sitting under an enormous umbrella with a large red hat on. Her skin was so pale I thought I could see the veins underneath. I felt a wave of courage, walked up to her and sat down, just outside of her umbrella.

"Hi Rachel," I said brightly. "Remember me?"

"Mariah," she said. She looked genuinely pleased to see me. "That was fun, last night. You have a pretty name."

"Oh," I said laughing. Then I told her the story of my name. She seemed fascinated.

"You've been here all this time. You must like it here." I got the sense that she wasn't too sure about it herself.

"We only come summers now," I said. "I wish we lived here year 'round."

"You do?" She was surprised. "I couldn't imagine it."

"You aren't a beach person, are you?" I said, taking in the umbrella and the hat.

"It's pretty, the ocean. From far away. But I didn't realize it was so…so loud. The waves…are so high here. Not like Nantucket."

"Is that where you usually go?"

"My family does, sometimes. But…I don't do so well in the sun." There it was, that weirdness again. Her eyes seemed far away.

"Oh well, you have fair skin," I said.

"Yes. And the sun…triggers my migraines."

"You get migraines?"

"Yes, they are very bad. I have to be careful."

I imagined that this girl was susceptible to a thousand dangers of which I never took any notice. I supposed I wouldn't be able to ask her to go for a swim with me.

So instead I said, "Wanna go to Pop's?"

"What's Pop's?"

"Just a hang out. We can play some games in the arcade, grab a soda."

She thought a moment. "Sure," she said. She still had that faraway look, but she followed me down the beach to Pop's.

We hung out the whole afternoon, playing Pokerino and Skeeball and stealing popcorn from the popcorn machine. I noticed she never actually ate the popcorn; she played with it, tossing it around and laughing and joking in that strange, unnatural way, as if she were acting in a play. When I asked if she wanted any lunch she said she wasn't hungry, which annoyed me because I was hungry but I wasn't going to eat if she didn't. Instead, we went to Sullivan's and tried on all the sunglasses in the rack until the shop clerk told us to stop. We moved onto the bathing suit rack, and I picked out a hot pink bikini I told her she should buy.

"This would look great on you," I said. She laughed and bought the suit, though I never saw her wear it.

At 4 we went back out to see Trey and Jack at the lifeguard stand. They still had another hour to work, but we hung around the stand, talking. Bowie, Trey's housemate, was the third lifeguard on the stand. He was older than Trey, with a big blond mustache and long, shaggy hair. It felt odd to be in the company of these cool, hip boys and this pretty girl. I was usually on the outside of such groups, looking in. It was thrilling and nerve-wracking at the same time.

I learned that Jack and Rachel had been dating for about a year. To me, that meant they were practically engaged. They went to the same private prep school, but Jack had graduated and was headed to Columbia for pre-med. He would be a doctor, like his dad, but he was not going into plastics. He wanted to be a heart and lung surgeon. Rachel had come to Avalon with Jack's family for a few weeks.

Rachel's parents were planning to come as well, though Rachel was vague on when that was going to happen.

The four of us went to Pop's for hotdogs when the guard shift was over. Jack took me aside. "Thanks for spending the day with Rachel," he said. "She's been kind of…lost here."

"No problem," I said, my heart beating fast. "I hope she had fun."

"She did. She seems a lot more relaxed than she's been in…awhile."

"Is she all right?"

He looked uncomfortable. "Her parents wanted her to come here, thought it would be good for her," he said. "That it would help."

"Help? With what?"

"Just stuff. She's had a rough year. She didn't want to come. She's not very good in…new situations."

"She seems fine to me."

"I'm really glad she met you, Mariah," he said. "You'll be good for her."

I smiled nervously. "I will?"

"Yeah. Because you're…normal."

My heart sank. "Oh."

"I don't mean that the way it sounded. Rachel just needs to relax. Let go. You know what I mean?"

"Oh, sure,'" I said. I loved the way he was protective of her. He wanted to give her shelter, and with all my heart I wanted to help him do that. I was his co-conspirator. I would be Rachel's guardian angel.

FIVE

I spent every day with Rachel, mostly on the beach. I even got her to go in the water once, though she was freaked out by the jellyfish and didn't last long. I told her they were harmless, but it didn't matter. The ocean was too "dangerous" for her. I didn't push it. In truth, she seemed a little too fragile for the rough ocean surf, the bed of broken shells. And then there were the sharks. We'd never seen anything other than the tiny dogfish sharks in Avalon, but *Jaws* had come out only 3 years before and it was still fresh in everyone's mind.

She liked sailing though, and when Jack or Trey had a day off we would go to Weatherby's wharf and rent a sunfish or a small sailboat. Rachel thrived on those small excursions, lifting her face to the wind and closing her eyes, a rapturous smile on her face

Sometimes we went to Sullivan's for sticky buns in the morning and then rented tandem bikes and biked up and down Dune Drive, from the inlet all the way through Stone Harbor to 110th Street. Somehow Avalon was the only place where a tandem bike seemed like a good idea.

In the evenings we would meet the other kids at the Pier. The Avalon Pier had seen better days — we didn't know it at the time, but 1978 was the last summer they would show movies there. Seeing a movie at the pier was always an adventure—at high tide the waves sounded as though they were coming right up through the floorboards. The movies they showed were mostly old—*Gone With the Wind* or *Casablanca*. The kids didn't pay much attention; they were there to make out. You had to stay away from the matinees, when the older folks went to reminisce.

I loved the Pier. It was so old and shabby, on the verge of falling into the ocean. But it was Avalon. It had been there almost 50 years. Decades of teenagers had fallen in love there, or at least thought they did.

Rachel told me about her family, how her grandfather and her father had both made their fortunes in real estate. Her father was a lawyer in a big time firm upstate and her mom taught English at a local university. This was so far out of my experience I could hardly imagine it. I knew that, had I met Rachel in the real world, she would never have been my friend. But here, in Avalon, I was her equal.

We did not talk much about our lives back home. What we did talk about was the South Jersey Lifeguard Championships, coming up in July. Jack and Trey were competing in rowing doubles. Jack had engineered it, convincing the Beach Patrol Captain he was ready for the challenge, despite the fact that he had never rowed in South Jersey before.

"I've been a crew champion for the last five years at home," he told us. I didn't want to tell him that crewing on a river was a little different from launching a rowboat off the beach into heavy surf. But Jack was the kind of person who seemed as though he could do anything; at least, he convinced all of us that he could.

They practiced every day before their shift began, launching the boat over and over through the breaking waves into the churning water beyond and then rowing to the buoy and back. Often they practiced after their shift as well, getting in a few more runs if the tide was good. Rachel and Miranda and I would sit on the beach and watch, lounging under Rachel's gargantuan umbrella with a cooler of drinks and Trey's old transistor radio so we could listen to the Jersey Giant on AM1340. Other girls started to join us, and it became a kind of impromptu beach party. Secretly, I would have preferred to be in the water with the boys. I was a good swimmer, I had swum in the State Final even, but here in Avalon girls were not allowed to be lifeguards.

"That's wrong," Rachel said when I told her of the rule. "That's discrimination."

"Girls are not as strong," I said, parroting what the patrol captain had told me. "You can't imagine how hard it is to swim against a rip current." I could do it, I thought, and I still bristled at the rule against girls. Even West Point was going to allow girls. That rule would crumble eventually. But not this year.

Usually after they were done, the boys would join us on our blankets to rest and eat our food. Trey would lie flat on his back on the hot sand, the water dripping from his body as his chest heaved slowly. Jack, who never seemed to get tired, would sit beside Rachel for a while then jump up and head back to the water to run or to swim. Rachel would trail after him, holding her wide-brimmed hat on the top of her head to keep it from flying off.

"Do you think he's ready?" I asked Trey as we watched them near the water's edge. Jack was trying to coax Rachel into a game of tag.

Trey shrugged. "He's good," he said. "He can row. He's strong and he's fast. But he's not as good as he thinks he is."

That would always be true of Jack Pendergrast.

The Avalon team held a rally the night before the championships at the pier, organized by Jack, of course. A band called "The Starving Artists" played and Jack grabbed the microphone and sang "We Are the Champions" in a Queen-like falsetto. I was amazed at how he could transform himself from preppy rich kid to rock star in mere moments. He soon had the crowd of lifeguards, girlfriends, parents and assorted supporters singing along with him. He finished with a rousing speech about how this was Avalon's year, how after four long years our time had come. No one really believed it, winning the Champion Cup was so completely out of the realm of possibilities that what we most often hoped for was simply not to finish last. But that night, Jack made as us all believe that we were, indeed, champions. That all we had to do was dream it, and it would come true.

The next morning we drove to Ocean City in Trey's jeep, following the boat trailers. Jack stood up the whole time, his body perched dangerously over the windshield, his arms splayed in the air like he was expecting to go airborne at any moment. Rachel and I sat in the back like homecoming queens, letting our hair tangle in the wind. Rachel wore a white blousy shirt and peasant skirt over her black bathing suit. She had actually gotten some color in her skin, despite her umbrella and hat coverage. I wore a two-piece with shorts. I wished I had chosen a skirt instead. Though I still felt like the Big, Friendly Giant next to Rachel, with my broad, swimmers shoulders, I had found myself, more and more, trying to mimic her: her dress, her mannerisms, her light, airy way of talking. More than anything, I wanted to *be* her.

Trey managed to find a place to park by wedging in between two broken down sand combers near the beach patrol hut. We got there early enough to stake out a patch of sand and lay down our towels.

Jack put up Rachel's umbrella, and Trey carted in the cooler. Miranda and several of the other girls met us there. Miranda had brought a boom box and soon had Queen blaring on the tinny speakers. We set up quite a cheering section for Avalon, though we got drowned out by the crowds that accompanied the other beach patrols. The party went on for almost an hour until the actual competition began; by then we were having so much fun we almost forgot there was a competition at all.

The swimming events were first. Trey won his race easily. Rachel and I cheered like crazy. The relay team got beat by Margate. After that came single rowing, and Avalon didn't win anything.

When at last it was time for the two-man crew, Rachel, who had been cheering loudly with the rest of us, suddenly grew quiet. We watched Jack and Trey ready their boat, shaking out their limbs. I looked at Rachel nervously.

"Are you all right?"

"Sure," she said, "I'm fine." She put her huge sunglasses back on, so I could no longer see her eyes. I felt her arm entwine with mine. We sat together on the beach blanket very still.

The boys lined up their boats along the shoreline. About 200 yards out in the water the flag buoys were placed, evenly spaced. The boys would have to row out to their flag, circle it, and come back in. The waves were unusually strong, made worse by the wind, which seemed to come from both north and east creating a difficult cross current.

An official on a jet ski motored out to a spot behind the flags and waited. The crowd on the beach quieted, waiting for a whistle. Trey was gazing fixedly at the water, nervous, I could tell, by the peculiar bend of the waves. Jack was looking around, joking with the guys from other teams, seemingly unconcerned. I felt a tiny spark of apprehension flare in my stomach.

When the whistle blew the boys flew into motion, pushing the boats out into the waves. Getting past the breaking waves was the hardest work, pushing the boat forward against the oncoming currents. I saw the muscles in Trey's and Jack's shoulders flex and tremble with the effort, but they were pretty fast, and after the first wave Jack jumped into the boat with pure, animal grace, grabbing the oars and starting to row in a single motion. Trey continued to push on foot until he, too, jumped into the boat, not nearly as gracefully as Jack, but then he was in deeper water. The boat immediately caught a heavy wave and lurched upward, almost vertical. Rachel gave a gasp, covering her mouth. Jack leaned back as Trey leaned forward into the wave, and Jack was grinning, we could see his big white smile even from this distance. The boat slapped down again, still upright and pointed toward the flags, a spray of water momentarily obliterating our view. Then they were back, rowing hard, in perfect unison. The boat lurched over another wave but they recovered easily, now clearly ahead of the pack, using the power of the waves to propel them forward.

Rachel suddenly burst to life, jumping to her feet and joining the other girls in a high-pitched chant.

"C'mon Jack! Faster! Faster!" she yelled. I could hardly believe her frenzy. She had even abandoned the umbrella. We watched the boat careen toward the buoy, the first one to get there. The crowd on the beach cheered. Getting around the flag was no easy task, especially with the conflicting current; the boat seemed to take forever to make the turn.

"Go! Go!" we screamed.

By the time Jack managed to get the craft around the flag he was a little off course, and Trey was shouting at him, rotating his own left oar to get back on track. Jack managed to get the boat righted, but he had lost ground in doing so, and the Wildwood team had caught up to them. The wind picked up in gusts, making more whitecaps on the water. The surf tossed the boats around like plastic toys. I could barely breathe with the suspense of it.

Suddenly a wave, one of those almighty double crested waves that seemed to come from both directions at once, hit the side of the boat dead on. It hit the other boats as well, but those caught it in the stern or a bow, some of them were pushed sideways, most were just propelled forward crazily, the rowers losing control for a moment. But Jack's boat, because it had turned almost parallel with the shore, seemed to flip into the air like a dolphin doing tricks, landing on its side in the water with a sickening slap. The boys threw their weight against the upside of the boat, hoping to tip it back, but it was too far gone. As if to seal their fate, another wave came to give it one final shove. It capsized, and they disappeared underneath.

The crowd gasped. Rachel grabbed my arm. When the wave subsided we saw the boat again, bobbing crazily, but we did not see either of the boys. Another wave hit hard, tossing the capsized boat closer to shore. I started running, running to the edge of the water. I saw others running as well, lifeguards, shouting at each other. I screamed at them. "Jack! Trey!"

As if he heard me, Trey appeared, to the starboard side of the boat, away from the beach. He looked around, frantically. There was no sign of Jack. He dove under again. Rachel was suddenly at my side, her fingers digging into my arm.

"What happened? Where is Jack?" Her voice was shrill.

"Don't worry," I said to her, trying for her sake to be calm. "Trey will find him. Don't worry."

Rachel could not speak. I could feel her whole body shaking through her fingers.

We waited, breathless, scanning the surface of the water for a bobbing head. It took forever, an agonizing wait. I wanted to jump in myself but dared not. There were more guards in the water now, diving under the boat. A moment later, there was a cheer from somewhere. Trey emerged, holding Jack above the surf. He was bleeding from the head and appeared unconscious. The other guards rushed into grab him, haul him to the shore. One of them helped Trey as well.

The guards on the beach pushed people away to make room as Jack was pulled onto the shore. He lay on his back, not moving. I pulled Rachel away from the scene, fearing the sight of Jack unconscious and bleeding would derail her for good. The crowd closed in around him, and they began emergency treatment immediately, these fun-loving boys who knew their business when it came down to it. Someone started CPR. Suddenly Jack was coughing, they rolled him over so he could vomit up water. The crowd cheered. I felt Rachel's grip even tighter.

"He's all right," I said to her.

I saw Trey get up and move away from the scene, his hands on his hips. An official went over to talk to him. Trey was just looking down, shaking his head. I couldn't hear what he was saying. Some of his friends went around him as well. A siren wailed and an ambulance drove through the crowd. EMTs jumped out of the ambulance and surrounded Jack. Rachel was pulling on my arm.

"No…No…"

"Don't worry, he's fine. He's alive. They're just going to take him to the hospital to check him out. You can go with him if you want…"

"No, you go," she said. "I can't go. I can't…"

I saw an EMT go to Trey to see if he needed help, he waved him away. I took Rachel's arm and walked over to him, sensing he needed something to do.

"Will you take Rachel home?" I asked him, pushing her toward him. "I'm going with Jack in the ambulance...She asked me to. You can come to the hospital in your car. All right?"

Trey nodded numbly.

I turned to Rachel. "You need to call Jack's parents. They're at a wedding in New York right?"

Rachel nodded.

"Great. I'll call you later. Don't worry. He's going to be fine."

I left them there and went over to the ambulance.

"I'm going with him," I said to the EMT. I thought I should just say it, like I had some authority, before anyone questioned me about it. The EMT just nodded. I followed the stretcher into the back of the ambulance. It all felt a little surreal, like I had suddenly jumped into someone else's body, was acting like a person I didn't even know, someone with confidence and certainty. I liked this new person, though I was scared of her too.

I sat down beside Jack on a small hard bench. He had an oxygen mask over his face and a temporary bandage on his head.

"Is it bad?" I asked the EMT tending him.

"Have to do an x-ray. Probably just a concussion. These boys do that all the time out here. Could be a skull fracture too."

Skull fracture. I shuddered.

"Hey, he was lucky," the guy said, noticing my expression. "Having a boat fall on your head is a nasty business."

It seemed like a long ride to the hospital at Cape May Courthouse, though in fact it was only six miles. Once at the emergency room they unloaded Jack and took him to x-ray. While I waited I used the pay phone to call Rachel, but there was no answer at the house. I called my grandparents. They were surprised to hear I was at the hospital. I told them I would call back if I needed a ride home.

Then I sat in one of the extremely uncomfortable plastic chairs in the ER and waited. Finally I saw them wheel Jack into a curtained area. I jumped up to see him, but a large nurse stood in my way.

"Who are you?"

"I'm a friend."

"Where's his parents?"

"They're in New York. But someone is going to contact them."

The nurse looked dissatisfied. "Well, he's got a hairline fracture of the skull. He needs to be admitted."

"I think he signed some sort of paper at the competition about medical treatment…"

"I'll take care of that." I turned to see Morey, the beach patrol captain, coming toward us with a passel of lifeguards, Trey included. He handed the nurse the necessary papers without looking at me.

"Fine then," said the nurse. "You can take that to the admitting desk. It will do for now. We'll take him to a room."

She walked away. Morey looked at me, mumbled something to his boys about getting back to the beach and left. Trey and the others lingered, uncertain what to do. I went over to them.

"He's going to be fine," I said to Trey. "So his parents are coming?"

"Rachel gave Morey the number for some hotel for the wedding so he left a message. He's got the police on it." He paused, looking down at the floor.

"It wasn't your fault."

He shrugged.

Jack was wheeled out of the curtain area. He opened his eyes and smiled blearily at us. Then he focused on Trey and said, "Did we win?"

Trey snorted. "No, but we lost with style."

"Right on." Jack smiled and closed his eyes. They wheeled him to the elevator.

I asked Trey about Rachel.

"She's pretty freaked. She's like…sensitive or something."

"You could say that," I said. "Hey, can you just go back and make sure she's all right? Maybe get some of the girls to go over there. I hate for her to be alone. I'll stay here until Jack's parents show up."

"Yeah, okay." He seemed relieved. "Thanks."

"Sure."

After all the lifeguards were gone I went up to Jack's room. He was asleep. I sat on the lone chair and stared at him for a long time, studying his face, so perfect in sleep, almost too perfect. I felt very tired suddenly, the stress of the whole situation bearing down on me. I closed my eyes.

I must have fallen asleep because I woke up to the sound of moaning. It was dark outside. I looked for a clock but couldn't find one. Must be after nine, I thought. Where were his parents? I went to his side.

"Jack! Jack! Does something hurt?"

"What time is it?" His voice was hoarse.

"Uh…I don't know. It's after dark. Your parents are on their way."

"Oh." That information did not seem to interest him.

"Jack. Do you remember what happened?" I wondered if the injury had knocked out his short-term memory.

"Something about a boat."

"Right. You had an accident, but you're in the hospital and you're going to be fine. You just need to lay still. Does your head hurt?"

"No…" he probably couldn't feel much with the pain killers. "I'm cold."

He was shivering. I felt his forehead. Dry and warm. Perhaps he was developing a fever.

I tried covering him up, but he continued to shiver. "Cold in here," he said over and over. Still he didn't open his eyes. I went out into the hall and looked up and down for a nurse. I saw no one. I went back into the room and picked up the call button that was attached to the bed.

Only I didn't press it. God only knows why I didn't. I only know that at that moment I saw two paths mapped out before me: one with Jack and one without. So I chose.

I dropped the call button, kicked off my flip flops and got in bed with him, pulling his body close to mine, wrapping my arms around him as tightly as I could.

I stared at the door, listening for footsteps, knowing I would have to bolt any moment. For a long time, it was quiet. I held him. His body slowly stilled. I turned to look at him, touched his face, his forehead. It was odd, being able to touch him, as if he were a mannequin or something. His head moved slightly, turning to me. His lips brushed against my cheek, fluttering, like the wings of a moth. I didn't pull away. I turned my head so that his lips would brush across my lips…

Footsteps. Voices. I jumped from the bed, my legs practically buckling under me. The voices grew louder, accompanied by the echoing click-clack of high heels. I backed away, toward the chair, nearly tripped over it before falling into it. I tried to steady my breathing. I was thankful it was still dark, that no one would see the intense blush on my cheeks.

A moment later Jack's parents appeared in the doorway, still dressed in wedding finery. Jack's mother was what my mother would have called a "brassy blond" — the kind of mom who would date her daughter's boyfriend. She rushed to the bed.

"Jack! Are you awake?"

"I am now."

I shifted and she saw me, startling at my presence. She had no idea who I was. Her husband moved into the room more slowly, staying behind her.

"Who are you?"

"I'm Mariah. A...friend." My heart was pounding so loudly I was sure the two of them could hear it. I tried to breathe slowly, look as normal as possible.

"Where's Rachel?" She sounded annoyed. Jack's father had moved in to look at his son, examining the wound without even glancing my way.

"Rachel was pretty upset," I said, "so I said I would come and wait...until you got here."

"It's all right, Mom," Jack said. Mrs. Pendergrast turned back to him.

"Jack, poor baby, how are you feeling?"

"Okay," said Jack. "Loopy."

"They said it was a hairline fracture," I offered. "They are just keeping him for observation, since they couldn't reach you."

"Are you a doctor?" She was staring at me with daggers for eyes. Jack had never treated me as if I were beneath his station, but this woman had sized me up in one look and decided I was definitely coach class.

"No...I just didn't want him to be alone."

"I'm going to look at the x-ray. And see if they did a CT Scan, though I doubt this hospital has one," Jack's father announced, marching out of the room.

Mrs. Pendergrast looked at me, softening a little. "Well...Mariah? Thank you for coming. Here's money for a cab."

She took a wad of cash out of her tiny purse. I almost laughed. She really wasn't from around here.

"That's all right. I'll call Trey. He'll give me a ride home."

"Trey?"

"He's one of the guards Jack works with."

"Oh, that." She rolled her eyes.

Her husband returned. "As I thought, no CT," he said, distain in his tone. "The x-ray shows a small linear fracture, but there doesn't appear to be any bleeding. He'll be okay. As soon as we can, we'll get him to a proper hospital."

"Well, I should go." I approached Jack's bedside. His eyes were still closed, but I had an idea he was more awake than he let on. "Bye Jack," I said. "Don't worry, even with a big lump on your head you're still the best-looking boy on the beach."

I thought he might have smiled.

Twenty-four years later, as I sat in the front pew at his funeral, it would occur to me how close to death Jack Pendergrast really did come that day on the beach. If the boat had hit his head one inch to the left of where it did, it might have burst that jumble of arteries and veins and triggered a fatal brain hemorrhage. So his survival that day was a kind of miracle. On the other hand, had that hospital possessed a CT Scanner, they might have discovered the existence of the abnormality and operated to fix it. Fate is funny sometimes, but there is no escaping it.

SIX

June 2003

I have always loved that first day at the shore, when the whole summer is before me, when the churning of the surf slips under my skin and into my marrow. I stand on the porch of the Pink Poodle, gazing at the blue ocean, letting the sensation of Avalon fill me, warm me, free me, as it has always done. It seems hard to believe that I have really been away so long; the time between has collapsed, sucked into a black hole of memory, as if it were simply another life altogether. I watch the seagulls dart and screech, hear a cicada on the wood siding of the house next door with its loud, electric keen, an eerie sound. When I was a child I thought that noise was bats snoring.

It is a spectacular day in early June, the first really warm day of the season, when I am certain that summer is here to stay. There are no clouds in the sky. A gentle breeze flaps the flags on the houses along the beachfront, telling which way the wind is blowing. The first thing my grandfather did every morning was check the flag and make the official announcement: either "sea breeze, all is well!" or "land breeze, grab the bug spray!" A land breeze brought the greenheads in off the bay to assault the beach dwellers, their relentless attacks usually sending us into the water or back to the house.

"Did you forget the key?" Caroline glares at me. She is holding her luggage, waiting for me to open the door. I dangle the key in front of her. She grabs it with an impatient huff. She has still not quite forgiven me for this summer.

I am nervous about going in. Shortly after my last visit Trey had called and said, "I have good news and bad news." "What's the bad news?" I asked, preparing myself. "Mold." I think I gasped. "What's the good news?" "I can fix it."

The mold was fairly contained, he said, to the kitchen and bathroom walls. He would have to tear out the walls, decontaminate the inside and replace the plaster with drywall. He promised to have it done. Still, I hold my breath as I walk through the door.

To my relief, the walls are all in place, everything freshly painted. Caroline runs to the sink and turns on the faucet.

"It looks like water!" she announces triumphantly.

I call Trey to thank him.

"You're a miracle worker," I say, feeling myself blush, even on the phone. "What did you have to do about the water?"

"Just replace the hot water heater. It was old, there was so much sediment in the bottom. A miracle it hadn't leaked."

"The pipes were good?"

"All copper. Your grandfather knew what he was doing. He didn't stint on materials."

"I must owe you a fortune."

"A small one."

"Can you drop by with your bill? I'd like to settle that with you."

"Sure. When?"

"Tonight. For dinner."

"Dinner?"

Oh dear, already I was offering to cook for him.

"It will be simple," I say.

"Okay. What time?"

"7:30?"

"Sounds good."

"Hey Trey! Thanks for the water!" Caroline calls from the kitchen.

"Did you hear that?" I ask.

"Yeah," he says, "so you talked her into it?"

"She didn't have much choice. It was either this or spend the summer with her Aunt Maude in Passaic."

"You're cruel, Mare."

As soon as I hang up, Caroline stands in front of me, arms folded.

"You invited him to dinner? On our first day here?"

I shrug. "I know, I know. I lost my head. Don't worry, he's not expecting a banquet. You unpack, I'll go into town and get a few things from the market."

We unload the luggage and boxes, and then I drive into town and get a new pot with a lid that actually fits, some groceries and fresh salmon. I had brought a small hibachi in the trailer with me from Raleigh, so I decided to make grilled salmon with horseradish sauce, one of Jack's favorites. I stop at the liquor store and pick up two bottles of white, which cost a fortune. I curse myself for not having brought any bottles from Jack's extensive collection at home.

By the time I return it is almost 4. To my surprise Caroline has set the table and even found candles in a cupboard. She shrugs when she sees me.

"Just to thank him for the water. The least I could do." Caroline likes to cook, a talent she inherited from Jack, so I ask her to make a salad so I can shower and change.

I put the salmon in the marinade and run upstairs to jump in the shower and put on clean clothes. For a moment I cannot find my suitcases; they are not in the master bedroom. They are not in Caroline's room either. I call down to Caroline, "Where did you put my suitcases?"

"I didn't put them anywhere!" she calls back, annoyed.

I wander back into the hallway, looking both ways, puzzled. Then I look up the narrow staircase. I can see the suitcases, jutting out from the doorway to my old room in the cupola, a door which had been locked for years, cast in the sharp edge of light from the cupola window. I feel the blood drain from my head; I grasp the stair rail for support, certain I am about to faint.

"Wanna hear a story?"

I sat with my grandfather on the porch swing. Grandpa was smoking his pipe and Grandma wouldn't let him do that in the house. "The smell gives me a fearsome headache!" she would say.

"Sure," I said. "The Lady of Asolat."

"Ah…Elaine…but that's a sad story."

"I know. I like sad stories."

Grandpa took a long draw on his pipe, blew the smoke through his teeth satisfactorily, then settled back to tell his story.

"Well, it all began when the Baron of Asolat decided to hold a tournament in honor of King Arthur, and Arthur and all his knights were invited. Lancelot was not at first planning to attend, mainly because Guinevere was sick and couldn't go. But then Guinevere got well and decided to go, so Lancelot changed his mind and journeyed to Asolat.

"However, he didn't travel with Arthur. Instead, he went to the Baron's castle. There he met the baron's daughter, Elaine, the fair Maid of Asolat. And Elaine fell madly in love with him. She begged him to wear her token in the tournament. Lancelot didn't want to hurt her feelings, so he said he would, as long as he could fight in disguise, for he knew Guinevere would be watching. So Elaine's brother Lavaine gave him the plain white shield he had and off he went to the tournament.

"When the melee began Lancelot took the field and beat back forty knights, including all of Arthur's Knights of the Round Table. But he was wounded by Sir Bors, who stuck a spear in his side and left the field before he could be declared the winner.

"Sir Gawain, one of Arthur's knights, went to the castle and Elaine asked him who had won the tournament. Sir Gawain told her he didn't know, but the knight had carried a plain white shield. Elaine knew it was Lancelot. She discovered where Lancelot was hiding, in the cave of a hermit, and went to him and tended him day and night until he was well.

"Meanwhile, Guinevere flew into a rage when she found out that Lancelot had worn another woman's token, calling him a traitor and other such names. Just like Guinevere, it's all about her.

"Lancelot recovered from his wound thanks to Elaine, and he returned with her to Asolat. Elaine begged him to marry her, but he refused, saying he would never marry. Instead, he offered to pay her for nursing him back to health! Elaine, naturally, was terribly insulted by this offer, and rightly so. She announced that if he would not marry her, then she would die.

"Lancelot did not know what to do. He consulted Lavain and the baron, who could offer him no advice. So Lancelot left, without saying goodbye to her, hoping that this discourtesy would cure her of her love for him. He went back to Arthur and Guinevere, who was not speaking to him either.

"Elaine, the Fair Maid of Asolat, wasted away, neither eating nor sleeping. She informed her father that she would die, insisting that it was God's will. She had her father write a letter which she dictated; she instructed that when she was dead the letter was to be bound up in her right hand, and her body should be placed on a bed in a small boat and sent up the Thames River to the palace at Westminster. The king and queen saw the strange boat from a window and hurried to the river's edge to see what it was. They found the fair maid, quite dead, dressed in cloth of rich gold. They noticed the letter and King Arthur had it read aloud…it was addressed to Lancelot, asking that since she had loved him and he had broken her heart, that he should bury her and pray for her soul. This Lancelot did, with humility and sadness. Then the queen called for him and apologized for having been so angry and jealous. Lancelot forgave her, though she didn't deserve it. Love is blind, and Lancelot the blindest of all."

Grandpa fell silent, smoking. Talk of Guinevere always got his dander up. I said dreamily, "Can a person really die of love?"

Grandpa laughed. "I suppose a person could die of anything that made them not eat or sleep for so long. But I've never heard of it really happening, not in the flesh anyway."

"What do you mean?"

"There are other kinds of death."

I knew what he meant, too clearly. I huddled closer to him, taking in the comforting smell of the pipe, dreaming about love.

SEVEN

"Mom, are you all right?"

I hear Caroline's footsteps on the stairs.

"Yeah," I say, scrambling to my feet before she can see what has happened. My head feels heavy and light at the same time. I have trouble focusing on my daughter's form coming up the stairs.

"Did you fall?"

"Just got—lightheaded for a moment. It's nothing. I couldn't find my suitcases. They were up there, at the top of the stairs."

"And you don't remember moving them up there?"

"No," I say. Maybe it wasn't me.

"You're getting old, Mom," she says, but her tone is not unkind. I think I actually scared her.

"Early onset dementia. Nothing to worry about." I fix her with a goofy smile.

"Yeah, I guess."

"Would you mind…going up there and getting them for me? I don't think I can do the stairs at the moment."

"Sure…" Caroline gazes at me another moment then goes up the stairs.

"And shut the door," I call after her.

A minute later she deposits my suitcases at my feet.

"Maybe you should lie down…"

"No, I'm fine…" I hear a knock at the door and then Trey's voice from the entrance, calling hello.

"Damn," I say under my breath. "Caroline, go and welcome him, will you? I'm not even dressed!" I grab the suitcases and dash into my grandparents' room, shutting the door, leaving Caroline to deal with Trey, with everything. I sit on the bed, breathing hard, counting, as my doctor had told me to do when the panic attacks started. I know the symptoms of onset by heart: shallow breathing, heat in my face, weakness in the limbs. My legs are shaking, my head swimming, I think I might throw up. I fumble to open the suitcase, retrieve the bottle of Prozac. I've been lax in taking my daily dose.

After a few minutes I feel able to stand, I go to the small bathroom and take a cool shower. I tie my wet hair into a messy bun and throw some makeup on my face and stare at myself, measuring how calm I look, how in control. I have lost twenty pounds since Jack's death, and it shows mostly in my face, the hollows of my eyes and cheeks. It makes my eyes look bigger than usual. I breathe slowly.

I rifle through the suitcase and find an old yellow sundress, smooth out the wrinkles and put it on. I look again in the mirror, seeing for a moment the girl from Avalon, a girl I thought no longer existed. I wonder if Trey will see her too.

Trey.

I sit back down on the bed, breathing again.

After awhile I get up and head for the stairs, wondering how I will explain away my long absence. Trey and Caroline are on the porch, Trey with a beer he must have brought himself, and my daughter with a coke, looking out onto the ocean and talking amicably. He's been telling her stories, I am sure, stories of our summers as teenagers on this beach. It's a part of myself that I had never shared with Caroline. Perhaps that is why she felt removed from me most of the time, deprived of a part of me that was absolutely essential, part of my soul.

I pour a glass of wine and go out to join them. Trey stands up instantly, and I see a trace of worry on his weathered face that quickly changes to relief.

"I'm sorry," I say, betraying my fluster, "it's taken me longer to get organized than I thought it would."

"No worries," he says. "We're fine here. Can I help?"

"No, let's just…sit a moment," I say. I sort of collapse into a chair. I can feel them both watching me. I smile brightly. "The air feels good."

Trey smiles a little. "Caroline was just going to tell me about Nags Head. I've never been there. Sounds a lot different from here."

Caroline nods eagerly. "It's not so congested. Houses are more spread out. You drive everywhere. You drive right onto the beach. And there are no beach patrols telling you where you can or can't swim."

"The surf can get pretty rough here," Trey says neutrally. "The beach patrol was originally formed to rescue people off of wrecked boats. That happened a lot."

"Seriously?"

"Sure. Later on it evolved into lifeguarding. People always complain about the beach patrol being too strict, but it comes from long experience. It's a tough surf here. Then there are the sharks," he says, glancing at me mischievously. "You know the movie 'Jaws' was based on actual shark attacks that took place on the Jersey Shore at the turn of the century."

"Wow. Did they ever catch the shark? Like in the movie?"

"Yeah. A guy in a little fishing boat caught it—he was a lion-tamer for the Barnum and Bailey circus. It almost sank his boat, but he somehow killed it with a broken oar he had found floating on the water. He didn't realize it was *the* shark until he got it home to gut it and body parts spilled out."

"No! You're lying!" Caroline exclaims.

"I am not. Look it up."

"So random."

"But that was North Jersey. Probably a mob shark."

She laughs. So do I. I drink my wine and gaze out on the glistening sea. My head still feels foggy, and the nearness of Trey is not helping. He doesn't seem to notice; he starts telling Caroline the history of the island.

"This island was all dunes and forests at one time. It was used mostly for grazing sheep, and for hunting. Like the Outer Banks, in fact. When the developers came in, they brought in loaders to haul out the dunes. There aren't much of the dunes left, except for the high dune area. The town was supposed to keep those dunes pristine, but instead they sold lots to wealthy people who built gigantic houses there. It was something that made the locals really mad at the time. That's when wealthier people started taking notice of Avalon."

"Are any of your friends still here?" I ask. "Like Dave...didn't you call him Bowie?"

"Yeah, everyone was a rock star back then. He still comes for a couple of weeks. He's a big time lawyer. Owns a house on 63rd."

"A lawyer? Dave? He was like a total beach bum!"

"Yeah. Who would have thought it, right?"

"What about my dad?" Caroline asks shyly. "What was he like? Was he a good lifeguard?"

70

"Your dad could do anything," Trey says. "He didn't much care for the patrolling part, too boring, but he loved the competitions. He was very competitive. And popular."

That was, I knew, an understatement. Jack had a supreme gift for attracting people to himself. Trey said he loved the competitions, but what he really loved was the *attention*. He thrived on it.

"I should get the salmon," I say, feeling the need to change the subject. "You two keep talking."

"You don't need to go through any trouble…" Trey says apologetically.

"It's no trouble. The salmon is marinated, I just need to throw together a salad."

"I did the salad, remember?" says Caroline, annoyed.

"Oh right. Then we are ready to grill!"

"You're going to grill on that?" Trey asks, pointing to the hibachi sitting on the porch deck. I had thought at the time it was a great idea. I look at it now rather forlornly.

"Sure…".

"Mare, have you ever started a charcoal fire before?" He is looking at me pointedly, no doubt surmising that I have been strictly a gas grill chick for all of my adult life. I shake my head sheepishly.

"It can't be that hard, can it?"

"Here, let me," he says, setting down his beer. He sets about expertly getting the charcoal going while I retreat into the kitchen to regroup. By the time I bring the salmon out for cooking, the coals are hot and ready.

"You've done this before," I remark idly.

"In Afghanistan, we cooked over an open fire, using a hubcap for a pan," he says matter-of-factly. "We didn't have much in the way of condiments, so we had to be pretty creative."

"Afghanistan?" Caroline asks. "You were in Afghanistan?"

"Yes. For twenty years."

"What did you do there?"

"Training, mostly."

"Training?"

Caroline waits for an explanation. Trey seems hesitant.

"We…the Americans…were helping out the Afghans in their war against the Soviets."

"Oh yeah, I think I remember that from history class. We boycotted the Moscow Olympics?"

"Yeah."

"Wow. So you were actually there? What was it like?"

"It was pretty bad. Women and children were murdered, whole villages bombed. The Russians didn't just go after the insurgents, they went after the people who gave them aid and comfort. They just underestimated their enemy."

"I thought we gave them rockets or something," Caroline says.

Trey slaps the salmon on the grill.

"Yes, we did that," he says, his voice carefully neutral.

"But you stayed there a long time." She is leaning forward, almost over him as he crouches over the grill, hanging on his every word. "Long after the war was over."

"Yes."

"Why did you stay so long?"

He doesn't say anything for a long time. I begin to feel uncomfortable and wonder if I should jump in and change the subject again. But I, too, want to know…

"It's a long story," he says finally.

"And you don't want to talk about it?"

"Something like that."

"I get it."

I am staring at Trey, at the change in him, more than just the wearied lines of this face. There is something different in his eyes, so blue and broken and emptied, and I wonder if this really is the teenage lifeguard I once knew. I feel the gulf between our life experiences widen, unbridgeable. My life has been all about country clubs and charity balls, his has been about war and tragedy and death. I see in his eyes the things he does not want to speak about, not yet, and I wonder what horrors he has witnessed, and how close he has come to death. I want answers too. But I will have to wait.

"It was a long time ago," he says dismissively. "I think this is ready."

"Oh, it smells good," I say brightly. "It's Sockeye, supposed to be the best. Do you want to eat inside or out? I'm afraid the deck out back is not very stable…"

"This is fine for me," Trey says. "It's a nice night."

Caroline and I go in to get plates, forks, napkins, the salad and the bread and haul it out to the porch, where Trey is waiting with the salmon. He puts a piece in each plate and we settle ourselves on the porch, Caroline and I in the wicker chairs, and Trey perched on the top step.

"I'm not sure how safe it is," I say, glancing at the listing steps off the porch.

"It's fine. This is delicious," Trey says.

"What did you eat in Afghanistan?" Caroline asks. I want to tell her to stop bringing up Afghanistan, that I can see this is somehow painful to him, but I don't intervene.

"A lot of bread," Trey says, "and tea. Sometimes fruit, pomegranates or oranges. Mostly…onions. You'd be surprised what I can do with a boiled onion." He smiles.

"Well, it's really pretty amazing," Caroline says, "that after all these years, you two are back here in Avalon. Must be karma."

"Karma?"

"Didn't you learn about karma? I thought it was big in Asia."

"The Afghans are Muslim," he says, "they don't believe in karma."

"What do they believe in?"

"Justice. The eternal kind."

"Oh, right," she says, uncertainly, "but still, don't you think it is an amazing coincidence?"

"Yes," he says, glancing at me. "Amazing."

I look away quickly.

"Caroline is going to try to find a job for the summer. Any leads you might have for her?"

"What kind of job do you want?" Trey asks Caroline.

"I don't know. What is there to do around here except scooping ice cream?"

"I have a friend at Uncle Bill's who would probably give you a waitressing job, if you are interested. It's a madhouse in there most mornings, but you'd earn tips and it closes at 2 so you could have the rest of the day on the beach."

"Really?" Caroline sounds ecstatic. "Ohmygod, that would be awesome!"

"How old are you?" he asked.

"Seventeen."

"That should work."

Caroline smiles broadly. "Cool. When can you talk to your friend?"

"Meet me over there tomorrow at 1, after the rush. We'll work it out."

After dinner Caroline volunteers to do the dishes, leaving Trey and me alone on the porch.

"Wow," I say, "I've never seen her volunteer to do a chore before. And so cheerfully. You must be having some kind of effect on her."

"I get the feeling she was daddy's girl," he says. I nod. I move to sit beside him on the porch step. It creaks under me, making me nervous.

"They did everything together. He went to all of her track meets, hanging around all day with the other parents, taking pictures. They ran together in the mornings before school. Ski trips to Aspen. They were very competitive with each other too — I'm sure you're not surprised. I think she wakes up every day and wonders why God took her father away from her and not me." The words are out before I can stop them.

"Why do you do that?" he asks. "Why do you beat yourself up over something you had no control over?"

"I don't know," I say simply, and laugh away threatening tears. "It's just the way I feel sometimes. I feel like I don't know what to do with her. Jack always knew. I could sit on the sidelines and watch and that was fine for me. This being in charge stuff...I'm not much good at it."

"This from the woman who manages armies of charity ball volunteers?"

I grin. "That's nothing compared to a teenage girl."

He reaches over and takes my hand. "You're doing fine," he says. There is no way he can really know that, but I love that he said it.

"Thanks for the vote of confidence. Are you sure you can get her a waitressing job?"

"Sure. Pat's an old friend. You'll remember him, I think, from the old days. She'll be fine, she'll meet some the kids, make some friends."

"It was very nice of you to offer."

"Pat owes me a few, anyway. I help him out with his...inspection issues. And there are only so many pancakes a man can eat."

I laugh, relaxing a little. We stare out, silently, at the whirling sea.

"I used to take Rachel to Uncle Bill's," I say, "just to try to get her to eat something. Thought I could fatten her up."

"Did she eat?"

"Yes, but then she'd disappear into the bathroom for a long time. After a while...I knew what she was doing."

"Oh."

"Sorry. I'm not sure why I brought that up. Being here, I am just remembering her again. I haven't really thought of her in years."

Rachel. She is still in my heart, after all these years. I still think of her as one of those watercolor drawings of woodland fairies, something gauzy and fragile that must stay in the shelter of the trees, never to come out into the sunlight. The one year she had come forth, into the sun, had proved her undoing. And I was part of that. Jack was too. We tried to help her, but in the end we shattered her.

EIGHT
July 1978

Jack returned to the lifeguard chair a week later, after a new set of x-rays showed no permanent damage. The fracture was still there, but it would heal on its own, as long as he didn't do anything to aggravate it. Of course, Jack completely ignored the doctor's orders. He wouldn't listen when Morey told him couldn't compete either. He would whether Morey gave his permission or not.

Trey and Jack resumed their early morning training sessions, though Trey was nervous and wouldn't let Jack go out in bad surf. Jack managed to persuade him to give him surfing lessons as well, since it seemed terribly wrong to him that an Avalon Lifeguard didn't know how to surf. Miranda and I resumed our morning vigils on the beach. But Rachel would not come out.

I would have thought Jack's parents would have objected to his activities, but his mom was busy with renovating the Grain Elevator, and his dad was upstate during the week doing plastic surgery and making millions of dollars, so neither one seemed very concerned.

I was more concerned about Rachel. I went to see her at Jack's house one day when I saw that his mom's car was gone — she was probably up in Egg Harbor shopping at the home stores. I did not want to meet up with Jack's mom again.

"Hey Rach," I said. She was sitting on the couch watching TV. There was a large bowl of popcorn in her hand, but the bowl was full, and I was certain she hadn't eaten a single kernel. She often did things like this, filling her plate with food or ordering several things at a restaurant, then playing with the food and pretending to eat, declaring she was full without having eaten more than a mouthful. At first I had been fooled by this; people with eating disorders were very good at deception. But I knew, now, what to look for.

"Whatcha doin?" I asked, plopping down beside her on the sofa and helping myself to the popcorn. "Anything good on?"

She was watching a soap opera.

"That's Clarissa," Rachel said, pointing to a woman on the screen with red hair. "She's in love with Burt. But Burt just got this other girl pregnant…I forget her name…and so Clarissa is plotting revenge by trying to get the other girl to sleep with her brother so she can tell on her to Burt."

"Sounds grand," I said. "Why don't you come down to the beach? It's a beautiful day."

"No, not today," Rachel said in the same, bland tone of voice she had used to describe the tawdry relationships in the soap opera. "Maybe tomorrow."

"Rachel, honestly, you've got to get over this. It's silly. There's nothing to be afraid of."

"I'm not afraid," Rachel said, genuinely surprised that I should think such a thing. "I just…don't feel like it right now."

I sighed. "Well, then, come to Pop's. We'll play some games. Get out of this house at least. Isn't Jack's mom driving you crazy?"

She smiled. "When she's around I stay in my room. But she isn't here very much. She likes to shop."

"Okay, so if you won't even come to Pop's, come to the Pink Poodle. We can read or watch old movies on the VCR. Grandpa's got a bunch of them. Abbot and Costello tapes. Really funny. C'mon, Rach."

To my surprise, she agreed to come to the Pink Poodle. We had to walk, but it was a nice day and we took our time, talking about friends back home and things we liked to do, avoiding the subject of the boat accident.

When we got to the house Grandma was out grocery shopping, but Grandpa was sitting on the porch, reading the newspaper and smoking his pipe, as he always did just before lunch. He was so pleased to have company he went into the house and made us both peanut butter sandwiches. Amazingly, Rachel ate a whole sandwich.

We spent the entire afternoon on the porch, playing checkers and Parcheesi, which Grandpa loved, eventually breaking out the UNO cards. When Grandma came home she made lemonade and brought out fresh cookies. I think Rachel even ate one, though she could have dropped it or hidden it, because she could do that as quickly as a magician.

Rachel stayed for dinner, and Grandma made fried chicken, which was too good even for Rachel to resist. Grandpa remarked that there was to be a meteor shower that night. I grabbed a blanket and dragged Rachel out onto the beach. I spread out the blanket and we lay down together, side by side, waiting for the meteor shower to start. She kept saying that we should go back to the house, but I insisted she stay, that when the stars started falling we needed to make a wish on them.

"What are you going to wish for?" she asked me.

"Oh, maybe for a car," I said vaguely. "What about you?"

"I will wish...for Jack's mother to eat a bad clam and have to go home." Then she started giggling, and I did too. I was glad to hear she felt as uneasy around Jack's mother as I did.

"That's sort of mean," she went on. "I just can't help it."

"Why don't you come and stay with me? You could sleep in my room. My grandparents won't mind."

"Maybe..." her voice trailed off. "There's one!" She pointed excitedly at the sky, but I had already missed it.

"Wish! Wish!" I said to her. She closed her eyes and concentrated hard, moving her lips slightly.

"Okay, all done," she said. "Your turn."

We waited with bated breath for the next one. When it finally appeared I claimed it for myself and closed my eyes and wished...wished for something I knew I shouldn't wish for. "Be careful what you wish for," I could almost hear my grandmother say. I didn't know then how right she was.

We watched for more, wishing on every one we saw, figuring that it couldn't hurt. Whoever saw it first got to claim it, though I let Rachel claim more than me, because she seemed to have so much fun doing it.

"Do you think Jack loves me?" she asked when the skies had quieted for a time.

"Of course he does," I said, hoping I sounded sincere.

"How do you know?"

"It just seems like he does. Don't you love him?"

"I guess I do. You can't *not* love him, right? But he makes me so crazy sometimes."

"You mean, like that stunt in the boat?"

"Yes...no. That's just Jack being Jack. Even his failures seem like successes. I don't think...I just can't live up to that."

"I don't think he expects you to live up to anything."

"I couldn't even go to the hospital with him."

"He totally understood."

"I know, he told me. But still, it's not right. It's not normal. He knows it too. He thinks he can...fix me."

"Do you love *him?*" I asked in a small voice.

She sighed. "I don't know what love is. I feel dependent on him, like I need him to breathe, to live. Like I couldn't exist without him."

"Tinker Bell," I said.

"What?"

"Tinker Bell...she started to die when she thought Peter Pan didn't love her anymore. I always thought that was so beautiful."

"Really?" She laughed a little. "It doesn't seem healthy, though, does it? It's like an addiction or something. When I thought he was going to die...I was sure I would too. I felt like I was suffocating."

"No, you're being dramatic. You were just scared. We all were. It was terrible. We all thought..." I didn't finish the sentence.

"You're really much too nice to me," she said, turning to look at me. "I've never had a friend like you."

"Me neither, with you I mean," I said, blushing.

"My shrink says I need more normal friends...like you, I guess."

Shrink? She had a shrink? Moreover, she must have had him a long time, because she used the term "shrink" rather than "psychiatrist" or "counselor." But probably everybody from upstate had shrinks, what did I know? I was a hick girl from south Jersey.

"So I'm normal?" I said with a laugh. "Boy, I'd hate to see your abnormal friends."

She laughed too. "You're funny," she said, in that way she had of making you feel like you just won the lottery.

"Mariah!" The voice was my grandmother's, coming from the house. I raised myself up onto my elbows.

"What?" I yelled. In the yellow glow of the porch light I could see two figures standing with my grandmother, looking out onto the beach. "Out here!"

Trey and Jack started jogging toward us. Rachel sat up, pulling the blanket over her shoulders and shivering.

"Hey, I've been looking everywhere for you," Jack said when they were close enough. I realized he was talking to Rachel, not me. "My mom didn't know where you were."

"We were here," Rachel said. "Playing checkers with Mariah's grandfather. He wins every time, so don't play him. I think he cheats." She giggled.

"We were watching the meteor shower," I offered. "Did you see it? It was amazing."

"No kidding? Cool. Hey, why don't you two come down to the Pier? Everyone's there."

Rachel yawned. "Not for me, thanks. I'm really tired. I think I'll just go home."

Jack looked at me. "What about it, Mariah?"

"Sure, I guess so, for a little while," I said. I glanced at Rachel, hoping she was not angry. She wasn't looking at me. She was still staring at the stars. "I'll have to go tell my grandparents."

"I'll take you home, Rach," Jack said, holding his hand out to her. She took it, and he pulled her up. But instead of leaning into him she pushed away and started walking toward the car.

"I'll meet you guys there," he said, following her.

"Bye Rach!" I yelled after her.

"Bye!" She turned quickly and waved.

I went to tell my grandparents I was going to the Pier. They were watching "All in the Family" reruns so they didn't really hear me, just smiled and waved. It was one of those times I was really glad my mother wasn't there. She would want to know everything, where I was going so late, who I would be with, and would I take my brother along with me? My brother, when he was not in his room with his Atari, was out on the basketball court skateboarding with his friends. I hardly ever saw him. I kissed them both, grabbed a sweatshirt and went out onto the porch where Trey was waiting. Since Jack had taken the car, we had to ride bikes the twenty blocks to the Pier. My grandparents had a large, rusty collection of bikes of various shapes and sizes, and pretty much every kid on the island knew about them and came by whenever they needed one. They always managed to get returned, making the Pink Poodle a kind of self-serve bike shop.

We rode in silence awhile. Being alone with Trey had become awkward, I realized, as if we both hovered under the awareness that we were not children anymore. We just didn't know what we were.

I asked him how Jack was doing. Trey said he was fine.

"Rachel looked better," he said. "We were kind of surprised you got her out of the house."

I felt a tremor of pride at this. "She's okay, just shaken up. It was traumatic for her. I think she's led a very sheltered life. She's never seen anything like that accident. And seeing Jack lying there in all that blood like he was dead..."

"But she's okay now? Jack was pretty worried..."

"She seemed to have fun today. Grandpa's peanut butter sandwiches are a cure for everything."

"Good thing you were there, Florence Nightingale," he said.

I shrugged, embarrassed. "I didn't do anything. You saved Jack's life. He would have drowned if not for you…"

"If not for me he wouldn't have been in that boat," Trey said, suddenly agitated. "I shouldn't have let him do it. Bowie was my partner, Bowie and I have been doing it for three years. Instead I told him I was going with Jack this year. It was completely stupid. I don't even know why I did it."

"Because Jack made you do it," I said softly. "He has that…that *way* with people. He makes them do things they don't want to do." Like being friends with Rachel, I thought to myself. I was doing that for Jack too. I really didn't need a difficult, moody, breakable friend, one that needed constant tending like a rare orchid. Rachel required all my energy, all my wit and will. And yet I had even invited her to come and live with me in the Pink Poodle. And it was all, I knew in my heart, for Jack.

Trey laughed. "It's true," he said. "But when I saw him lying on the beach, I thought he was dead too…and, honestly Mare, I was never so scared in my whole life."

"We were all scared," I said.

"I've never been scared before, not in the boat. I could do it in my sleep. But I felt responsible for him, and I let my concentration slip."

"You did? I saw the whole thing, Trey, it was the wave…"

"No, I should have seen it. That was my job. But I wasn't watching the wave. I was watching him. Damn it, Mare…I couldn't take my eyes off him."

It seemed strange to hear a boy say this, but I understood instantly what he meant. It was the power of attraction, how some people had it, and some people didn't. Trey, for all his sun-kissed beauty, didn't have it. Neither did I. But Jack Pendergrast did. He drew others to him like mosquitoes to a porch light. Even Trey, who seemed to be immune to everyone else, was not immune to Jack.

As soon as we got to the Pier, Trey joined his circle of lifeguard friends and their girls, a circle in which I was not included. I found Miranda and Tanya and we started dancing to someone's boom box, which was playing reggae music. Reggae was new to us, but we loved its relaxed, groovy beat, like the motion of the sea, and we found all new ways to move our arms and legs and toss our hair. Beneath us, the tide washed up against the pilings, the sound incessant and soothing in the quiet moments between songs. We bought lemonade from the concession stand and talked about the boys, most of the girls pressing me for information about Jack.

"Where is Jack anyway? With Rachel?" Miranda asked.

"He took her home. He's coming here though. He said he was."

They were circling me now, the only one among them to have inside information. I felt supremely powerful in my scant knowledge. I longed to tell them about that crazy night in the hospital room. But that was a secret I would not share with anyone, except maybe someday I would tell Jack, who seemed to have no memory of it at all.

I had hoped that that particular event would bind us in some celestial way, that he would feel something between us, a connection, a flow of energy. I was probably imagining it, I knew, imagining he noticed me when really he didn't. Now, with Rachel home in bed, I thought I might have a chance to jar his memory.

But I didn't see him. Perhaps he had stayed home after all, to keep Rachel company. The kid with the boom box went home, and the party drifted out to the beach, where the stars were still falling. I went out as well, needing a breath of cool air, along with Miranda, who was still dancing to her own beat, doing a goofy Bob Marley impression. "Hey, mon…hey mon…"

There were kids all over the sand, making out, prone shapes like beached seals. We walked gingerly between them, trying to see faces, who was kissing whom. I saw heads bobbing in the waves, knew there were even couples out there in the ocean probably doing more than just kissing.

"Let's go swimming!' I said impulsively, pulling my shirt over my head. I still had my bathing suit on. I ran for the surf tossing my shirt carelessly into the sand. Miranda was laughing.

"No way Jose!" she shouted at me. "Mariah!" Her voice held a note of warning. I didn't look back. I was feeling weird and crazy all at once, I needed to dive, to swim. I had spent the day with Rachel, and it was a rare day that I didn't go into the waves. I suddenly felt the need for the cold ocean, the stinging salt, the swirl of seaweed. It was a part of my body almost. My grandmother had called me a fish when I was younger. Now I wanted to be one, to swim on and on, darting down and diving, shooting to the surface, it was like flying.

I dove in, feeling the cold wave crash against my face, the shock of it radiating to my core. I swam underwater in total blackness and then came up, breathless, past the breaking waves. I looked around to see where I was. At first I couldn't see anything, then the salt water cleared from my eyes and I could make out the lights of the boardwalk. As long as I kept them in view, I would be all right. I floated with the swells for awhile, lying on my back, paddling idly, then turned over and dove again, hitting the sandy floor and coming back up, tossing my hair back dramatically.

I was pretty far from everybody, including the kissing couples, who had stayed close to shore so as not to lose their footing. I swam some more, back and forth, turning and twisting, floating. I could hear the girls calling me to come back. I turned, reluctantly, and headed toward them, bobbing over the heavy swells, taking my time.

86

I heard a sound in front of me and looked up, saw someone swimming out to me with a hand buoy, the kind the lifeguards use. I saw a dark head break the surface, twisting left and right to shake off the water, and I saw it was Jack.

"What are you doing out here?" he asked.

"Went for a swim," I said, as if it were a dumb question.

"The girls thought you were drowning."

"Did you come to rescue me?" My voice sounded different to me, throaty and brazen, as if the sea had freed me from my inhibitions, my girlish fears.

"Do you need rescuing?" he asked me in the same voice, a voice of testing, of knowledge.

I thought for a moment.

"Yes," I said. And I promptly pretended to drown.

In a second he had his arms around me, pulling me to the surface, his face close to mine, my body pressed against his chest. He held me there a moment, a moment that seemed to go on forever, for I couldn't breathe, couldn't bear it. Then he kissed me, his salty mouth covering mine. I didn't know what to do, I had never been kissed before, not like that, slow and searching. That kiss burned down my throat into my stomach and beyond, to the place where kisses go. I wrapped my arms around his waist, forgetting even to tread water, thinking that if he let go of me at that moment I would sink to the bottom of the sea.

He pulled away finally, and his lips formed words in my ear.

"That was for the hospital."

So he had remembered after all.

He turned and swam with me toward the shore. I heard cheering, realized that the girls had thought I had actually been rescued. That annoyed me a little, for everyone knew I was a strong swimmer. But in the next moment, seeing their rapt faces, the hint of jealousy, I didn't mind it anymore.

We swam-walked the rest of the way to the beach, the girls surrounding us, asking if I was okay.

"Of course I'm all right you ninnies," I said to them. "You didn't have to send the Marines in after me."

"You looked like you were struggling! We thought you were being attacked by a shark!" Tanya said almost hysterically. It was the *Jaws* effect again.

"I'm sorry they scared you," I said, turning to Jack. "I was fine, really."

"Well, You shouldn't go out in the ocean at night," he said in his "beach patrol" voice, the one lifeguards used to warn the public about the possibility of a strong riptide. It was as if the kiss had never happened. I was still shaking from it, my tremors masked by the shivering, and yet it seemed to have no effect on him at all. Was it only for the hospital? Was there nothing else between us? Or was he simply masking his true feelings in front of these gossipy girls so that Rachel wouldn't get wind of it?

"Thanks Jack, you're our hero," said Tanya, sidling up to him. "You saved our silly Mariah from death! How can we thank you?" It was clear she had an idea how to thank him. Jack played along.

"No thanks needed, ma'am, just doing my job," he said in a mockingly deep voice. The girls convulsed in a fresh round of giggles. Trey walked over to us. He looked me over and smirked a little. He was carrying a towel.

"Took a dip, Mare?" he asked. Then he threw me the towel. "I borrowed this from Pop." I wrapped the towel around myself quickly, still shivering.

"Can you give me a ride home?" I asked him.

"Sure. What about the bikes?"

"Just leave them. I'll get them tomorrow."

We walked over the boardwalk to the parking lot, which was relatively deserted except for the skateboarders. We got in Trey's jeep and drove down Avalon Avenue, and I apologized for getting his car seat wet.

"What was that all about?" he asked me finally.

"Nothing. I just wanted to swim."

"Really? In the dark?"

"It's just been one of those days," I said. "I was with Rachel all day, and it kind of wore me out. I just needed to…do something."

There was a pause.

"You've got a thing for Jack, don't you?" he said.

I looked at him, open-mouthed. "Why do you think that?"

He shrugged. "I'm observant," he said. Then after a moment, "Be careful, Mare."

I suddenly didn't care what he knew or what he thought. "Sure I like him. Everyone likes him. But Rachel is my friend and I would never hurt her. She…she's messed up."

"Messed up?"

"Yeah…she told me she doesn't think she should be with Jack. But she can't let him go. It's a weird Jack thing, you know."

"Yeah, I know."

Trey dropped me off, though he didn't get out of the car to see me to the door. I slipped in the screen door and shimmied up the stairs before either of my grandparents could emerge from their room to see me. I went to my attic room, undressed, put on warm pajamas and crawled into my narrow bed, letting my hands roam the places that Jack had touched, as if I could recreate the feel of him against my skin, my mouth, keep that forever in my memory, share it with no one else. Ever.

NINE

June 2003

In the early morning, with the sea shrouded in mist, Avalon looks the most like the ancient isle of Arthur, or at least how I always imagined it. Then the sun peeks up from the streaked horizon and the mist begins to evaporate, revealing the wide blue sky, the breadth of endless ocean, the eternal whitecaps lurching to the shore. It is that sense of eternity that stirs the soul here, as it did even in Nags Head, the rhythmic throbbing of the waves as constant and unending as time itself.

I lie in my grandparents' old iron bed, watching the sea, waiting for it to appear in the mist. I am remembering as well, remembering that first taste of Jack in the black ocean under the black sky, the soft, salty sweetness of his mouth. Whenever I was angry at Jack or disappointed in him I would close my eyes and recreate that moment when he had, literally, swept me off my feet. It was twenty-five years ago and yet it seemed like yesterday, the memory so fresh and alive that it makes him alive again. I turn, as if I would see him there in the bed with me, reaching for me as he often did in the early mornings when I was barely awake, pulling my hips against his. I feel a swift, sudden yearning for him, as I have not felt in years. I roll over on my side, fighting back tears, tears I had not been able to summon even at his memorial service. Why now? Because I am in the place where we began. Did I come here to live it all again? To imagine one can go back to the beginning? All I could experience now was a vast and terrible sense of all I'd lost.

I decide it's a good time to take a walk on the beach. I get up and rifle through one suitcase (I still haven't unpacked) and pull out a bathing suit and swim shorts, grab my iPod and head downstairs. Caroline, I'm sure, is still fast asleep. I make a pot of coffee and putter around impatiently while it percolates. I really need to get a drip coffeemaker. When finally the bubbling and gurgling of the pot has slowed I pour some into a cup, add some milk, and take it out to the front porch. This is the other reason why I love mornings in Avalon, that first cup of coffee on the porch. There is nothing like it in the world.

The sun is higher now, casting long shadows of the houses along 6th Street. I see the early joggers on the beach, the old men walking their dogs, the fishermen on the rock jetty casting their lines. It is a lovely, peaceful moment, when all is right with the world. It is easy, in Avalon, to forget the rest of the world exists. To never want to leave. That's why Arthur hasn't left to return to the real world, I suppose.

When my coffee is gone I put in my ear buds and head out to the path that leads through the dunes to the flatter sand of the shoreline. It is low tide, the beach is a wide stretch of hard, flat sand, as perfectly smooth as a concrete walkway. I start to walk, but take the ear buds out of my ears, preferring to listen to the sound of the ocean, to watch the bubble-laced streams of water lash at my feet.

The lifeguard stands and the boats are lined up every three blocks or so at the top of the beach, just as they always have been, ready to be hauled down to the water in a few hours when the guards come out. I see a few boats in the water, lifeguards practicing for an upcoming competition, and I cast my thoughts back upon that fateful boat race. Everything had changed that day, for Jack, for me, but especially for Rachel. She might have married him and lived happily ever after, if not for that day. Even now I still look back and wonder where it all went wrong.

1978

The day after the kiss, it rained, one of those drawn out, all day rains when you know you just better settle in and find something else to do. I was glad for it. I looked forward to spending a day in the Pink Poodle, just me and my grandparents and my rarely seen brother, reading or playing solitaire. Grandma made pancakes and I ate a whole bunch, not caring how many calories were in them. Then I went into the sunroom and read more King Arthur stories while Grandpa took his morning nap. My brother yelled that he was going to his friend Brian's house; I heard the door slam. The rain streamed down the windows of the sun porch, beating on the tin roof making a terrible racket, but a racket so familiar and comforting that it soon lulled me to sleep.

I was awakened by my grandmother standing over me, shaking my shoulders and calling my name.

"Mariah, Mariah…Rachel is here."

I sat up quickly, staring at Rachel, who was soaked to her skin, looking thinner and paler than ever, her wet hair sticking to her scalp. My grandmother had given her a towel, which she had wrapped around herself, but she was still shivering.

"Did you walk here?" I asked, amazed.

"Yeah," she said.

"Where's Jack?" I heard the fear in my own voice. I thought for a moment that he had told her everything, how he had kissed me, how I had responded, and that she had come to confront me, to accuse me of betraying her friendship. But instead she shrugged.

"He went to the doctor with his mom," she said. "In the city."

"New York?"

"Philly. His dad found a specialist there."

"Is he all right?"

"Yeah, it's just a check up."

"Why didn't you go?"

She shrugged again. She was still standing there, shivering. I hadn't offered her a chair or anything. "I told them I had a headache and just wanted to stay in bed. But that was kind of a lie…I decided to come here…do you mind?" She must have noticed my lack of enthusiasm. I didn't want any company today. Truth be told, being with Rachel wore me out, and I needed a break. A day of doing nothing.

But I said, "No, of course not. I'll get you some dry clothes."

I did not take her to my room. I went up and found a sweatshirt and shorts that I had worn when I was 10 or 11 and brought them down to her. She changed in the bathroom, and I got her a hairdryer so she could dry her hair. After awhile she stopped shivering.

Despite my misgivings Rachel seemed to understand my mood. We sat in the sun porch wrapped in blankets and read quietly while the rain came down. She seemed perfectly happy to do this, not needing conversation but just wanting to be there, in the Pink Poodle, with me.

My grandmother made us peanut butter sandwiches for lunch. Then Grandpa challenged us to a game of Monopoly and we played for the entire afternoon. Rachel was more at ease than I had ever seen her, laughing and silly, so unlike the stilted society girl I had seen when I first met her. Maybe it was my grandfather's lame jokes. More likely it was the plainness of our lives, the lack of expectation, of watching other people, waiting for them to make a mistake. I didn't know her parents, but I imagined her father was a powerful man who made inordinate demands upon his children, and her mother was a fancy socialite who cared more about public image than private happiness. Was that why she needed a shrink?

Later that day I did take her up to my room, "Mariah's Aerie" as my grandmother called it, and we sat on the bed and talked for a long time.

"It's nice here," she said finally. "Very pink. I like your family. What're your mom and dad like?"

"My dad is great, really easy going. My mom is…tougher. She thinks it's her job to make sure my dad doesn't make any mistakes."

"They don't like Avalon?"

"My dad loves it. But he works all summer. He's a contractor. And my mom does his bookkeeping. They'll come for Labor Day, probably."

"You don't miss them?"

"Sometimes." I looked at her. "Do you miss your parents?"

"Yes," she said. "They're coming next weekend, soon as mom's done with summer classes."

"Are they staying at the Pendergrasts'?" I found I couldn't say Jack's name aloud.

"No, Jack's dad got them a suite at the Windrift. My dad wants to go to Atlantic City. He loves to gamble. Just for fun, though. Jack's dad does too—they have a lot in common. Our moms do too. I guess it was natural that Jack and I would end up together."

"You went to the same school, right? Is that how you met?"

"Sort of. I mean, I'd seen him around, everyone knew him, but he was a year ahead of me and so we didn't actually meet until his parents invited us over for a barbeque. They were in this Bridge club and met once a month or so. So we went. Jack was in the pool when we got there, doing back flips off the diving board, showing off for everybody. Jack is always showing off, though it doesn't seem like showing off. It seems like he's just doing what he does, and people happen to be watching. Like on the boat…" She broke off.

"Do you think he was showing off on the boat?" I asked, surprised that she would think that.

"Sure he was. Trying to prove he was the best. He always knows he's the best at everything. He can't stand for anyone to be better than him at anything." She paused, smiling a little. "It's not a bad thing, I guess. He's just very…competitive."

"So you met at their house?" I asked.

"Yeah. He came over to me and started talking, introducing himself and all, he said he'd seen me at school and that he wanted to meet me. That he knew our parents were in this Bridge Club…"

"So *he* made the plans to have your family come over," I finished for her.

"Yeah, it was his idea. And what Jack wants, Jack gets." She laughed a little.

"What about what you want, Rach?" I asked quietly.

"Me?" She looked surprised at the question. She had a pillow in her hand, one of the little throw pillows I had made in sewing class,

96

and she was pulling on the fringe, straightening out each piece and lining it up so each strand was the same distance apart. I watched her, though she seemed unaware of what she was doing. "I just want…someone to love."

To this day I was certain she meant "Someone to love *me*," that she had left off the "me" on purpose, because she could not confess that need, even to me. Isn't that what we all want, after all? I remember in Sunday School, asking my teacher the question, "Why did God make Adam and Eve? After all, if he knew everything, he knew they would screw up and disappoint him and that the whole human race would end up being a terrible mistake. So why bother in the first place?" And she had answered, "God made people because He wanted someone to love Him." Whether or not it was true I have always loved this explanation, as my faith waxed and waned I returned to it time and again, thinking often of Rachel and her terrible need, my own need as well. If God could create the human race for that same need, why should it not be the desire of our hearts as well?

TEN

2003

Caroline is seated at the table when I return from my walk, a cup of coffee in her hand. She looks at me blearily and asks what we have for breakfast.

"Oh, I didn't get anything," I say. "There's cereal in the cupboard."

"I was hoping for something more…interesting," she says.

"Get some sticky buns," I say. "Mallon's on 24th. Buy a half dozen bagels too. I'm going to the beach."

I grab a chair, a towel and a book from the sunroom and head to the beach, where I decide I will plant myself for the entire day. I rarely went to the beach in Nags Head, absorbing myself in house projects instead. I had an enormous house project still awaiting me right here on 6th Street, but I figured I could put it off for a day. The house had managed to survive all these years without me; it could wait a little longer.

After awhile Caroline joins me on the beach.

"Where's my bun?" I ask.

"Oh, did you want one?" she asks innocently. "Don't forget, Mom, we have to go to Uncle Bill's to see Trey's friend today."

I had forgotten. "You don't need me there. Trey will do the talking. You just look neat and talk smart."

"You're not coming?"

"I have a date with this beach chair all day."

"But I think Trey…" she stops mid-sentence. I open one eye and glare at her.

"Yes?"

"Oh, nothing. It's just that…he might want to see you too."

"He knows where I live."

"Is this like how you grownups play hard to get?"

"What?"

"Never mind."

"Caroline, honestly, Trey and I are old friends. He's like a brother to me."

"A brother? Mom, give me a break. I see how you look at him. That is *not* brotherly love, no way."

"I don't know what you're talking about," I say obstinately, closing my eyes again.

"Man," she says, annoyed, "I'm going for a run."

She runs off, headed down the beach. I watch her, admiring her long strides, her runner's body. She is a beauty, like her father. I wonder if she will catch the eye of some lifeguard…I was sixteen the year I met Jack, younger than she is now. The thought makes me quiver with a familiar fear. Sixteen seemed so old then. I thought I was grown up. Now I realize I was more a child than even Caroline is, less certain of the world and of my place in it.

In the end I do go to Uncle Bill's with Caroline. Trey is there when we arrive, sitting in one of the vinyl booths with a heavy set, balding man he introduces to us as Pat Garridy. The name sounds familiar.

"You don't remember me, Mariah?" he says with a strong Jersey accent I suddenly recognize. Pat had been one of the summer kids, a little older than Trey, though I never would have known him.

"Good grief, Pat!" I say belatedly, giving him a hug. "I didn't recognize you."

"This is what pancakes do to a guy," he said, patting his ample belly. "Do you want some?"

I introduce him to Caroline, and he smiles and hands her an application.

"Just fill this out. When can you start?"

"Tomorrow?" she ventures, glancing at me.

"Great. I'll put you on shift with Margo. She'll show you the ropes. Tomorrow is Tuesday, should be fairly slow, you can get the hang of the place."

Caroline seems pleased, aware that she has already been hired without even completing the application.

"How's business?" I ask Pat.

"Great, as always," he says. He has a waitress bring water and menus. I realize that we had better order lunch, at least. I sit beside Caroline and Trey sits across the table next to Pat. I order some buckwheat pancakes and Trey gets the same. Caroline asks for a diet coke.

"This is the same menu they had when I was a kid," I say, handing them back to him.

"Nothing ever changes at Uncle Bill's," he says with a laugh.

"Thank God for that," I say under my breath. "I mean, things are changing so fast around here."

"Yeah, can you believe it? Hardware store's gone, the deli, the drugstore, now we got all those fancy shops and condos. Crazy. But that's life. You still got that Pepto Palace up there at the inlet?"

I smile—I'd forgotten that particular nickname. "Yeah. Trey here is going to fix it up."

"To sell? Wouldn't bother. Buyer just tear it down anyway."

Trey and I exchange glances. "We know," Trey says. "But Mariah thinks she can get it on the historic register, make it bomb proof."

I had thought no such thing, but I am grateful for Trey's quick response.

"I doubt that, but go ahead and try," Pat says with a snort. "Nothing sacred around here. But I got connections at the Inquirer — if you could get one of those journalist types interested in the early architecture of Avalon, you might have a shot."

I thank him for the advice. Trey offers that the house is sound, other than a few minor issues. Like the roof. And the floors. And the deck and porches. And the water damage in the ceilings. And the ancient wiring. And the lack of air conditioning. Minor stuff. I go over the list in my head. Once again I get the feeling I have made a colossal mistake. For this I have given up the house that Jack built, the perfect house by the perfect shore, out of some sense of nostalgia borne of grief. And Trey had been the one to tip the scales. Had he not been there, I probably would have listed the house without looking back. As it was, looking back was all I could do.

ELEVEN
1978

Jack's trip to the doctor's was uneventful; the doctor did another x-ray to be sure everything was healing as it should and that getting a CT Scan was not necessary. It had been, Jack told us, just an excuse for his mom to spend the day in Philadelphia and shop for more house stuff. The pickings were slim on the Seven Mile Beach, he said, and Egg Harbor didn't have anything that was to her taste.

He told us this while we hung out on the Boardwalk in the early evening. The rain had finally stopped, though the smell of it still lingered. I liked the evenings after a long rain. There was something fresh and renewing about them, a cleansing. People were starting to move about again, bundled in sweatshirts against the cool, rain-tossed air.

We bought hot dogs and cokes and then decided to go in for the movie. Miranda and Tanya and some other kids arrived loaded with popcorn they'd stolen from Pop's machine. The movie that night was "Yours, Mine and Ours," and so we sat in the back row and laughed in all the wrong places and threw popcorn in the air and tried to catch it in our mouths until the usher, a boy named Pat, told us to stop because we were making a mess. I don't know how he could tell, since the floor of that place was so caked with layers of popcorn grease and sticky, dried up soda that you could use a surfboard to get down the aisles.

When the movie was over we wandered out onto the boardwalk, and I started thinking it was time to head home. I was tired, and being the third wheel with Jack and Rachel wasn't that much fun. I said goodnight, grabbed my bike from the lot and rode home.

I sat on the front porch, not going in for a long time, staring out at the black ocean, listening to the steady roar of the waves. The Pink Poodle's front yard butted right up against the sea wall, so it seemed, at high tide, like the waves would crash right up onto our porch. On stormy days you could feel the spray from the breakers on your face. There was something dangerous in this, as if we all knew that the house was built on the cleft of a rock, which would hold out only so long against the power of the sea. During big storms I would see my grandmother, sitting in her rocker under the reading light in the living room, stiffen every time a wave hit the wall, as if waiting for the one that would finally break through and crash right into the house. I had grown so used to the sound that for weeks after going home to Merion I would not be able to sleep because of the lack of ocean noise. My mother finally found a machine at a yard sale that would simulate the ocean, but the sound on that machine was paltry compared to the real thing, and so I would still lay awake. It was as if the heartbeat of the world had stopped, and all I could hear was my own heartbeat, and I would wait for that to stop as well.

I heard the slam of the screen door and looked up to see my grandfather ambling out onto the porch, pipe in hand, banished from the house as usual.

"Mind?" he asked me, indicating the pipe. I shook my head. I loved the smell of his pipe, at least at first, before it got stale and flat. He sat in the rocker, settled himself in comfortably and lit the pipe, taking several long draws. The rocker creaked reassuringly.

"You're up late," I said.

"Ah, don't like to go to bed too early. Then I wake up in the middle of the night and can't get back to sleep. One of those 'getting old' issues, I suppose." He sighed. "It was nice having you and your friend here today. Rachel. Nice girl. Very…fluttery." I laughed at the description. "Glad you're making friends. Your dad used to do that — run off with all kinds of kids all the time. Good kids. He was like you."

"I wish he could come down," I said.

Grandpa sighed again, a heavy sound, full of regret. "Not your mom's cup of tea, I guess. But they'll be down for Labor Day. That'll be something to look forward to, won't it?"

"Yeah." I don't often miss my parents, but at that moment I missed them both terribly. I felt weirdly lonely, desolate, needing to see their faces. I thought about going home. But I knew my dad wouldn't be able to drop work to come and get me, and my grandparents would not want to drive me back to the city. I'd have to wait.

"Did I ever tell you about the night you were born?" he asked.

"Yes, Grandpa," I said patiently. "About a hundred times."

"My what a storm that was," he said as if he hadn't heard me. "The waves came crashing off that sea wall like they were going right over the house. I thought we were goners, I surely did. Your ma was in there having you, and I just couldn't believe it. What kind of child is going to come out of this storm, I wondered. Your mom, you know, she loved the ocean until that night. Even though you were born safe and sound and the house stood, she didn't trust it. She didn't trust the ocean either. But you can't trust the ocean, can you? The ocean'll kill you soon as look at you. The ocean is a power beyond anything else there is on this earth. It's like God's power, you know? It seems really regular, predictable, it can get shoved into the background, a regular rhythm, and we just learn to move around it, sleep with it, eat with it, go about our own lives as if it weren't even there. But then every once in awhile it rises up and shows us who's boss. Then, watch out. Get what I mean?"

I nodded, feeling a chill in my bones at his words.

"Yeah, I've been living by the ocean a long time. I love the ocean, but I fear it too. That's the thing you gotta do. I used to take the boat, go out into the bay, do a little fishing; I don't do that any more. Don't know why. Nothing scary out there. Though there was a guy I knew once who claimed he saw a shark in the bay once. Almost caught it too. Don't know if I believe it. But one day I just woke up and realized that I wasn't going out there anymore. It's like I needed to let go. Let go of your nets, that's what Jesus said to the disciples. Let 'em go. So I've been letting go of a few things. Except for this house. Can't let go of it, yet."

"I hope you never do," I said, fearful that he might be thinking of selling.

He smiled at me. "Not yet," he said. "Not yet." He paused. "Who would buy this silly old pink house anyway?"

I laughed. "I love this silly old pink house," I said. "I want to live here forever."

"Then I'm gonna give it to you when I die, Mariah." That's all he said.

But he didn't give it to me. He died less than a year after that conversation, he died before the next summer began, and I think he knew that it would be his last summer sitting on that porch. It wasn't the ocean that killed him. All his life he had been waiting for the ocean, for those waves to crash into his house and claim him, but he wasn't anywhere near the ocean when he died. He was driving his car down Route 9 on the way to pick up groceries for my grandmother when he hit a tree. The autopsy said he had a stroke. But I think he must be in heaven, still dismayed that it was a tree that got him, of all the natural forces with which to do battle, one so mundane as that.

My grandmother closed up the house and moved in with Aunt Julia, my father's sister, in Scranton. She couldn't go back, she said. After that summer, after what happened with Rachel, I realized I couldn't go back either.

But that night, sitting next to my grandfather on the porch of the Pink Poodle, I felt certain that I would live there for the rest of my life; that nothing could separate me from the Jersey Shore, from this particular beach. The little drama of Jack and Rachel seemed small and unimportant; like the tide, there was nothing any of us could do about it. Events would happen with or without our consent, hearts would move where they would. My own heart was still unknowable to me. I wanted so many things but never at the same time. I kept going back to the kiss, which seemed to me like a dividing line in my life, a crossroads. Perhaps Jack gave it no further thought, but I could not think beyond it. That kiss happened because it was meant to happen, because even if Jack didn't know it, I was the one he would love.

I got up, kissed my grandfather on the top of his head and went to bed.

TWELVE

2003

I awake to the sound of demolition, the ripping of wood, the smashing of planking. I look at the clock, 7:30. I roll over, covering my ears. I had been up late the night before, unable to sleep for a violent thunderstorm that had shaken the windows. I look out. The rain has stopped, but the sky is still grey and overcast.

I throw on a sweatsuit, pull my hair into a ponytail and descend to the kitchen, where I can see Trey outside with a sledgehammer, knocking down the remnants of the rotted back deck. I open the door, and he stops, wipes his forehead, and waves.

"Coffee?" I ask.

He nods. "I need to get this cleared out before the guys come with the lumber."

"I didn't know you were starting today."

"No time like the present. We have a lot to do." He throws himself back into the work. I shut the door and blearily make coffee, annoyed once again at the lethargy of the percolator, remembering I was going to get a real coffeemaker. I should make a list, I think, and sit down to write one, though I cannot find a pad of paper. That would be first on the list.

When the coffee is finally done I pull out the last of the sticky buns and invite Trey in. He says he's too dirty to come in and would I just bring the cup outside. He is standing on the wood frame of the decking, his legs spread, pulling up planks. It looks precarious. There's no way I can reach him. He sees my dilemma and comes over, still straddling the frame, taking the cup and the sticky bun.

"Thanks," he says. "Caroline go to work this morning?"

"I assume so. I didn't hear her leave. Her first day of training. She's not usually an early riser."

"I hope she likes it there."

"She'll be fine. It will keep her busy. That's the important thing. She'll have less time to mope. So what should I be working on while you are demolishing the deck?"

"Call the roofer. Here's the number."

"You don't do roofs?"

"Definitely not. These Victorians need special equipment anyway, the roofs are so steeply pitched. The windows should be replaced as well. But you can wait on that for awhile."

"Good Lord," I am adding it all up in my head.

"You might want to think about air conditioning too." It seems a sacrilege to even mention the word in this house. Trey looks at me and shrugs. "Just a thought."

"I'll think about it," I say, though I doubt I will. I am still wondering why I am bothering with all this anyway. This was not my home anymore, yet I was planning to restore it as if I were going to stay, to live here "for the rest of my life" as I had told my grandfather twenty-five years before.

"What else?" I ask, though I really don't want to know.

"I have an electrical contractor coming over to evaluate," he says. "Even without A/C this house will have to be brought up to code."

"This was all a mistake," I say, throwing up my hands. "I must be crazy."

"Sure you are, Mare, we both are. We're here, right? Thanks for the coffee." He hands me back the cup. "What's for lunch?"

All I have is canned tuna and mayo, so I make him a sandwich a few hours later. Shortly after that the "lumber guys" arrive and start rebuilding the deck. Trey is making it bigger than before, so it will fit an outside table and chairs and even a grill. Another thing for the list. I decide to go shopping, to escape the noise of construction. I hope Grandpa will be pleased with Trey's renovation. I'm half afraid the work will awaken the ghost in the house, make him angry. Pure nonsense.

I head to Stone Harbor to check out the shops, which look fresh and chic and expensive. I browse through some home stores, then end up at Hoy's for new beach chairs and a coffee maker, and then to the Fudge Kitchen for the best fudge in the world, served up by kids imported from Eastern bloc countries. When my meter runs out I head back to 6th Street.

I see Caroline when I pull up, sitting on the front porch with Trey, who has a beer in his hand. He looks sweat-stained and relaxed. He salutes me.

"You're finished?" I ask.

"Told you it was a one day job. That's the easy part," Trey says. Leaving the car I follow them to the back porch, where the rickety screen door from the sun porch leads out to a beautiful new deck facing east, toward the ocean. Trey has replaced the railings with benches to provide extra seating. There's plenty of room for a table and a grill, which I still, as yet, don't own. Trey has set up a card table from the house there with the card table chairs, a comical touch. I feel a strange affection for him at that moment; that he would think to add this little detail.

"What do you think?"

"Oh, Trey, I love it!" I proclaim, and I throw my arms around his neck and kiss him. The kiss surprises both of us, because I kissed him on the mouth, though I had been aiming for a cheek, and it was the first kiss we had ever shared in all the years we knew each other. It was a quick, darting thing, over in a flash, but it lingered there between us, hovered like a shadow, and I felt a laugh bubble up from within me, the kind one gets when one wants to smooth over an awkward moment. "What do I owe you?"

"I'll send you the bill," he says, disengaging from me. "The rest of the house may fall down, but this deck will still be here."

I get Mexican takeout, and we eat at the wobbly card table, enjoying our first meal on the new deck. Caroline tells us about her first day at Uncle Bill's, which she seemed to enjoy, though it was harder than she thought it would be. After some of the girls from the restaurant had invited her to the beach.

"Any boys?" I ask.

"Mom," she says giving me that teenager look. Like she would ever tell me if there were. "We just laid out and mostly slept. This getting up at 6 is going to kill me."

"You'll survive."

After dinner we sort through the hardwood floor samples I have brought and pick one, a natural cherry, that I think goes best with the house. We then pick out tile for the bathrooms as part of the "future" projects for the house. I have lost some of my sense of doom at the house project—there is nothing like picking out colors and materials to absorb a person, make them forget that what they are renovating is an old, ugly house that no one in the world would want. For some reason I had begun to imagine Trey there, as incongruous as he looked in an old Painted Lady; I had begun to feel him as a part of the house, as its permanent resident. I didn't see myself there yet. My soul had not yet settled down, found a place to light. This was not yet my place of rest.

Afterwards, Trey suggests a walk on the beach. Caroline begs off, saying she is going to bed with her iPod — she needs it to drown out the surf so she can sleep. I grab a sweater, for the evening is chilly, and head out onto the beach with Trey.

"I remember when you taught me how to body surf," I say. It is nearing the summer solstice so the sky is still fairly light. "I couldn't get the hang of it for the longest time. How old was I? Eleven? Once I did, though, you couldn't get me out of the water."

"I remember," he says. "You wore me out."

"Then the boogie boards came along and ruined everything," I say. "Anyone could do it then."

"Yeah, you were mad about that."

We walk awhile in silence. The sky grows darker, the sun setting behind us. There are a few people out on the beach, ambling about aimlessly. A man is throwing a ball into the surf for a rambunctious dog. The wind is brisk; I pull the sweater closer around me.

"You're cold. We should head back." Trey starts to turn back. I put a hand on his arm.

"No," I say. "I'm fine. It's nice out here." I look at his thin T-shirt. "You aren't cold, of course."

He smiles. Neither one of us knows what to talk about, away from the specter of the house, our mutual project. He still has said almost nothing about the tragedy he had lived through, his murdered wife. I want desperately to know.

"This is the Avalon I remember," he says. "Quiet. Sort of empty. When everyone's gone in and it's just us and the seagulls…We sometimes came out and repaired the boats this time of day. Or did some late surfing. Not often. It's a very strange light, isn't it? Sort of light and dark at the same time…"

He's right, of course. The sun sets on the opposite side of the island, so there is no orange glow here, no bright light on the edge of the sea.

"Trey…" I say finally, "what made you decide to…come back here?"

He doesn't speak for a long time. When he does his voice is different, faded, gray, like the darkening water.

"I had a son, Mare. He was seven. He was with us at the marketplace that day in Kabul."

I stop walking, stricken. "Trey." It's all I can think to say.

He is not looking at me. He is looking out to the ocean, the eternal, mighty, ocean, as if he can see the place where he had been, where he had put down his roots, had his branches ripped away. Trey had a child. And that child was dead.

"Tell me what happened," I say.

He shakes his head. "I can't do that. Not right at this moment. But I will, I promise." He takes a breath, changing worlds again. "I came here because I couldn't think of anywhere else to go. My dad died a few years ago — I wasn't even here for his funeral. My mom remarried and moved to Hoboken. She wanted me to go there, but I thought Hoboken would be a little too much like Kabul. This place was the only place I really remembered."

He pauses, glancing at me. "I took a job with a ready-mix contractor, something I remembered how to do. One day I saw the ad for Avalon Building Company. I thought it was…kind of like what your daughter would call karma or something, I had money saved from my military service, money I never used…so I bought it." He smiles, and his smile seems more real now. "It was a way of…being connected…I guess. To this beach, to my past, a time when I remembered being happy. To you."

"To me?" I look at him, surprised.

"Yes, well, I believe you still owe me a game of Skeeball."

I feel a burst of laughter from the bottom of my throat. "You're on," I say.

We walk down to the arcade. It is dusk, and despite the cool evening the arcade is hot and smells of sticky bodies and Coca-Cola. We play Skeeball until we run out of quarters, and I am certain that Trey let me win a few games. I haven't played in years and it shows. In the end I concede to him for good and all the title of Supreme Skeeball Champion of the Universe, after a tense death match which seems to have the entire population of the arcade standing on tiptoe around us, hearts in throats.

In truth, I was too distracted to play well. I was watching Trey, playing this ridiculous game with the tiny wooden balls, and trying to imagine him in his other world, the one with the bombs and the bloodshed and dead children. I tried to imagine him storming a fortress commando style, automatic weapon aloft, shouting "clear" or shooting men dead. I could not wrap my brain around it. I still see the boy in the lifeguard chair, swinging a whistle around his finger, watching the girls parade before him, tossing their long hair in case he was watching. This is where he belongs. If only he had stayed here. If only none of us had ever left Avalon.

THIRTEEN
1978

Jack decided he wanted to throw Rachel a birthday party. A surprise. On the week *before* her birthday, so she wouldn't suspect: August 5. I told him in no uncertain terms that it was a terrible idea.

"She'll hate it," I said. "She hardly knows anyone here except me and Trey. She's not comfortable in crowds. Let's just take her out for dinner, the four of us. We can go to the Crab House…"

"She's allergic to seafood," Jack said. He wasn't looking at me. He was in the lifeguard chair, watching the kids playing in the surf. He wasn't supposed to be talking to me at all, but he never took his eyes from the water.

I had spent the day hanging around the beach, mostly alone. Rachel had a headache and didn't want to be out in the sun. Her migraines seemed to be getting worse; she would spend the day in bed or in the bathroom throwing up. Miranda had gone home to attend a family reunion, and no one else seemed to be around. It was the first time all summer that I didn't have anyone to hang out with.

Trey was off that day, working for his dad pouring concrete. Like most of the lifeguards, Trey had other jobs to supplement his income. On Friday and Saturday nights he worked as a bouncer at Phil's Rock Room, along with some of the other guys. He didn't hang out at the Pier as much as he used to.

"Then we'll go somewhere else," I said, exasperated with him. "Rachel hates parties…"

"Rachel *loves* parties," Jack said.

"Not when she has to be the center of attention. She doesn't like that kind of pressure…"

"Don't worry, she'll be fine. It's going to be at the Princeton," Jack continued, as if he had not heard a word I said. "I rented out the Banjo Room. I got a DJ too, in case you want to show us your Yvonne Elliman impression again."

The Princeton! That must have been pretty expensive. Jack looked down at me and winked; I felt my stomach flutter.

"Could you help me out? In my duffel there are a bunch of flyers about the party. You know where everyone lives, so could you just ride your bike around and stuff them in mailboxes? That would help a lot."

Of course, my liege. Your wish is my command. I opened my mouth in an attempt to refuse, to tell him I would not conspire with him in making Rachel's life miserable, but of course nothing came out. I said instead, "Whatever." He gave me one of his heart-stopping smiles. I whacked him hard on the shins in return.

I found the flyers and spent the rest of the afternoon stuffing the mailboxes of everyone I knew. I could not help but feel slightly uneasy about doing this, as if I were participating in a kind of social lynching, an act of cruelty disguised as a glowing tribute. The flyers specifically stated that the party was a "surprise." I wondered if I should tell

Rachel anyway, give her the option of not going. But that would be cruel to Jack, who wanted to give his girlfriend a party in her honor, and I thought that might be even worse.

After I finished with the flyers I rode to Sullivan's where I saw Trey getting a coke. He was wearing jeans and a T-shirt, caked with cement dust.

"Hey," Trey said when he saw me.

"Hey," I said. "Did you hear about the party?"

He glanced at me. "What party?"

"Jack's throwing a surprise birthday party for Rachel. Didn't he tell you?"

"No."

"What do you think?"

Trey shrugged, throwing his bag over his shoulder. "I think it's cool."

"You do?" I was annoyed. "You think she'll be okay with it?"

"Who? Rachel? Sure. Why not? I'm going down for a swim." He started walking toward the boardwalk. I followed at his heels.

"I really think it's a bad idea," I said.

"Mare, you're making a big deal out of this. It's not." I stopped, watching him as he walked away from me, feeling hurt for some reason. Normally he would have challenged me to a Skeeball match. But that day he just walked away.

August 5th dawned clear and sunny, without the paralyzing heat of most August days. I was not surprised, of course. I had had little to do with the party plans; I tried to keep myself aloof from it all, my slender act of protest against this monstrous idea. And yet I had conspired with Jack to bring Rachel to the party. I was supposed to tell her that it was a birthday party for one of Trey's friends and that all the lifeguards and their girlfriends were going. Jack, I was to tell Rachel, had promised to help Trey unload the keg and get stuff ready, so he had sent me to collect her.

"I don't really feel like going," Rachel said when I went to the Grain Elevator to fetch her. I was dressed in a polka-dotted beach dress and flip-flops, and had pulled my hair into a braid to control the frizz. Rachel was sitting cross-legged on the floor of her room, reading a book she borrowed from my grandfather, Tennyson's *Idylls of the King*. She was wearing a T-shirt and baggy pajama pants, even though it was 5 in the afternoon.

"You have to get ready," I said.

"I'm really into this poem. It's so…majestic."

Tennyson was my least favorite Arthurian writer. His poetry was way too flowery for me. Besides, it irked me that he had changed Guinevere's ultimate fate from burning at the stake (which is what she deserved) to fleeing to a convent where she repents of all her sins and becomes miraculously "good." Tennyson felt Guinevere was worthy of redemption, but I didn't.

"I think I will do my senior thesis on the *Idylls*. The words he uses…when I say them out loud they taste like pearls in my mouth."

"I was never much into the poetry," I said. "But we really need to go…"

"Do we have to? Why don't we go to the Pink Poodle instead? I want to talk to your grandfather about this book…"

"We can do that later," I said, "I promise. But Jack really wants you there."

"Why didn't he come to get me then?"

"He told Trey he would help set up. Look. This is no big deal. We'll stay for an hour and then go to my house. Okay?"

Finally, she agreed. I went out into the living room and waited while she got dressed. She took her time. I was sitting on the living room couch, staring around me at the white, plastered walls of the Grain Elevator, still devoid of artwork or color of any kind, when Mrs. Pendergrast came into the kitchen from the deck. She was wearing a two-piece white bikini, which looked amazing on her, with an oversized white shirt and a big white floppy hat. I thought of my own mother, wide-hipped and pallid from spending her summers in my father's basement office, doing his books, trying to keep his business afloat. The two of them were probably the same age, I thought, early forties.

Mrs. Pendergrast stared at me as if I was a meteor that had just crashed through her roof. Then I saw a flash of memory cross her tanned brow. She was in on the joke, of course.

"Is she…?" she asked, her eyes flickering toward Rachel's door.

I nodded, feeling increasingly miserable about the whole thing. *She's going to kill me.* This was the first time I had chosen sides in our three-way relationship. I had chosen Jack.

I stood up and went to the kitchen, where Mrs. Pendergrast was refilling her glass with water and fresh lime slices.

"I was thinking," I said nervously, "that this is maybe not such a good idea. I think we should tell Rachel what is going on, so it doesn't come as such a shock…"

Mrs. Pendergrast looked at me as if I had an extra eyeball. "Don't be silly. Everyone always wants to coddle her. That's part of her problem. Here Jack is doing this wonderful thing for her, and you talk as if it is some form of torture. The girl needs to stop being so *sensitive*."

She returned to the sun deck. I stared in her wake, aghast at her words. Rachel *is* sensitive, I thought. Sensitive to light, to heat, to the very air around her. She was like one of those blown-glass Christmas ornaments that would shatter if even nudged against another ornament in a box. These were things that needed to be protected, wrapped in miles of tissue paper and packed delicately in their own little velvet-lined case. One could not make them tougher or more resilient. It was ridiculous to think that exposing Rachel to more naked experience in her life would make her stronger. But everyone, including Jack, seemed to think otherwise.

Rachel finally emerged from her room. She spread her arms to show off her long, gauzy peasant skirt of light pink, designed to make her look bulkier, with a white peasant blouse of flowing, wing-cut sleeves. Her hair was pulled back in a half-pony tail, accentuating the hippy look, something she could wear well, for her pale thinness was the hippy mantra. Next to her I was way too big, too clumsy, too colorful. As usual, I felt as though I did everything wrong, that no matter how much time I slaved in front of my mirror, I could never get it quite right. And just at that moment, for the tiniest instant, I did not feel too badly about delivering Rachel to the lions' den.

"You ready?" I asked her a little too brightly. She put on a brave smile for me, and instantly I felt bad again.

"We can go to your house after?" she asked again. I bit my lip.

"Sure," I said. "Grandpa would love it. There's nothing he likes more than talking about King Arthur with someone who's actually read some of the books."

She smiled, relieved. My heart sank.

"Goodbye Clarice," she called to the sculpted shape still tanning on the deck. We heard an indistinct "Have fun," and giggled a little. We walked down to Dune Drive, arm in arm, chatting amiably.

"Don't you think it's weird living with your boyfriend's mom?" I asked her. "And you call her Clarice?"

"Yes, she told me to," she said. "'Mrs. Pendergrast is my mother in law,' she says. It's hard to say her name without laughing though."

"Awkward," I said.

"It's going to get even more awkward when my parents get here."

"Why?"

"Because they all act like we're getting married…like tomorrow or something. My parents just think Jack is perfect for me. He's perfect anyway, right? They are like chomping at the bit to see me married off before I'm twenty."

"But why? Don't they want you to go to college first?"

"Oh, they want me to go to college, but they think we should get engaged first. Jack is going to Columbia, so of course they want me to go to Barnard. How perfect, I guess. The perfect couple, the perfect life."

"Don't you want to go to Barnard?"

"Not really…I'd rather go to Columbia."

"I don't think they take women."

"Well, that will change soon. They let Barnard women take some classes at Columbia now, so it can't be much longer. Columbia is the last of the Ivys to be all male. It will fall before my senior year, I bet."

She was, in fact, completely correct about that.

"What about you, Mariah? Where do you want to go to college?"

"I haven't thought about it," I said, which was sort of true. I wasn't sure I even wanted to go to college, though my mom was pretty insistent about it. She had not been able to go to college, so she was determined that her children would.

"I'm not sure I could afford it," I said lamely.

"I bet you could get a swimming scholarship," Rachel said. "Didn't you win the State championships last year?"

"I came in third," I said. "In the 400 medley."

"Well, that's still really good."

She said it as if she were genuinely impressed. I figured she was just being nice, trying to support me. That made me happy, and a little mad too.

We arrived at the Princeton and could hear the throbbing of the music even before we got to the door of the Banjo Room. I took a deep breath, preparing myself for Rachel's reaction to this. "It'll be fun, I promise," I said, and opened the door.

It took a moment to adjust to the darkness. I took Rachel's hand subconsciously as we passed through the foyer and into the main room, a fairly large room with tables, a dance floor, a stage for the band. I didn't really have time to register anything else, for the first thing I saw when I entered was a large banner hanging over the stage. It said: "Happy Sweet Sixteen Mariah."

Mariah?

I stared at it, uncomprehending.

"Happy Birthday Mariah," Rachel said to me, and squeezed my arm.

"But...it's *your* birthday," I said to her.

"No, actually my birthday's in May. Sorry about that." She grinned at me.

Suddenly Jack was onstage with a microphone, saying, "Hey everyone, let's hear it for our guest of honor, Mariah Murphy!"

And everyone cheered and yelled Happy Birthday in unison. And they laughed. Because I was still standing there like a deer in headlights, unable to understand what had happened.

"You told me you didn't have a sweet sixteen party," Rachel said. "So I thought, well, Jack and I thought, it would be nice to give you one."

I looked at her, and then I was laughing, and we were hugging, and everyone was clapping. I couldn't think of anything to say, all I could do was laugh. The DJ started to play and Rachel grabbed my arm and dragged me to the dance floor. Jack met us there, and I hugged him, still laughing, wildly happy.

"What about the flyers? I said. "I passed them out…"

"We passed out the real ones before that."

"So everyone knew…?"

"Pretty much." He grinned at me. "Happy Birthday, Mariah."

The music thrummed against my temples, I just went with it, not knowing what else to do. People gathered around wishing me happy birthday, laughing at how completely I was taken. I felt utterly foolish and thrilled beyond measure. The music pulsed in my stomach, in my throat.

Jack did this.

I said it over and over to myself while kids came up to wish me a happy birthday, still laughing at my complete surprise. *Jack did this*, I thought. *For me*. Well, maybe it had been Rachel's idea, but Jack had done all the work. That he had taken so much time to think about me, about what I would like, about how to totally surprise me, filled me with such a wellspring of love I could barely contain it. That's what it was, I knew. I was in love with Jack. I did not want to love him. I knew it was wrong, and dangerous, but he had forced me into it. His kiss still echoed on my mouth, in my throat, I still awoke with it every morning and went to bed with it every night. Now I would have this as well. A sweet sixteen.

I started to dance. I barely registered who was there, but I had been in Avalon for a long time and I knew all the kids, though I didn't realize until that night that they knew me as well. Rachel danced her funny, angular dance, in her own little circle of imagining. I could not stop laughing. I couldn't help but be amazed at the depth of kindness that had gone into giving me a party like this. My sixteenth birthday had passed virtually unnoticed at home. My mother had promised to take me to New York for a weekend, but it never happened.

I danced my way over to Jack, who was watching by the DJ stand.

"Jack," I said, "I don't know what to say…why did you…?"

"You've been a really great friend to Rachel, Mariah. And we are all…grateful for how you've helped her this summer."

I began to see that the Pendergrasts had an ulterior motive for inviting Rachel to Avalon for the summer: not just to cement her relationship with Jack, but to see if she had the right stuff to be a Pendergrast, if she could handle the pressure. The Rachel I saw that night was equal to the task, every inch a princess in the making. She could do it, if she really wanted to. But I wondered if she really did.

"This," I said, indicating the room. "This is amazing. I will never forget this."

"You deserve it." He kissed me on the cheek, a light, tender sweep of a kiss. I felt myself blush deeply.

After a few sets of disco the band switched to Reggae and the mood mellowed considerably. I went to the bar for a soda, saw Miranda and some other girls there and we talked and giggled and I told the whole story of how Jack had fooled me.

"Wow, Mariah," Miranda said archly, "he must have a thing for you."

"No, it was Rachel's idea, really. He just helped her."

Miranda gave me a funny look. "Yeah, she has a thing for you too. It's pretty weird."

"What do you mean?" I asked, perturbed at her tone.

"Nothing."

"I didn't even know you were back," I said, trying to change the subject.

"Sandy called me and said they were doing this thing. Sounded like fun."

"Are you back for good?"

"Yes, unless I don't get invited to the Lifeguard Ball."

"You will. I bet Trevor will ask you. He keeps asking me where you've been."

The Ball was the last big party of the summer thrown by the Beach Patrol at the Pier. Everyone in Avalon wanted to go, but you had to be invited by a lifeguard, which made it a very exclusive event. My friends and I had never been old enough to attend before, and so far as I knew, none of us had been asked.

"Hey." Rachel appeared from nowhere, smiling benignly at Miranda and me. I wondered if she heard any of our conversation.

"Hey Rach," I said warmly.

"So you were surprised right?" she said.

"Totally."

She smiled, looking genuinely happy.

"Look, Trey's here," Miranda said, pointing. All the girls looked, including me. It was the natural thing to do when Trey came in. To our surprise, he had a girl with him. We all gasped. Trey had a girlfriend? Since when?

She was petite, a good foot shorter than Trey, and cute rather than beautiful, with a pert expression, large blue eyes, blond hair pulled into a high ponytail. Very tanned, very fit. Trey had his arm around her, was leading her through the crowd toward a group of his friends.

"Wow," Miranda said. "Perky." We all laughed.

"Do you know anything about her?" I asked.

"She's a professional surfer, I heard," said Julie, one of the other girls.

"She looks older than him," said Miranda.

"Yeah, a couple of years anyway."

We all tried to absorb this information.

"She's totally wrong for him," Rachel said, her voice surprisingly harsh. We all giggled at that. No, she was not the Amazonian warrior princess I had always imagined.

Trey caught my eye and started toward me, working through the crowd, the girl attached to his arm.

"Here they come," Miranda said. "Tanya, stop staring!" We giggled again.

"Happy Birthday Mare," Trey said, kissing me on the cheek.

"It's not really my birthday," I said, watching the girl to see how she reacted to the kiss on the cheek. It was a big brother kiss, but still, her face showed only pleasant apprehension.

"Then it's your very first beach birthday party," he said. "This is Robin. She's visiting from California."

"Hi," Robin said cheerfully, shaking my hand. "Happy Sweet Sixteen!"

California? Trey had a girlfriend in California? That made her a "California girl." The kind the Beach Boys sang about. How did he meet a girl from California?

As if she knew what I was thinking, Robin answered. "I met Trey when he came out for surfing camp last winter," she said very pertly.

"Wow," I said, "so you're a surfer?"

"She's the best female surfer in southern California," Trey said with genuine admiration. Robin blushed. "She taught me everything I know."

This was shocking news. That Trey learned to surf from this pert older woman in California was something I would never have dreamed.

"We tried to get him to stay for the summer last year," Robin said, inching closer to him, "but he insists on coming back to Avalon. Don't know why."

She did not mean to be insulting, but it still came out that way.

"That's nice that you came all this way for my birthday," I said with a straight face. "But you really didn't have to."

She laughed, predictably. "I have an aunt in Jersey. I mean, doesn't everyone? Seriously, I thought I should come visit her." She glanced at Trey. "Not just her, of course," she said, with a giggle I found a little tiresome.

Trey gave me a "well-you-asked-for it" look.

"Well, you'll be disappointed," Miranda said. "The surfing's not much here."

"Trey promised me to teach me to surf ages ago," I said. "But he never did."

"Why don't you come down to the beach tomorrow, and I'll give you a lesson," Robin said in a very friendly, non-threatening way. Miranda made a noise, maybe a laugh, and I glared at her.

"Uh, sure," I said.

"Tide's in a 7am," Trey informed us.

"Seven too early?" Robin asked me.

"No, that's great." I never got up before ten, but I wasn't going to tell her that.

"Great. I told Trey I would give Avalon a try. Should be fun. Bring your friends. Do you have a board?"

"I can get one," I said. Our neighbors had several surf boards that stood unused in their shed most of the summer.

"You're on your own," Miranda said. "Seven is too early for me!" The other girls seemed to agree.

We were interrupted by the arrival of the cake, which was shaped like a sandcastle, naturally. Jack took the mike and sang Happy Birthday a la Beach Boys' "Merry Christmas Baby"—just changing the words. Everyone joined in. I turned to Rachel to give her a hug, but she was gone. I looked around. It was like she had vanished into the air.

Jack coaxed me to come to the stage to open some silly gifts, a large inflatable shark, a plastic tiara, which I was to wear for the rest of the evening, some water wings (in case I decided to take a midnight swim), and lots and lots of homemade cards. I felt myself blush crimson, overwhelmed and deeply moved. I wanted it never to end.

I went home that night to my little room in the cupola, all my gifts and cards clutched in my arms, as if I carried my whole life with me, everything that mattered to a sixteen-year-old girl. And I fell asleep, curled up with my stash, Jack's kiss on one cheek and Trey's on the other, and hoped I would never have to wake up to an ordinary day again.

FOURTEEN

2003

I settle into the rhythm of life in Avalon, a slow, steady cadence, as regular as the roar of the waves heaving against the shore. I wake up early to the whispers of the ocean, put on the coffee and go for a walk on the beach. I cool off on the bracing water, return to the house for a cup of coffee and a bagel or crumb bun, if there are any left. Caroline sleeps in late on her days off, but she goes for a run before breakfast, so I have a few minutes alone on the deck to watch the sea. Sometimes Trey comes by, if there are workmen expected, to tell me what will be demolished or repainted that day. I make phone calls, mostly to accountants and lawyers and real estate agents, trying to divest myself of Jack's properties, liquidate some assets so I can pay for this senseless renovation I have undertaken.

If Caroline is home I try to get her to have breakfast with me, to tell me about her day, her new friends, trying to assess how she likes it here. She doesn't talk much. She likes the beach, surprisingly, but I can see she is rather lonely. She spends half her time texting her friends in North Carolina.

To cheer her up I take her shopping, letting her pick out things for the house, something she loves to do. We have gone to some of the pricey home stores in Avalon and Stone Harbor, but lately we find better deals and more selection inland, along Route 9. Caroline has a wonderful, eclectic sense of style. She knows what will look right in an old Victorian, what will make it seem more up to date without being out of place. She's much better at this than I am.

On days she works I go alone to the beach and read as much as I can, rereading the Arthurian legends of my grandfather's collection as if I could conjure his ghost back again, a ghost that has been silent since our arrival, since the day of the misplaced suitcases.

But the memory of my 16th birthday party stirs something in me, and I screw up my courage and make the trip up the narrow stairs to my old room in the attic. It looks so much like the day I left it that I am nearly breathless for a moment, but that could be due to the stifling heat. How did I manage to sleep here for so many years?

Everything is pink, an explosion of pink. Posters of disco stars peel from the walls. My inflatable shark, very deflated, lies dejected by the bed. I pull aside a pink shag throw rug on the floor and remove a couple of boards to pull up a faded shoebox, so dusty I can barely read the "Buster Brown" on the cover. Inside are all the cards I had received on that magical day of my sweet sixteen, as well as several pictures someone had taken and given to me. Among them was a picture of Trey and Robin, his arm around her, her wide California smile filling the frame. I wonder why I had saved that picture. There is another one of Rachel and me, arm and arm, mugging for the camera. I look at my narrow face and wild, frizzy hair and grimace. I notice, too, that even though I am grinning madly, my eyes look sad. My eyes droop slightly in the corners, so they always look a little hangdog. But why, on this, the happiest day of my life, did I look sad?

"Whatever happened to Robin?" I ask Trey one morning. He has come to supervise the roofers, making sure they used the materials we had ordered. But he isn't doing much supervising, and we lounge on the deck, drinking lemonade, while the work goes on over our heads.

"Robin?" he says, as if he doesn't remember. Then it seems to dawn on him. "Oh." He smiles. "Robin. The surfer."

"From California," I add.

"Right. We spent time together when I was out west. But it wasn't a...long-term thing. I don't know what she's doing now." He takes a sip from his glass.

"Remember the surfing lesson she gave me?" I ask.

"Yeah." Trey laughs. "You were pathetic."

"She was a bad teacher."

"You just didn't like her."

"Well, none of us did. Though I admit it was pure jealousy. Even Rachel hated her. And Rachel never hated anybody."

Trey doesn't answer; he is looking up, at the debris coming off the roof and crashing to the ground all around us. "Maybe this isn't such a good place to hang out."

I stand up to take a look for myself and just at that moment a large plank comes sliding down the roof. There is a loud, scraping sound and my eyes fill with dust and roofing particles and someone above yells "heads up!" I put my arms over my head defensively, but I don't get out of the way in time. I feel the roof crash against my wrist and head, and I fall in a shower of shingles.

"Mariah!"

I feel Trey's arms around me, lifting me, carrying me into the darkened living room. He puts me on the couch. My arm feels paralyzed, shot with pain.

"Does your head hurt?"

"No, my arm…"

I open my eyes, still stinging with dust, to see his anxious face close to mine. He wipes dust and strands of hair out of my face.

"I think your wrist is broken. You might need stitches too. I better take you to the emergency room."

I try to protest, but Trey lifts me up, and I ride in his arms to his truck, my head pressed against his shoulder. How often had I dreamed of this? Well, not quite this. My head is pounding. My wrist throbs. I notice the workmen standing around watching while Trey opens the side door and slides me into the seat. He shuts the door and goes to talk to the roofer, who looks at me nervously and nods. Then he gets in the truck and starts the engine.

"Hang on Mare…are you okay?"

"Yeah," I say. "I feel like an idiot." My arm is throbbing. I close my eyes for a while, holding my wrist cradled against me like a newborn. I feel blood trickling down the side of my face. I think of Jack, of the headache that had turned monstrous, lethal. Is this how it feels when your head is about to implode? He died in terrible pain. I try not to think about that.

"The foreman said that piece slipped," Trey says. "He's very sorry. Didn't realize you would be sticking your head out from the deck at that exact moment."

"My luck," I say. "Do you have a phone? I should call Caroline…"

"I'll call her when we get there."

The hospital emergency room is busy, this being high season. I walk into the lobby, leaning heavily on Trey, dimly aware of the dingy yellow walls and redolence of disinfectant. The attendant at the desk takes a cursory look at me and decides, apparently, that I will live. She hands Trey a bunch of forms and directs us to the plastic chairs to wait. Trey leads me to a seat. I am still holding my arm. The pain is worse, making me feel rather nauseous and warm.

"Sit here. I'll go and call Caroline," he says.

"Tell her I'm fine."

I wait impatiently for him to return.

"I left a message at the restaurant," he says, sitting beside me. "Pat said he would tell her right away."

"Okay."

I lean against him, my head on his shoulder, hoping he won't move. His arm is around me, holding me close. I glance around the wide room, at people waiting, gazing into space, leafing through old copies of Reader's Digest. They have a glazed look, as if they have been there for years, have no hope of getting out. None of them look particularly sick.

"I'm so stupid," I say, tears filling my eyes.

"Stop saying that."

"Remember the last time we were here? With Jack?"

"Yeah."

"It feels like another lifetime." I say.

He pulls a tissue from a nearby box and wipes my eyes for me. His touch is very gentle, as if he were afraid I might break.

"Yeah, maybe it was."

"Feels like it," I say. "Jack is dead, Trey. He's really dead. Sometimes I just don't believe it. I wake up and think maybe he's just gone to work early, or he's off on one of his golfing trips. It doesn't register. I've been living in a dream world, thinking I can go back to the way it was. That's why I'm holding onto the house, I think. Trying to go back to the way things were. When we were young and innocent and had the world ahead of us. I don't feel different. I feel like I'm that same person with the frizzy hair who danced on the beach and played Skeeball and hung around the lifeguard stand, hoping you would talk to me. Oops. Did I say that? Never mind. I'm such an idiot."

"God, Mariah, you are an idiot," he says, laughing at me. "You talk too much."

"I know. Do you remember my Sweet Sixteen party?"

"Yeah."

"That was the best night of my life. Jack did that for me. And Rachel. I want that again. I want that for Caroline. To have some moment in your life that you can look back and remember as truly happy, when you felt really loved."

Before he can respond, I hear my name called. I look up and see a nurse gazing at me sternly, and I wonder if she is the same nurse who was here twenty-five years ago when I came here with Jack. She looks the same. I have a weird sense that she recognizes me.

She takes me to a curtained area, then glances at Trey.

"Are you her husband?"

"No."

She gives him an assessing look and decides to let him stay with me. She asks me a series of questions, takes my temperature, briefly examines my wrist and my head and tells me to wait for a doctor. Another twenty minutes goes by before the doctor, a young Indian woman, pushes aside the curtain, smiles and examines my wrist and head.

"Looks broken. But your head looks okay. We'll clean that up."

She orders an x-ray, and when the wrist fracture is confirmed I am sent to another curtained area, where a PA plasters me up, cleans up the gash in my head, gives me a shot for the pain, hands me a prescription and tells me to come back in three weeks to have it removed. He also tells me to not get it wet and have a nice day. Then he is gone. We are alone.

I look at Trey and smile wanly. "I guess we're done."

"What about pain meds?"

"I've got Advil at home. It'll hold me for awhile." I think longingly of my Prozac and my AmBien. I think I even have a few Percocets stashed somewhere. "Let's just get out of here."

He nods, helps me off the gurney and out of the ER. The pain in my wrist has lessened, but my head hurts more. I lean into him, already dizzy from the shot.

"Mom!"

I look up to see Caroline running up the sidewalk. I stop, blinking, wondering how she got here. Then I see a golden-headed boy walking a little behind her wearing a beach patrol T-shirt. I feel my breath catch in my throat.

"Mom, good God, what did you do?" Caroline is saying. She is out of breath. The boy catches up, and I realize he is not as young as I first thought him to be. He is just slightly taller than Caroline, blond, slim but very fit, very tanned. A lifeguard. *Oh Lord*, I think to myself. *What now.*

"How did you get here?" I ask, ignoring her question.

"Ben drove me," she said. Then, "Oh, I forgot. Mom, this is Ben. I met him at the restaurant. And this is Trey Bennett, her…friend."

"Nice to meet you, Mrs. Pendergrast…Trey." He takes my hand, smiling. Then he looks at Trey and hesitates, as if unsure what to do. Trey puts out a hand to shake, though he too looks hesitant.

I guess him to be in his mid-twenties. He is completely adorable, with a kind of young-Brad Pitt twinkle in his creamy brown eyes. I wince, slightly, pretending it is from the pain.

"What happened?" says Caroline.

"I was in the wrong place when the roof was coming down," I say. There is an awkward silence.

"Which beach are you on?" Trey asks Ben.

"24th right now, but they move me around. I'm like a…fill-in."

"Are you off today?" I ask, perhaps a little too pointedly.

"Yeah…I was just at the restaurant when Caroline got the message, so I offered to give her a ride."

Convenient.

"That was nice of you. But Caroline can ride with us back to the house."

"Okay, sure," Ben says easily. He is smooth, I think. He gets it. "See you later Caroline." He smiles winningly at me.

We get back into the truck, all three of us in the front seat, me in the middle. The heat is suffocating. Trey starts the engine and opens the windows. He shifts and pulls out of the parking lot.

"He just gave me a ride, Mom. Don't have a coronary," Caroline says before I can get a word out. "He was being nice."

"Did I say anything? It was very gallant of him. He just seems…a little old for you."

"He's only twenty-four."

"And you are seventeen. What's a twenty-four year old doing on the beach anyway? Shouldn't he have a real job by now?"

"He's in law school. He took a year off to travel. He's been all around the world doing amazing things."

"Sounds fascinating," I say. "You two have had a lot of time to talk."

"Mom! You are way overreacting!"

"Well, that's my job."

Trey, through all this, is completely silent. "Sorry," I say to him. "You probably don't need to hear all this."

"No problem," he says. He sounds abstracted, as if he has not even been listening. I gaze at him, wondering what he is thinking about, trying to imagine what it is like for him, to never hear the sound of his own child's voice. I fall silent, feeling guilty for the way I am talking to Caroline, wishing I could take it all back.

We ride the rest of the way in silence, and as soon as we are back at the house Caroline gets out of the truck and slams the door, running into the house. I don't move, too tired to think of going in after her. Finally, in the dim, humid silence, Trey speaks.

"All the summers you spent here," he says, "your mom never knew what you were doing."

I look at him. "So I should just let her run amuck?"

He laughs. "She's smart. And grounded. I don't think she would do half the dumb things we did as kids."

I sigh. "I know. But something about that boy…he's much too old for her, don't you think?"

Trey is silent a moment. "He seems…like a good kid," he says finally. "Caroline was right, you know. You did overreact."

"I know. I just…I panicked. She's never had a boyfriend before. I just haven't dealt with the whole boy thing yet. I was hoping for a little more time." I blush, embarrassed.

"Maybe it's nothing. Maybe they're just friends."

"Really?" I almost laugh. "Have you seen him on the beach?"

"No," Trey says. "But I don't spend much time on the beach anymore. Morey's been trying to get me back as a trainer, but I told him no."

I could understand. After you've trained wild Afghan warriors to shoot Russian gunships out of the sky, how do you go back to showing college kids how to paddle a boat?

"Oh Trey," I say, "I'm sorry about unloading all that stuff on you in the waiting room. It seems so stupid and ridiculous now."

"It wasn't stupid."

I am beginning to feel the effects of the pain shot. I know I should get out of the truck right now before I say something I will regret. "I always could talk to you. You seemed to get things other kids didn't."

"We were Avalon kids," he says. Poor, he means, I guess. There is something behind his gaze that worries me. I try to imagine what he is seeing, the hundred horrors of life in Afghanistan, the story of his lost family that I still have not heard.

"You know I have always...loved you, Trey."

Did I really say that out loud? I am really losing it now.

"And what about now?" he says. I look at him, surprised. His eyes are earnest. He looks so different...exposed. I feel my eyes sting with tears; I try to wipe them away with my bad wrist and almost knock myself out. Trey laughs at that. He pulls me toward him, his hand on my neck. I think he is going to give me a hug, but instead he turns my face to his and kisses me, very slowly and deliberately, on the mouth. I am stunned, too stunned to respond at first, a mad panic rising in my chest, like jumping off a step and realizing it is a cliff a mile above water. I feel myself falling, with only his hand on my neck to keep me from crashing. My heart is pounding so hard I think he must feel it too.

He draws away very slowly, as if surprised by his own action. His thumb brushes across my cheek; a gesture of utter tenderness. I am helpless.

"I wanted to do that when I first saw you," he says, his eyes peculiarly light, shining. "I was expecting a sixteen year old girl with frizzy hair. But you grew into a woman, Mare. I never realized how beautiful you were."

"I'm not," I say, embarrassed, heat in my cheeks, my mouth still burning.

"All the more because you don't even know it."

"Trey," I say. "Neither one of us…"

"I know. It was just a kiss. Not a marriage proposal."

I laugh, the sound locked in my throat. I desperately need a tissue.

He is looking at the house. "I have to go up to Hoboken for a couple of days, see my mom. Looks like the roofers will be back tomorrow to finish. Do you think you can stay out of their way? Or should I send an ambulance just in case?"

"Very funny." I start to open the door but he stops me, gets out and comes around to help. I am glad of it, for I am still shaking so badly I'm not sure I can stand. He leads me to the house, up the steps and onto the couch in the living room.

"Do you have to go?" I ask as he straightens.

"Well…no, I guess not… What about Caroline?"

"Up in her room probably, with headphones on. She'll be mad for awhile."

"I see. Can I make you some dinner?"

"No." My stomach is still lurching. "Talk to me, Trey. Tell me. About Afghanistan. Please. I need to know this."

He is silent a long while, deciding. I wait, watching his face. Then he takes a seat on the chair opposite me. His eyes get that look again, a thousand miles away. Finally, he starts to talk.

FIFTEEN

"I spent my life living on the coast," he begins, "so it's ironic that I should end up in a country as landlocked as Afghanistan, a land with almost no water. A mountainous desert. A man once asked me how to get to America, and I told him you had to cross the ocean. He didn't know what an ocean was. He thought I was making it up. It was more than just going back in time, it was like living on another planet.

"How did I end up there? It's a strange story. I joined the army, then was recruited for the Green Berets. I loved it, the challenge, the adventure. It was like there were no rules, I could do anything. The military spends a lot of time and money making guys like me feel like we're invincible. I was sent into a lot of bad places to get rid of bad people. It was a little like lifeguarding. I felt I was doing something, I don't know, noble.

"After about three years I was recruited to join the paramilitary arm of the CIA, to help with the training of the mujahedeen in their war against the Soviets. It was considered the most dangerous mission there was, so everyone had to be volunteers. It was also really secret, which made it even more intriguing. So I volunteered. There was a real war going on over there, and I wanted to be in on it.

"That's when I got my first glimpse of Afghanistan. I was hooked. Don't know why. It was a hellhole, war torn, bombed out, miserable. Groups of mujahedeen would come to our camps to learn tactics and get weapons training. We were giving those Muslim fundamentalists an amazing concoction of weapons. It would cost us later on. But at the time we thought we were heroes, doing the right thing to defeat the Commies, make the world safe for democracy.

"Really, I think I learned more from them, at least about what was worth fighting for. Freedom. It's something we in America just don't think much about. We don't care about freedom. We want the government to do things for us, give us health care, bail us out if we default on our mortgages, pay us if we don't have a job. But freedom we take for granted. The Afghans would have probably fared better under Communist rule. The Soviets pumped money into the country for schools, hospitals, infrastructure. The Communists were liberating women, putting them in the workforce, allowing girls to attend school. Many people thought these were good things to have. But the Afghans didn't want a foreign nation coming into their land and bossing them around, no matter how many schools it built.

"They were untrained, unorganized guerrilla fighters, some of them way past their prime, armed with World War 1-era bolt-action rifles against the most sophisticated army in the world. But they totally believed they would win, because Allah was on their side. The more time I spent with them, the more I saw that this was not blind faith at all. Their faith had serious results. Because of it they refused to give up.

"Well, you don't want to hear my preaching about it. The Soviets withdrew eventually. I was discharged from the CIA and the Green

144

Berets. I came back to the States for a couple of months, but I couldn't stand it. So I went back with a contractor group who was doing reconstruction. They were based in Kabul. Kabul did not see a lot of fighting, so it was relatively untouched by the war. And more modern than people think. Women often held jobs and went uncovered there, probably due to the Soviet influence.

"That's where I met Arya. She owned a small teashop. It's hard to describe her. She was young but had an old soul, you know what I mean? She was gentle and graceful in a land with very little gentleness or grace. Her husband and brothers had been killed in the war. Her mother was sick, always sick, and Arya spent her life taking care of her. She had lost everyone she loved, her brothers, her father, all dead in the war. Yet she was not bitter. She believed in God absolutely, she believed God had a plan for her life. I had been impressed with the muj and their faith, but I always thought 'that's not for me.' I didn't need a higher power. I *was* a higher power. I could do anything. But she made me see that my view was very…small and self-centered. I wanted her sense of peace in the storm, something I could not find. Some people might look at a place like war-torn Afghanistan and say, 'there is no God.' Arya looked at it and said, 'This is why we need God.'

"She looked a little like you, actually. She had black hair and greenish eyes. Her skin was lighter than most Afghans—I think there must have been a westerner in her lineage. Which is not uncommon. We got married, secretly, through an imam she knew. It might not even be considered a real marriage here, but to us it was real. We lived above her shop with her mother for awhile. Civil war had broken out between the various political groups, and we made love in this little dingy apartment while bombs fells and gunfire rattled the windows. It was almost…romantic, I guess. We would lay huddled together and listen to bullets fly around outside, some of them hitting the walls of her shop in bursts. Once a bottle grenade broke the front window of the shop, but it didn't explode. Arya said God was protecting us.

"I wanted to take her out of Afghanistan, but she wouldn't leave her mother. So I stayed with her. Then, we had a son. We named him Robbie, after my father. I told Arya we needed to leave, to take Robbie to America so he could have a better life. She finally agreed with me, but it was too late; I applied for visas, but then the Taliban took power and the borders were closed. The government denied Arya an exit visa. I wrote to the Embassy in Islamabad, to the government in Washington. They told me I needed to leave, no American was allowed in Afghanistan, but I couldn't leave her, so I hid. I didn't think the Taliban would last. I just decided to wait it out.

"Things got worse and worse. Women were no longer allowed to own shops or to move about freely, so Arya lost her teashop. They just came in one day and shut it down, after taking anything of value. Farmers were forced to grow poppies for opium. Women had to wear burkas and were beaten if they showed their ankles. We survived...I don't know how. We scavenged. We stole. My years of clandestine work made me a pretty good thief.

"But we were mainly scared that the Taliban was taking young boys from their families and indoctrinating them in their own camps. It was worse than the Communists. We knew that sooner or later they would come for Robbie.

"Then Arya's mother died, because there was no hospital care to speak of in Kabul, especially for women. We decided to try to leave, to sneak across the border into Pakistan. I had many contacts in Kabul, people who could smuggle us out of the country, for a price. We hired a man to take us in his van, but he betrayed us, for opium, probably.

146

We were imprisoned for awhile. Arya was severely beaten. That was the worst thing…seeing that…"

He stops then. I see his body heave a little with the pain of memory. I wait, unable to say anything, allowing him to continue.

"Then there was 9/11, and the US invaded Afghanistan. Kabul fell in November, only two months after that. We had hope then, hope that we could finally get out.

"The city was a madhouse. I never saw so much destruction — the Taliban had tried to take it apart before they abandoned it. But the Pakistan Embassy was still standing. We had to wait in a line for three days to get in. We were then put on a waiting list. They said we could leave in three weeks for a refugee camp in Pakistan. From there I could find a way to get us out of Asia altogether.

"I was hopeful then that everything was going to be okay. We had survived, we had made it through the worst of it. Arya was just happy to be able to walk the streets again. She wanted to be out all the time. She had spent almost five years locked inside a house. It was wonderful for her, despite the destruction that surrounded us, the horrible state of the city. People were trying to rebuild their shops and houses from whatever they could find in the wreckage. That was the spirit of the Afghans — you knock them down and they get back on their feet and carry on. No whining. No complaining. They have been oppressed and abused for hundreds of years, but they never give up. They survive and survive and survive. They will be around long after the rest of us are gone.

"The marketplace went back to business, with women and men selling fruit and scarves on the street. It was our only entertainment, so we went every day. The day it happened, I remember, it was cold. Early December. I was thinking of Christmas back home, something I hadn't celebrated in twenty years. I was beginning to have a great longing for home, for America. It was the first time I could remember such a longing. I can't recall much about the blast. I remember…I was holding Robbie's hand and then all of the sudden it wasn't there anymore, and I felt as though I were flying through the air, and all I saw was blood, everywhere, nothing recognizably human. I heard screaming, horrible screaming, and I was screaming Arya's name, and Robbie's name, but I couldn't hear their voices…I couldn't see anything, there was so much fire and smoke and screaming. It was like nothing I had ever heard before. I found out later my eardrums had been blown by the blast. I woke up later…I don't even know how much time had passed.

"It was how I imagine the end of the world would look…just chaos and confusion and screaming, smoke and fire and crying. Lots of crying. Soldiers came, thank God they were Americans. They started organizing the bivouacking of the wounded. I tried to look for them…but I never found them."

I feel a great knot in my chest, a horror and rage and pity mixed in one giant stew. Trey has not moved, as if he has been transported to that place and he is not even present in his own body anymore. I think perhaps he has never quite moved on from that moment. I wonder how he has been carrying this around, silently, for so long, acting as if everything in his life was perfectly normal, with only an average amount of tragedy, like most of us.

"The Americans medivacked me to Ramstein where I spent a few weeks in the hospital, burns and the concussion and blown ear drums. Then they shipped me home. It still doesn't feel quite real to me…like I've just woken up from a 20-year nap, like Rumplestiltsken.

"It all seems so unfair. To have survived so much, and to be almost to the end of the journey, to have the goal in sight… Why didn't I see that bomber…I used to spend all my time on the streets studying people, looking for the suspicious ones. I had a sixth sense for trouble. But I wasn't paying attention that day…I let my guard down for a moment…this is what it cost me."

His eyes close, and I see in the set of his mouth how he would give anything to go back, to do that one moment over. As if he could have stopped it. I don't know what to say; tears are streaming down my face. I want to go to him and hold him, but I feel curiously unable to move at all.

"Trey," I say finally. "I'm…so sorry."

He doesn't say anything, as if he is played out, too exhausted to speak.

"Thank you for telling me," I say. "I know that was hard."

"Yes," he says. Then he sighs, pushes up out of the chair. "I'd better go."

I start to get up but he stops me. "Take it easy," he says. "I'll see you in a few days, okay?"

"Okay."

He leaves, and I am alone. I watch the light move slowly across the rug to the sofa, aged and yellowed. It must be long after seven. I feel steadier, and I decide it is as good a time as any to apologize to Caroline.

She is lying on her bed, fiddling with her iPod. Her phone is beside her, and I assume she has been texting her friends in Nags Head, reporting my latest atrocities. I stand in the doorway until she notices me and pulls the ear buds out of her ears.

"Hey," I say.

"Hey," she says. "Feeling better?"

"I'm okay," I say. "Good pain killer."

"Great."

I go and sit on the edge of the bed. She makes room for me without really looking up from the iPod. "Caroline. I'm sorry."

"For what?"

"For sounding like I was coming down on you. You were worried about me, you came to see if I was all right, and I didn't…greet you very well."

"It's okay."

"So Ben is in law school?"

"Yeah."

"Where?"

"Rutgers I think."

"Oh. Right up the road. Has he been coming to Avalon a long time?"

"No. Some of his old college friends got him to come. Because they needed good swimmers. For the competitions."

"So he swims?"

"Yeah. He almost went to the Olympics."

"Wow."

She is smiling now, talking of Ben, and I can see real admiration in her eyes. She has forgotten how angry she is with me.

"Yeah. When he didn't make the team he got pretty depressed. That's when he went on his travels. He wanted to do something amazing, you know, to prove to himself that he still could, even if it wasn't swimming. And he did cool things. He worked with relief organizations in Bangladesh, India, Pakistan, all over. One of his jobs was to run medicine from airports to these remote villages, and he had to find all kinds of ways to do it, borrowing vehicles, motorbikes, hiking, rickshaw, anything he could find, because they couldn't afford to give him a truck. He ended up getting a truck for them, though. From the US government! He has an uncle in Congress, apparently."

I listen in silence, watching her eyes as she speaks. Ben has opened her up to a world outside her small, safe universe. Something I wish I had done for her. I had built a stronghold around her, as around myself, thick stout walls to keep out trouble, to keep out pain. I had tried to inoculate us both against any sort of real experience. I thought I was doing the right thing. But she had seen the world and its possibilities. She wanted more.

"I saw him kiss you," she says suddenly. I stare at her. "In the truck."

"That was nothing."

"It didn't look like nothing to me, Mom."

I sigh. "Things aren't always what they seem, Caroline."

"Yeah? Well, that's what I'm trying to tell you. Ben's nice, and he's smart, and he's fun to talk to. And I think you should try to get to know him a little better before you jump to conclusions."

I nod. "Fair enough. Invite him to dinner."

She looks alarmed. "What? Here?"

"No, we'll go out. The Princeton. Friday. Ask him."

"Are you sure you're up for that? With your arm and all?"

"I can still hold a menu," I say.

"Is Trey going to come too?"

"Do you want him to?"

"Yeah, sort of. I mean, it would be less pressure on Ben, I think."

"You mean, if your mom had a boyfriend too? Look, Caroline, whatever you saw happen, it was just…one of those moments. That's all it was."

"Sure Mom." She sounds a little less frigid. I take a chance and edge closer to her. "Are you still mad at me for bringing you here?"

She shakes her head. "I guess not. I still don't get it though. Why are we here? Why did you want to come back to this crummy old house? And this thing with Trey—I mean, I like him, and all, but God, Mom, Dad hasn't even been dead a year yet…"

A year and three weeks, I think to myself. But who's counting.

"I know it's crazy. I think I *am* crazy most days. But this house, this island…it is so much a part of me. I had forgotten how much. This was home, Caroline. I know that's how you feel about Nags Head, but without your father there…it just seemed so empty."

"Yes, I know," she admits. "But I didn't think you'd care. You and Dad…you were always going in opposite directions."

Did she really notice this? It's true, I realize. He had his practice, his golf, the undying love and affection of our only child. I had the house, the book clubs, the 9-holers, the ladies' luncheons. Jack was always happy, though. He thought it was the perfect life. He didn't understand my discontent. What more do you want? he'd ask. Then he'd buy another house, or car, thinking that must be it. He lavished gifts on both Caroline and me. Every Friday a dozen roses were delivered to my door. My neighbors thought I was the luckiest woman in the world, to have such a romantic husband. For me, those roses were more like treats proffered to a favored mistress. I told him to stop. I didn't need gifts. But it was his way, the only way he knew of expressing his love. His father had been the same, and his mother had lived for what she got in return, the beach houses, the ski houses, the fur coats, the jetting off to the Alps. It took me a long time to realize that what I really wanted from him he could not give me. Jack collected people, and I was part of his vast collection, more privileged, perhaps, but otherwise not very different. What I needed was to feel like a real person, capable of something in the world. Perhaps this house, this project, was my way of asserting myself, of saying for once and all that I have something to offer the world, even if it doesn't count for very much. But I was failing at this, as I was failing at parenting Caroline.

"I thought…you just wanted to get away from him. And get me away too," she says softly.

"No, no…" I say, reaching a hand to touch her face. She pulls back only slightly. "I felt closer to him here than I ever did there. This is where we began, your father and I."

She shrugs. "You never told me about it."

"Do you want to hear it?"

"Sure."

So as the sunlight slides away and the room darkens I tell her about Avalon in 1978, about meeting her father on the beach, about Rachel, the boat accident, about everything…almost everything…I can remember. Twenty-five years later that summer still shines bright and real in my memory as if it were yesterday. I play it like a movie in my head, over and over, the summer I chose the path for my life.

SIXTEEN

August 1978

The college kids would leave Avalon around the middle of August, and things would get pretty quiet after that. Jack was going to Columbia. Trey had never mentioned college, or any plans at all. I wondered if he would join the army, as his father had done. Vietnam was over, so many guys were thinking the army might be a safe career path now. Of course, he might just stay in New Jersey and take over his father's business, maybe even take over Morey's job someday. I still could not imagine him anywhere else but this beach.

The only thing left to look forward to was the Lifeguard's Ball. In the early years it was a fancy, dress-up affair, but now it was just a giant party attended by the lifeguards and whoever they wanted to invite. I was finally old enough to go, but I wasn't sure if anyone would ask me. Trey took a different girl every year, usually friends of his sister Rita. But Rita and most of her friends did not come to Avalon anymore. Rita had gotten a real job in New York City. And as far as I knew, Robin had gone back to California.

I spent the Saturday before the ball at the Wildwood Lifeguard Championship with Rachel and Miranda and Sarah. Tanya had a new boyfriend and sat with him on a towel, kissing through the entire competition. Miranda and I thought it was disgusting. Rachel just stared at them.

"Who is that guy?" she asked me. "He gives me the creeps."

"No one knows," I said.

She looked away finally. "Want to go for a walk?"

"Sure." Neither Trey nor Jack would be up for awhile. We got up and walked down the beach, and Rachel made a game of scattering the sandpipers. She thought they were hilarious, the way they dashed toward the sea when the tide went out and then ran madly back up the beach on their spindly little legs when the ocean came back in.

"Kind of what we do, all the time," she said. "I really just wanted to talk to you, alone."

I waited, my heart hammering. There was something in her voice that told me I would not like what she wanted to talk about. Did she know about my feelings for Jack? Was she finally going to confront me about it, once and for all?

"I've decided to…do it," she says.

It took me a minute to realize what she was talking about.

"You mean, with Jack?"

She didn't answer.

"Why?" I said, kind of incredulous. "Do you feel like you have to or something?"

"Well…no…and yes. I don't know. That's why I'm telling you. Because you are the only person in the world I could think of who I could talk to. You know? You're like the big sister I never had. Not that you're older than me, but you're wiser, and you seem to have your head together, which I definitely don't."

156

"Wiser? Than you? Are you kidding? I've read your poetry, Rach. I know you're way smarter than me."

"I'm not talking about that kind of smart. But you really do underestimate yourself, don't you? No...I'm talking about wisdom. Making good choices, as my shrink would say."

That sent me into a swirl of panic. Why would she tell me this? I didn't want to know this. More than that, I needed to stop it from happening somehow.

"Well, if you want my opinion, then don't do it. It's a bad idea. You could get pregnant, for one thing. Or you could get...something else. But more than that...are you totally sure you really *want* to? Because Rachel, listen to me, once you do that thing, you've given away something you can't get back."

"Yeah, I know."

"No, it's more than *just* that...it's something so special and secret...it's a piece of your soul. Are you really ready to give all that to a boy? Do you love him that much?"

She shrugged. "I feel like I won't know if I do or not until I...do it."

"I don't think it works that way."

"So you speak from experience? You've done it?"

"No, of course not."

"Then how do you know?"

"I just do. Anyway, you asked for my opinion. So there it is."

She was silent awhile. Then she started to sing, kicking at the tidal pools as she went...

Bobby Shaftoe's gone to sea,
Silver buckles on his knee;
He'll come back and marry me,
Pretty Bobby Shaftoe.

She did that sometimes, break into nursery rhymes. She seemed to know a lot of weird ones. Those were the times when I thought I was losing her; that she was losing her grip.

"Maybe you're right," she said finally, sounding fairly sane. "Maybe I should wait." She looked back toward the competition. "I think the boys will be up soon. Let's go back."

2003

The Princeton is packed. The crowd is not as young as it used to be back in the day. I think the same people who came here as lifeguards and college students still returned, while the new lifeguards and college students had found someplace newer and hipper to hang out. It looks its age, dated and homely, the kind of place that teenagers were forced to rent when they "had" to get married. The walls are still paneled in dark brown, the rugs are red, the tables that chunky wood found in "Steak and seafood" places, the kind that put "Cocktails" in neon on their road signs.

Not that Caroline seems to mind. I made reservations but we are still waiting twenty minutes after we arrive, and the hostess seems in no hurry to seat us. I stand by the hostess station, jostled by people trying to get by me, determined that she will not forget our existence. Trey is standing near the coat racks, grinning like a Cheshire cat at me. Caroline and Ben sit together on the waiting area bench, smiling foolishly at each other.

Finally, I walk back to where Trey is standing and glare at him.

"What?" I say.

158

"It's just funny seeing you...in your element," he says, trying to suppress his grin.

"You mean me fuming because I'm not getting my way?"

"Something like that."

I huff. "Don't you have any friends here you could talk to?"

"I'll see what I can do." He disappears into the crowd, and minutes later we are called to a table in one of the private dining rooms, those reserved for special events. Trey doesn't say anything about it, and I decide it is better not to ask. At least, I think, it will be quieter, and we can cross-examine Ben in relative peace.

I say "we" because I assume that Trey will be on my side in this. Seven years is a big age gap when the girl is only seventeen. And despite the fact that Ben is obviously a decent, grounded young man with seemingly honorable intentions, I am still uneasy.

We order drinks and laugh a little at our sudden elevation to royal status while the waitress goes to fill the order. Ben is particularly impressed.

"So you must be kind of a big shot around here, Mr. Bennett," he says to Trey, who I think actually blushes.

"No, just a lot of the guys from the old days are still here, working at these places, and they all owe me favors. I unplug a lot of toilets in this town."

We all laugh. Caroline, I think, laughs a little too much.

"Morey still talks about you," Ben says. "You and the guys from that time, the seventies. That was like some kind of golden age for the Beach Patrol, I think."

"Yeah, that's what we think anyway. I used to meet the old-timers at the lifeguard parties and hear all about the real glory days, the forties and fifties. An Avalon Lifeguard back then was really king of the beach. And those guys were tough, let me tell you."

"Yeah?"

"Go over to the museum sometime and check out the pictures. Some of their old surfboards are there too. You should see what those guys surfed on—you'd know how tough they really were."

"Cool."

The drinks arrive and we toast and take sips. The waitress takes our order, writing things down nervously. She is very young and I think this is her first day of waitressing. After she is gone I turn to Ben, deciding that the small talk has gone on long enough.

"So tell me how you two met," I say. Caroline glares at me, but I ignore her.

"Well, we met at the pancake house…the guys usually go there in the morning before the shift starts…honestly, Mrs. Pendergrast, I thought she was a lot older…"

I have heard this before, but he seems sincere.

"So where are you from?"

"Upstate…Princeton."

"Are your parents still there?"

"I lived with my grandparents."

I want to ask about that, but decide not to. I glance at Trey, who is staring at his drink.

"So…where did you do your undergrad? Princeton?"

"No, Penn State. I wanted to get out of Princeton. It was kind of…stuffy."

How ironic that we should be in a restaurant called "The Princeton." But I seem to be the only one who notices.

"Now you are at Rutgers? Law School?"

"Well, I took a year off, but I plan to go back in the fall."

"Oh yes, traveling, Caroline told me. So how did you find your way here?"

"Some guys I knew from Rutgers recruited me. Said they needed swimmers. I needed a place to live. So it's worked out pretty well. We're renting a house, six of us, it's messed up. But I like it. So Mr. Bennett, what was it like back then? Was Morey the same bad ass he is now?"

Trey laughed at that. They talk more about the beach patrol, Trey recounting some of his more memorable rescues.

"I rescued a dog once," he says.

"I thought dogs weren't allowed on the beach," Caroline says.

"They aren't, but sometimes they got on anyway, and this one dog, some kind of lab, it was running all over the beach and no one could catch it. You should have seen us all, chasing this stupid dog. Finally, it goes charging into the surf—I think someone threw a Frisbee—and before you know it the dumb dog is out in the waves and way over his head. I dove in after him. By the time I got to him he was pretty much exhausted, so I grabbed him around the neck and hauled him back in. Everyone had lined up along the beach to watch. They all cheered when I brought this dog in. Best rescue I ever did."

The food finally arrives and we all start eating. In the ensuing silence I want to ask questions I know I shouldn't ask: why does he live with his grandparents? Are his parents dead? Divorced? Drug addicts? What are his intentions with my daughter? Why does he have to be so gosh-darned likeable? My job, as Parent, is to uncover his deep, dark, ugly secrets, to prove to Caroline that he is no good for her. Other than the dropping out of law school (for noble reasons) part, I'm finding this exceedingly difficult.

"Do you see your grandparents much?" I ask, hoping his answer will give me a glimpse into his family life.

"My grandmother is coming up in a few weeks," Ben says, not very helpfully. "My grandfather has not been feeling good, so I don't think he's going to come with her."

"Well, that's a shame," I say. I try to think of another probing question, but Trey interrupts to ask about some upcoming race, and they are off again. I glance at Caroline, who is gazing at Ben, clearly entranced. I remember that, the look on her face, I remember feeling as she feels now. For a moment, I think I am even envious of her.

After dinner we stroll down Dune Drive, commenting on the shops and the attractions, reminiscing about what used to be there. Trey and I vigorously disagree on this, which Ben and Caroline seem to find extremely funny. We stop for ice cream at Avalon Freeze then Ben bids us goodbye and takes off down 23rd toward the bay. Caroline looks at me hopefully.

"What do you think?"

"He's nice," I say. "And smart. And cute. And twenty-four. That's the part I have a problem with."

"Mom…" she says, exasperated.

"Hey kid," Trey says, "just take it slow, okay?"

She looks wide-eyed at him, as if he had betrayed her deeply. "But you like him, don't you?"

"Sure," Trey says. "But he's still a guy, after all."

He grins, but his meaning is clear. Caroline purses her lips. "Well, I'm not going to do anything stupid," she throws at us, as if *we* are the ones who are stupid. I had forgotten that, at seventeen, she knows everything.

We get in the truck to head back to the Pink Poodle. The ride is very quiet. Caroline is out the door before Trey has even rolled to a stop.

"Wanna take a walk?" he asks me, smiling. I nod. We get out of the truck and head toward the beach path.

"I just don't get her, I guess," I say as we walk. "Seems like no matter what I do or say, it's going to be wrong."

Trey laughs. "Isn't that the definition of teenager-hood? She's just finding her way. You push, she pushes back."

I sigh. "I'm overprotective, I know. She was an only child, and it took us so long to have her, so many procedures, tests, miscarriages…I was in bed for seven months. But I made it to term with her. She was our miracle baby. Jack was beside himself. I thought he might mind that she wasn't a boy, but it didn't matter to him. And as it turned out, they had so much in common. Jack indulged her every whim. She wanted a horse, she got a horse. She wanted to go skydiving, they went skydiving. Meanwhile I was just…afraid, most of the time. She fell off the horse and broke her arm and I was apoplectic…"

"Stop it," Trey says. "You'll drive yourself crazy."

"I did. I drove both of them crazy too. But she was fearless, like Jack. Fearless. With no thought of…consequences."

"That's a good word for him," Trey says.

"He was so full of life…so full of himself," I say. "There really wasn't room for me."

Trey stops, looking at me. I see his expression.

"I don't mean he ignored me. It's just that he…*consumed* me. I felt like I didn't exist when he was in the room. Do you know what I mean?"

He pulls me to him, cradling my bad arm. His embrace is so warm and comfortable and I want to crawl inside it and curl up and sleep. "I'm sorry," I say, still babbling, "I shouldn't be laying all this on you. You were his friend, for a time anyway." I pull away, looking into his eyes. "I had hoped you would come to the wedding, but I guess you were already gone by then. Jack said he called but couldn't reach you."

"I got his message," Trey says. "But…well, it was a bad time. I'm sorry I missed it. How did the two of you finally hook up anyway?"

We are walking again. We hit the sand and I take off my sandals. I pull my wrap tighter around me, in protection from the wind, from him.

"At Columbia," I say. "I went there, one of the first classes to accept women. It was Rachel's dream — I ended up living it for her."

"You went to Columbia?"

"Yeah, Jack encouraged me to, actually. We'd been writing, back and forth. No one thought I could get into Columbia. But I got in, and I even got a scholarship. The money from the rental of the Pink Poodle paid for the rest. I kind of always wondered if Jack had pulled some strings to get me in there…but he never told me.

"I didn't like New York at first. But every day I could walk to Riverside Park by the river, and it felt sort of comforting…I think I will always need to be near water.

"One thing led to another, as they say. Jack and I started dating, officially, much to his parents' chagrin. We never talked about…what happened. It seemed to me that Jack had simply erased it from his memory. He could do that. He was great at denial.

"We got married right after he graduated. He went to Cornell med, because that's where his father went. It's in New York, but on the east side. I ended up quitting school. I just didn't see the point, I guess. From the moment I first saw him all I ever wanted to be was…Jack's wife."

We get to the end of the beach by the rock jetty, watching the waves crash against the stones. Trey seems lost in thought, his mind somewhere else. I study him, remembering how he once looked, the golden boy on the beach. I am caught by memory of us as we were then, young and tanned and full of promise, straining toward the world before us. Now we return in middle age, world-weary and broken-hearted, looking to recapture something we hope is still here, in this place. But everything is different now.

I start to turn away, to head toward the house, but he stops me. He takes hold of my arm and draws me in, and I am stunned again, at the suddenness of his presence, his mouth on mine, his hand against my neck. I put my good arm around him, steadying myself, sure that I will fall, spinning, like Alice through the looking glass, my vision clouded with starlight and wind and Trey. I pull away from him, gasping for breath, my whole body seeming to melt from under me. He holds me still, pressed against him. I whisper softly:

"Why did we ever leave Avalon?"

He doesn't answer.

SEVENTEEN

August 1978

The stars were out that night. Pegasus, the winged horse tamed by Neptune and used to carry thunder and lightning across the sky. Sagittarius, the centaur, who changed himself into a horse to escape his jealous wife Rhea. Cygnus, the Swan, stricken with grief over the death of his friend. Lyra, the lyre, used by Orpheus to charm Euridice, to draw her from the pit of Hades. Andromeda, the maiden in chains, sacrificed to the sea monster by her own mother but rescued by Perseus, rescued for Love. What a story of love and sadness the stars tell.

My grandfather was fond of constellations, as he was fond of all magical, mysterious things. He had a telescope he kept in his cupola, and on clear nights he cast it out to the eastern sky of Avalon and told me the stories of the stars. I could not always see the shapes myself, they are the fanciful conjurings of ancient people, but I loved the stories, the tragic romance, the noble deaths. Like Arthur and Guinevere, those are the stories that endure.

I stood on the boardwalk and stared at the stars in my silver high heeled sandals and white eyelet summer dress with spaghetti straps, a dress my mother had bought me out of the blue, one day, on one of her rare visits to Avalon. It wasn't a fancy dress, but it felt right for this night, and I felt like a real girl wearing it. My mom had been surprised to hear I was going to the ball, and especially that I had been invited by Trey, though I was quick to point out that we were just going as "friends." Trey had only asked me because he knew I wanted desperately to go, and apparently he didn't have anyone else to ask. Still, it was a dream come true for me; I would walk into the Avalon Pier on the arm of Trey Bennett. No one needed to know the rest of the story.

"Mare?"

I turned to see Trey staring at me quizzically. I flushed, wondering what sort of expression had been on my face as I stared at the heavens.

"Hi," I said.

"You looked a little spaced."

"Yeah. Well, I was trying to find Scorpius," I said quickly.

"Scorpius?"

"The god who killed Orion. Well, you see, Orion was a great hunter, but he was always bragging about his hunting skills, and the other gods got kind of sick of it, so they sent Scorpius — the Scorpion — to kill him. Orion didn't take Scorpius very seriously, because he was such a little creature, and so he was killed by the scorpion. But his last wish was that he would never be placed in the sky with the scorpion, so that's why Orion is only visible in the winter, and Scorpius in the summer."

Trey smiled. "You sure do know a lot of useless stuff."

I shrugged. "I think it's interesting," I murmured.

"Those stories never seem to turn out very well though," Trey said grimly.

"That's what makes them beautiful."

We looked at each other for a moment. Then I started to laugh.

"I'm so weird," I said.

"Got that right." He stuck his elbow out so I could take it. "Are you ready, m'lady?" He said mockingly. He didn't know how much I thrilled to hear him say it.

"As you wish, Sir Knight," I said, and burst out laughing again.

The dance floor was already packed by the time we got into the hall, with disco lights spinning crazily around the room, making the normally drab, peeling vanilla walls burst with motion. The band, the *Screaming Meamies,* certainly lived up to their name, so that it was impossible to hear anything or anyone else. Trey led me through the crowds, which seemed to part before us, faces turning to him and smiling, greeting him. Some chanced to look at me too, but not many. I scanned the crowd for Rachel and Jack, but I saw no sign of them.

Trey greeted his housemates and was soon absorbed into their midst, leaving me alone. I felt a nudge in the middle of my back and turned to see Miranda. She grabbed by arm without speaking and led me off to the side.

"Big news," she said. "Rachel's not coming."

"Yes she is, I talked to her like, an hour ago," I said, annoyed with Miranda for her constant disparagement of Rachel.

"Uh uh. Jack told Trevor that she locked herself in her room and won't come out."

"Oh God. I better go and get her," I said, turning to leave.

"You're going to get her?" Miranda sounded incredulous. "Why?"

"Because she's obviously upset and needs help," I said. *What did Jack do to upset her?* I wonder. I thought, fleetingly, of my conversation with her on the beach, and I had a sinking feeling in the pit of my stomach. "Do me a favor, go and tell Trey I had to go get Rachel, and I'll be back as soon as I can."

"What's the point? She's crazy, everyone knows it." Miranda said.

"She's not crazy!" I said, angry. "She's just…confused. She needs a friend."

"Man, Mariah, you are so…delusional."

"Just please go tell him, will you?"

I turned away and made my tortuous way back through the hall and down the main exit stairs to the boardwalk. In truth, I was glad to be out of the heat and noise of that place, though my ears were still ringing. I took the wooden stairs down to the street and walked the five blocks to the Grain Elevator. I could hear noises from within, terrible noises, like the sound of breakable things crashing and doors pounding and the thin cries of a girl. I stood there a long time, listening, wondering if I should knock on the door at all.

Just then the door opened. Jack stood in the portal, his face flushed with what seemed to me to be terror. He grabbed my arm and pulled me inside.

"Go talk to her," he said breathlessly. "Please. She's gone nuts."

Stunned, I stumbled up the stairs to the main floor, in the direction of the crying. Jack followed a short distance, then stopped, letting me go alone. In the kitchen I saw his mother, leaning against the counter smoking a cigarette and blowing the smoke up, her chin jutting out as she did it. Her eyes were on Jack, her expression blank.

I looked away from her and moved toward the door. I stood there a moment, listening. Then I knocked.

"Go away!" Rachel shrieked from within.

"It's me," I said.

A moment later, the door opened. I slipped through, shutting it again behind me. The room was a shambles, clothes and books everywhere, a broken lamp and pictures half hanging on the walls. Rachel herself was dressed in her gown, a shimmering gold confection I would have died to own, let alone fit into. Her hair, done into an Audrey-Hepburn upsweep, was in disarray, her mascara running, her eyes swollen with tears. I didn't know what to say, so I held out my arms and she fell into them, her whole body rattling with sobs.

"Rachel, what happened? What's wrong?" I asked. "Can you tell me?"

She clearly couldn't.

"Is this about…what we talked about on the beach?"

I felt her head move against my chest. After awhile I pushed her gently away from me and looked into her eyes.

"Rachel, talk to me. Please."

"I can't go out there…" she whispered in my chest. "I just can't. I can't even look at him."

This was worse than I thought it would be. I tried to think of something to say, something comforting. But what I felt was anger. Anger at Jack. Anger at myself. Anger at…something. I gripped her shoulders and pushed her away from me.

"Rachel," I said, "I know this is hard, but you have to clean yourself up and go to that ball. If you don't, everyone will be talking about you and there will be all kinds of rumors and you don't want that. You need to get yourself together, and I am going to help you."

I took her into her bathroom and washed her face and applied fresh makeup. I fixed her hair as best I could, using as much hairspray as her thin hair could hold. Her eyes were still red-rimmed, but her face looked smooth and pale as always.

"Just say you stabbed yourself with the mascara and that's why your eyes are all red. And you couldn't see for a while because your eye hurt so bad. And…you think you are coming down with a cold. Okay?"

She nodded slowly.

"Are you ready to go out there?"

She didn't answer, but she breathed deeply, the spasms subsiding. She seemed suddenly completely calm, composed. I was amazed at her transformation.

"Let's go," she said.

I opened the door and we walked out together into that soaring living room. Jack was where I had left him, standing by the couch with his hands in his pockets, looking sheepish and alone. I glanced into the kitchen, but his mom was gone. Jack looked at me with deep gratitude, then went to Rachel, putting his hand out for her to take. She hesitated, then took it, breathing deeply.

"Are you ready to go?" he asked.

"Yes." I saw that she could not look directly at him. "I'm sorry," she murmured. "I had some…hair trouble," I looked at Jack and saw that he was enormously relieved.

By the time we got back to the Pier the band was taking a break, and the crowd had dissipated somewhat. Someone had finally opened the windows along the sea side so the air felt cooler, more breathable.

Jack's entrance was instantly acknowledged; the two of them were engulfed by a crowd. I hung back, forgotten. I felt a touch on my arm and turned to see Trey looking down at me. He looked worried.

"Everything all right?"

"Yeah. Rachel just needed some help…with her hair. One of those hair emergencies, you know." I told him the mascara story too, for good measure.

Trey looked dubious. His gaze drifted to Jack and Rachel. "Well…I'm glad you were able to help," he murmured.

"Sure, no big deal. Maybe you could get me some punch or something?" I offered, nudging him with my elbow. "It's the least you could do."

He looked at me blankly a moment, as if he had forgotten who I was. "Sure," he said.

I followed him to the "under 18 bar," where several huge punch bowls stood with little plastic cups stacked beside them. He poured a cup and handed it to me without really looking at me.

"I'm going to grab a beer, okay? I'll be right back." With that, he disappeared into the separate room which housed the "over 18" bar. I waited, feeling awkward. Trey did not come back for a long time.

The band started to play and I decided to dance. Miranda and Tanya were already out there, so I marched out to join them. As usual, the girls were dancing, and the boys were drinking.

I pulled the pins out of my hair and let it go free, filling my body up with the disco beat, screaming the lyrics at the top of my lungs. This was pure forgetting, pure energy, pure emotion. I didn't think about Trey or Jack or Rachel.

During a break between numbers I ran up to the bandstand and begged for them to play "If I Can't Have You," which they did. Miranda and Tanya and Sarah and I danced as we had that first night, huddled in a circle, our arms draped around each other, shouting out the lyrics:

If I can't have you,
I don't want nobody baby,
if I can't have you…

Once the song was over the front man of the band, a handsome black guy with long dread locks, started speaking into his microphone, saying how they wanted to slow it down for a bit and that all the couples should hit the dance floor. The band started to play "Precious and Few" and the girls and I groaned in disappointment. We shuffled off the dance floor to make room for the couples. I looked around for Trey, but he was nowhere in sight. Dumped by my date. It was humiliating.

"Mariah."

Someone touched my shoulder and I swung around to see Jack before me. I was suddenly aware of my sweat-drenched skin, my disheveled hair, the white dress sticking to my ribcage. I pushed a lock of curls out of my face self-consciously and tried to smile.

"Dance with me?"

I opened my mouth. "What about…"

"She doesn't want to dance."

"Oh."

He didn't wait for an answer, and I didn't resist as he pulled me onto the dance floor with other couples, most of whom were hanging on each other in that boneless way teens do. I felt the blood rush to my face so that I thought I might be coming down with prickly heat. Neither Trey nor Rachel were anywhere in sight. Tanya and Sarah were drinking punch and waving at me. Miranda was smirking.

"I wanted to thank you," he said, once we started swaying together. "You saved my life."

"I didn't do it for you," I said sharply, angered by his self-centeredness. "I did it for her. What happened, Jack? What got her going?"

I doubted he would tell me the truth. But he looked troubled, his eyes searching. "I don't know. I was sitting in the living room, talking to my mom, waiting for her to come out of her room. But she never came out. I went and knocked, but she just screamed at me to go away.

Then we started to hear her crying, breaking things. The guys were waiting for me out on the deck, so I just told them to go on without me, that we would be a little while. I tried to talk to her, my mom tried, through the door, but nothing seemed to work. I didn't know what to do. I was thinking of calling the EMTs…when you showed up."

"And you have no idea what brought it on?"

"She seemed fine all day."

Could he really be that oblivious? I guess he could, I thought. He had no idea what he had done to her.

"Jack, is there anything that has gone on between the two of you…something that might have upset her?"

"I don't know. We went to the movies the other night, and she started crying during the movie and when I asked her what was wrong she ran out of the theater. We were watching *Grease*, which I didn't think was all that sad or anything…so I figured it was just her time of the month or something…well, she can be a little crazy sometimes."

I wanted to be angry with him, to turn and walk away from him, to even throw what he had done in his face so that he would have to live with the shame and the guilt of it forever. But I looked into his dark eyes, eyes that seemed genuinely confused and sad, and I found I could not move from his embrace, that to be there, in his arms, was all that mattered to me anymore. Rachel faded from my mind.

"Well," I heard myself say, "she is so much more sensitive than the rest of us…"

The song played on.

Precious and few are the moments we two can share….

Quiet and blue like the sky I'm hung over you…

The song ended and we stopped moving, standing awkwardly in the sea of sweaty bodies. He kissed me on the cheek. Then he walked me off the dance floor and delivered me into the company of my friends. The band started playing reggae, and Miranda wanted to dance again. But I could hardly stand. "You go ahead," I told her. "I'm going out onto the deck for a bit."

"Sure, cool down," Miranda said, laughing. The other girls laughed too. "You're not fooling anyone, you know." She fixed me with an accusing stare. I turned away without saying anything.

I went out to the deck, sucking in the salty air as if I'd just surfaced from deep water, my head reeling from love and pain and an inner sickness I could barely endure. I looked out to the ocean. It was almost completely dark except for the lights along the fishing pier that seemed to disappear out into the black water.

"I'm sorry."

I turned. It was Rachel, standing alone in her gold dress.

"I'm sorry for being so crazy. I'm sorry for causing you so much trouble. You and Jack. And everyone. I'm a big pain. I'm sorry, Mariah."

"You shouldn't be sorry for who you are," I said. I reached out to take her hand. "You're special, Rachel. You should be treated…special."

She laughed. "I'm not that special. I think Jack has had enough of me. I think we're going to be done, after tonight."

"No, Jack loves you," I said, and a part of me really meant it.

"You were right, Mariah," she said with the same eerie softness, "you were right, about losing a piece of your soul. You can never get it back."

I saw a quicksilver tear track down her cheek. She turned her face to the wind, leaning over the railing, dangerously, I thought: she is so light she could be swept up in a little gust and carried off.

"I wish we could go over to the Pink Poodle now and put on flannel pajamas and pink fuzzy slippers and play checkers with your grandfather," she said. "Life is so much simpler at the Pink Poodle."

"Yes," I said softly.

"I finished the *Idylls*," she said. "So terribly sad. *'Late, late, so late! and dark the night and chill! Late, late, so late! but we can enter still.'* Why do stories have to have sad endings, in order to feel real to us? I'm so tired, Mariah. I'm sixteen and I feel like, it's already too late for me."

"No, you're missing the point of the story: *'we can enter still.'* It's never too late, that's what she's saying. No matter how dark it gets. It's never hopeless."

Rachel shook her head. "It was kind of hopeless for Guinevere."

"No, because Arthur forgave her, and he set her free. She lived for three years in peace. Probably the only peace she ever knew in her life."

"Free? But she was in a convent."

"Freedom is not about walls. It's something inside you."

"Oh. I see."

The doors from the hall opened and the music seemed to explode outward onto the deck. A group of girls came out, giggling, their hands over their mouths.

"Come in and dance," I said. "It will get your mind off…all this stuff."

"You go on. I like it out here. The sea air smells good for once."

"Ok. Talk to you later?"

She nodded, giving me a brave smile.

"I'll tell Jack you're out here," I said.

Inside music seemed to have gotten louder, the floor slicker, the heat now so intense I could feel the makeup melting off my face. I looked around for Trey but he was nowhere in sight. Getting drunk, maybe, with the guys in the bar. I was mad that he would leave me alone. Miranda pulled me back to the dance floor, and I tried to forget about Trey and Jack and Rachel and just have fun. It *was* fun, too, dancing made me lose myself. I lost track of time, for then the music stopped, and I heard screaming instead. Everyone was running. To the windows. I tried to follow, but I had trouble moving through the press of bodies. "What's going on?" I screamed at Miranda, but she didn't know.

A horn blew. *The* horn. That could mean only one thing. Someone was drowning.

I shoved my way through the screaming teenagers to the bank of windows. I couldn't see anything at first, then a glimmer of gold, a tiny fleck, appeared in the glare of the lights off the fishing pier, just above the water. I stood riveted, feeling all the blood drain from my face, my limbs useless, frozen. I knew exactly what that fleck of gold was.

EIGHTEEN
2003

There is a picture of me in the white sundress I wore to the Lifeguard's Ball, the one and only time I ever attended. I find it in my old room, stuck behind the oval mirror on the wall with a yellowed piece of tape. Why did I put it there? Did I hate it so much? I look at my tanned and smiling sixteen year old self with my broad, sloping shoulders and frizzy hair sticking out in all directions from my attempt at a bun, that shining light of hope in my eyes, and I want to laugh and cry. My mother must have taken the picture; she had come to see me off, but she had not stayed. Still, I remember that as one of the few times my mother took an active interest in my life, apart from criticizing me about my hair or my clothes or my posture. When I called her the next day to tell her how things had gone, she seemed to be barely listening, as if once again consumed with the problems of her world, my father's failing business, the ever growing piles of bills. This was a world I tried not to think about. I remember winters as dark and depressing with endless worries about clients who didn't pay, employees who didn't work, and bankers who cut off their credit. I remember the cold of those winters as well, the bone-cracking cold of the seventies, along with the tumbling economy and the cluelessness of the President and the long gas lines and horrendous fashion choices which made that decade seem like the darkest of Dark Ages. But the music was good. I miss the music.

I am in my old room in Avalon. The ghost is gone. There have been no more weird occurrences like the books or the suitcases. But Rachel is there, and Jack too. I am imagining her as she looked that night, a vision in shimmering gold, drifting down to the end of the fishing pier and throwing herself in the ocean, the dirty, dangerous ocean that frightened her so badly, that almost took her boyfriend. She had given herself to the ocean that night.

I remember sitting huddled with the rest of the party-goers in the dance room for hours while the police and the ambulances and fire trucks came, along with hysterical parents and town officials shouting for everyone to calm down. I was the last person to talk to her, so the cops questioned me for a long time. What could I tell them?

I remember Jack, sitting in a chair with his head in his hands, his friends clustered around him protectively. Trey was not with them. He stood with the police, telling them what happened. He'd been in the Over 18 bar, which was on the ocean side, and had seen something out the window, something gold and shiny, a movement that did not seem natural to the ocean. He knew the ocean, knew its every flickering color. He went out to investigate and realized someone was in the water. Had it not been for him, Rachel would have died.

I wonder if he did her a favor, saving her like that. I wonder if she was grateful, or angry. I never found out, because I never saw her again. I heard that she was taken to a hospital in Philadelphia and then whisked up north, to Vermont, to some kind of sanitarium. Jack and his family left the next day as well. A few days later we all saw a FOR SALE OR RENT sign on the Grain Elevator.

It's gone now, the Grain Elevator. I first realized it when I was riding my bike up Dune Drive a week ago. Funny how I had not even looked for it before, so focused had I been on the Pink Poodle. At first I could not even remember where it had stood; was it 34th or 35th? I drove back and forth several times before realizing it was really gone, in its place a clean-lined beige "traditional contemporary" — a name I always found terribly funny. The soulless, impersonal modern movement did not last long in Avalon; people wanted their houses to breathe in the rhythm of the tides, to move with the cadence of the undulating dunes. Attempts at bucking tradition failed in Avalon, or at least failed to sell.

At any rate, the Grain Elevator was gone. I felt a throb in my chest at that realization; a sense that the last bit of Jack that held any connection for me was gone with it. There were no pictures of him on the lifeguard wall of the Avalon Museum, there were no records of him in the lifeguard journals. It was as if he never existed at all.

I think about calling Jack's mother, of telling her that the house is gone. I won't, of course. Though my relationship with her had been cordial at best, I don't believe she had ever been able to look at me without thinking of Rachel, and I believed, in my own insecurity, that she thought I was to blame for what happened.

"Mom, what are you doing up here?" I look up to see Caroline standing in the doorway, gazing around the room with a mixture of fascination and horror on her face. "So this is it? Like an oven in here."

"Oh," I say, as if she caught me naked. "I was just going through some old stuff."

"Wow. You liked pink, didn't you?"

"Haha. It went with the house." I think about showing her the pictures but decide against it. Another time.

"Oh, well, I was wondering…"

Here it comes, I think. She's being way too friendly.

"…if I could go down to Wildwood tonight."

"With whom?"

"With some kids."

"And Ben?"

"Yeah, he's going too, but…"

"Sure, go," I say, cutting her off.

"Huh?" She is clearly surprised. I get up and leave, tripping down the stairs. "Be home by midnight. No drinking. And stay with the group. Do you have money?"

She follows me down the stairs. I turn to look at her and see that she is staring at me as if I just walked out of a space ship from Mars.

"Take some money out of my purse." I go into my bedroom.

"Thanks, Mom," I hear her say.

"Have fun," I say. I close the door and wait until I hear her footsteps going down the stairs. Then I go to the window and look down on Ben pacing the driveway in front of the house. Parked behind him is his yellow jeep with two other kids in the backseat. After a moment I see Caroline race down the steps to greet him. He looks happy. He jumps into the driver's seat and she jumps in beside him, and they are off, laughing, hands in the air to capture the breeze.

I must be crazy, I think to myself. To let my 17-year old daughter go out with a 24-year old man I barely know, to Wildwood of all places, that hotbed of vice and greasy pizza. There is something terribly wrong with me.

With nothing else to do I call my dad in Florida.

"How's the house?" he asks when he finally comes to the phone.

"It's coming along," I say evasively. "The roof is done, and the porch. I wish you could see it. We'll be starting on the kitchen floor soon."

"Did you get an estimate for air conditioning?"

"Yes, but it's ridiculous in an old house like this. It would be like wallpapering the Sistene Chapel."

"I figured."

"I did put in some new fans though. And I'm thinking we will need to re-side the house. The wood is pretty rotted."

"Siding? Then it wouldn't be pink anymore," he says. He sounds forlorn.

"No, probably not…Why don't you and mom come up for Labor Day? It would be nice to spend a weekend here, like the old days."

There is a pause on the line. "I'll talk to your mother," he says finally. I know what that means.

"Tell her it will probably be the last time. Anyway, it's got to be beastly hot down there in the 'gater swamp."

"How hot is it up there?" he asks.

"90 in the shade."

"Sounds refreshing."

We talk awhile longer, and he brings me up to date on all the doctor visits and outpatient procedures he and mom have had since the last time we talked, and I get the feeling that they live their lives from appointment to appointment, from one condition to the next, and that they might even be competing to see who can have the most medical issues at any one time. My dad was never a complainer, but it appears now that he doesn't have much else to talk about except the weather (in Florida it is either too hot or too rainy) and joint pain. It is a reminder of how strange life is, that my parents can go on living, seemingly forever, with a myriad of physical deficiencies, and someone like Jack, so eminently alive and healthy and unstoppable, could be dead from a tiny cluster of misplaced veins. Life is so fragile, people would tell me, but for some it is endless and unbearable.

I once visited my grandmother in the nursing home when her health and her memory began to fail, and though it was a fairly cheery place and the people who worked there caring and upbeat, the sight of so many people sitting in wheelchairs, waiting to die and yet seemingly indestructible, depressed me deeply. They would go on like this, I thought, forever and forever, their heads permanently sunk to their chests, their mouths half open, their eyes glazed, being diapered and fed and put to bed. My grandmother had become surly there, angry that she had been lumped in with so many "old" people. She got old quickly in the nursing home, and died as soon as she could manage it, which was three years later.

We hang up and I think, with an afternoon to myself (Trey is working elsewhere) I will just go to the beach. I go up to my room and put on a bathing suit and search the clean clothes bin for a towel.

The doorbell rings. Trey? I wonder idly. Perhaps he got off work early. He came over at odd times, whenever he felt like it, and we had accepted his presence almost as if he lived there too, though he never stayed over. He had never pressed the issue, and for that I was grateful. Though my heart still skipped when I heard his voice, and my body longed for him in the small hours of the night as I lay in the big bed alone, I knew that to cross that line would be a mistake, both for myself and for Caroline, who needed more than ever a good role model. I knew she was watching my every move.

I throw on a coverup and run down the stairs to let him in. But it is not Trey standing there. A small woman, elderly but well preserved, slim and beautifully dressed, is standing in my doorway. She looks familiar to me, but I can't place her. Her hair is silvery brown and

perfectly coiffed, quite short. She has beautiful brown eyes that crinkle
when she smiles at me, though the smile is rather tremulous, as if on
the verge of tears.

"Mariah?"

"Yes," I say, feeling foolish for not knowing her. I wait
expectantly.

"I hope you don't mind my stopping by. You obviously don't
know me. I'm Amanda Rosen, Rachel's mother."

I feel as though the floor has opened before me, and once more I
am falling, the walls and air spinning upwards, out of sight. When I am
able to focus again I see that she is still standing there, patiently,
waiting for this information to process. It seems like a long time before
I can speak at all.

"Mrs. Rosen…How did you find me?"

"Well, it's rather a long story. May I come in?"

"Oh…of course!"

I step aside and let her come into my house, just as Rachel had
done twenty-five years before. Her voice was light and sweet,
childlike, so similar to Rachel's. I should have known her from the
first.

I invite her to sit and ask if she wants some tea. She says yes,
probably not because she wants tea but she knows I need time, I need
to think, and I need to be busy. So I put the tea pot on the stove and put
a bag of Earl Grey into a cup that I hope is clean. What is she doing
here? I fear the worst: Rachel is dead. What else could it be, I wonder.
But she could have sent a letter. She did not have to come personally
to tell me that.

I take several deep breaths, then carry the tea to the living room
where Mrs. Rosen is sitting quietly on the massive sofa, looking so

tiny and out of place. She smiles at me again as I hand her the mug and sit opposite her in the easy chair. She takes a small sip.

"Mariah," she says. "It's nice to meet you…finally."

"Yes," I say. "Rachel…?"

"Oh, she's fine," Mrs. Rosen says.

Now I am really confused. "Then…"

"I came to Avalon to see my grandson, Ben."

I let a long moment pass.

"Ben is your grandson?" I repeat the words stupidly, as if I don't even know what they mean.

"Ben is Rachel's son," she says. "Rachel's…and Jack's."

For a long time I cannot speak. She sees this and continues.

"I'm sorry if this shocks you. Ben does not know. Rachel never told him. When he told us his friends had invited him for the summer…I became concerned. I didn't say anything to him; of course, I did not know you were still here…"

"This is my first time back in 25 years," I say.

"Oh my. That is…something of a coincidence, isn't it? Well, a week ago he called, and he told me about meeting you…and your daughter…well, naturally I was alarmed."

"Oh God," I say. I curl up, holding my stomach, sure I will be sick. "Oh my…God." This cannot be happening.

"I'm sorry, Mariah, for telling you like this. I never thought I would have to. We found out she was pregnant at the hospital. She hadn't told anyone. Perhaps she didn't even know…"

"She had to have known," I hear myself say. "That's why she did it."

"Perhaps. She had so many issues, of course. We really don't know the cause. Her father and I had tried to ignore it, thinking she just needed to get away for a bit, meet some new people. We all loved

Jack, we thought he would be good for her. And you…she told us about you, and you seemed to be such a good friend to her. You were really helping her…"

Helping her by stealing her boyfriend, I think. I am sick.

"The doctors wanted her to have an abortion. They said in her condition, with her eating disorders and her migraines, she would not bring a baby to term. But Rachel would not do it. Nor would she let me tell Jack about it. She planned to put the baby up for adoption. But after he was born…she couldn't go through with it."

"So…Jack didn't know?"

"He had no idea. He tried to call her several times, but she would not take his calls."

"But how could she…?"

"She put a false name on the birth certificate."

I say nothing, letting all this wash over me like a tsunami. I am drowning.

"He's a strong young man," she adds, her smile more solid now, "he's very grounded. We all have high hopes for him…"

"What do I tell Caroline?" I say, suddenly awash in fear. "How can I tell her she can't see him without telling her the truth?"

"You could just tell her that Ben is too old for her, which he is," Mrs. Rosen says with her former pragmatism. "I have already told Ben as much. He won't do anything dishonorable. And I'm sure, once the summer is over, they will lose touch, and it will be of no matter. There is no need to tell her anything upsetting, is there? They can be friends. And one day, perhaps, they can know the truth."

When I am dead, I think she meant.

"Mariah," she says in a different voice, "I want to thank you, for being her friend, all those years ago. I think it was because of you that she was so good that summer, so much better than she had been. She told me that you had warned her against doing anything she would regret, and she even said she wished she had listened to you. I wish I could have told you about all this sooner. Had you known, you might have been able to help her. And perhaps…"

"I wouldn't have married Jack," I say, finishing her sentence. But I wonder if this were true. I remember my rush of passion for Jack, it went against anything reasonable and right. I wonder if I would not have married him anyway. "I figured you all must have hated me for doing that. Rachel must have hated me too."

Mrs. Rosen smiles at me, a small, sad smile. "Perhaps you did her a favor."

I cannot answer her. I can only stare into space, too shell-shocked even to cry.

"I should go, I'll see myself out," she says.

"No," I say, "please tell me about Rachel. Tell me…how is she? Is she well?"

"She is…doing as best as she can, I think," Mrs. Rosen says after a long moment of considering her answer. "She lives in a commune up in Vermont."

"A *commune?*"

Mrs. Rosen sighs a little. "Yes. Maple Grove. It's quite famous. Her father was furious, as you can imagine. He hasn't spoken to her since. But in a way she seems…quite happy. Ben stayed with her until he was twelve, then he came to live with us. It was his choice, he wanted to go to a regular school, but he still spent his summers there with her."

She is leaving out so much, but I can see she doesn't want to tell me everything.

"Does she know you are here?" I ask.

Mrs. Rosen blinks. "I haven't told her. I don't speak to her very often. She doesn't have a phone of her own. I email her on occasion. Do you want me to tell her?"

"I don't know," I say. "Probably not. But if you decide to, please give her my love, will you?"

"Of course." She rises, setting her mug on the coffee table. I get up as well, my legs still wobbly, my head fuzzy. "I am so sorry, for your loss, by the way," she says, taking my hand in her bony one. "I should have said that first. I remember Jack as a…a life force. I was truly shocked to hear of his death."

"Yes," I say, numbly. "Thank you."

She smiles and turns to the door. Then she stops again, glancing around. "So this is the Pink Poodle," she says, a kind of wonder in her voice.

"It's seen better days," I say. "But…not much better."

"She quite loved it here. She often talked of it. She seemed to find peace here. That is all I have ever wanted for Rachel: peace."

I feel a great well of a sob rise up to my throat; I fight to hold it down until she is gone and the door is closed. I lean against it, the worn, fibrous wood pressing into my cheeks, and I weep.

NINETEEN

After awhile I go to lie down on the couch, my arm flung over my eyes, which sting from crying. My stomach aches, like it is being squeezed, my lungs contracted, I can hardly breathe.

It is all making sense to me now. Rachel's suicide attempt, her refusal to see Jack again, or me. She had to make a clean break, I guess. She had to keep her dangerous secret to herself.

I should have tried harder to see her, to talk to her again. Had she spent all the years thinking we abandoned her? Like this house, I think, a house that had longed for love to dwell in its heart, and had gotten only summer renters, using and abusing it, griping about its leaky roof and its heat-trapping walls and splintered porch, leaving at the end of the allotted week with hardly a look back. Is this how Rachel felt? Like she too was not worth saving?

Trey calls. I tell him about Amanda Rosen, in between my hiccups. He is silent for a long time on the phone. Then he asks if I want him to come over. I tell him no. I need to be alone for a while. He does not protest.

I have to get out of the house, so I decide to go to the beach, since there is no place else to go. It is crowded, the height of the summer season, and the cries of children compete with the shrill screaming of the seagulls. It is not the summer haven I remember, this beach. I don't remember so many mammoth umbrellas packed together, so they seem to form an unbroken tapestry of jarring color. I try to find a bit of sand that has not already been claimed by towels and boogie boards, and I stare, shamelessly, at the lifeguards. The swimsuits have changed, but how much the boys of summer have stayed the same, browned and muscled and self-assured, presiding over their small domains. The lifeguards of Avalon were always more zealous than the other beaches; patrons constantly complain that they huddle the swimmers in such a small area, restricting their every move, blowing their whistles incessantly. It was one of the reasons (ironic as it seems) Jack gave me for building on the Outer Banks: no lifeguards.

I have a book, but I cannot read, cannot concentrate. So I watch people. There are not as many teenagers as there used to be; there are more generational families, women, sisters with their passel of kids and their aging parents, a few dads who seem to be in constant motion, digging holes, dragging toddlers into the surf, setting up umbrellas and tents, sorting out chairs. The women sit in the chairs, books in hand, calling out to their children, who do not listen. Beyond the swimmers there are wave runners and, farther out, dolphins play, unacknowledged. One or two sailboats sit serenely on the horizon. The teens are absent — gone to Stone Harbor, perhaps, where the crowd is more youthful and hip.

At five the lifeguards leave their stations, and the surfers come out. The beach begins to empty, the mothers packing up their children and their troves of toys and collected shells, shaking sand out of towels, collecting garbage in little grocery bags to be tossed in the cans on the way up the dune walks. This is timeless and familiar, a ritual untouched by the hazard of years, and I feel grateful for it. Seagulls forage in their wake, screeching over spilled goldfish crackers. My brother and I used to make a game of targeting the seagulls, shooting at them with loaded water pistols if they came too near our compound. The seagulls of the Jersey Shore are the most villainous on the east coast; they have been known to snatch sandwiches right out of the mouths of innocent children. They seem to be the only creatures on the shore that have actually prospered here.

The spectacle of children and gulls distracts me for a time from the hard lump in my stomach, the terrible knowledge I wish I could somehow un-remember. I have a wild desire to run into the water, to splash through the waves and dive under them, to swim until I have no breath left. But I cannot swim, because of the cast on my wrist. I content myself with wading in the shallows and walking, walking, walking, up to the 30th Street beach and past it, where the beach widens so that you can barely see the dunes from the edge of the shore, and the houses get bigger and farther apart and more distant, lost in a haze, like houses in the dream. I walk until I don't know where I am, exactly, but I have passed the steeple of the Catholic church. Then I turn around and walk back. It is growing dark already. How quickly dusk comes at the end of summer. The beach is empty but for the ever-vigilant seagulls and families in matching T-shirts who come down to take photos with the boats and the lifeguard stands.

I pick up my chair and my bag and head back to the house, which is still empty and silent. I call Trey, but there is no answer. Caroline will not be back for hours. The thought of so much time alone in this house fills me with horror; I don't know why. I can think of nothing, no one, except Jack, the Jack I knew on this beach, and my imagination goes to dark places, to him and Rachel, together…where were they that night? There were not many nights that I did not spend with one or the other, but that night they had planned to go somewhere…the movies, I guess…that is what Jack had told me. But it must have been before the movie, because Jack told me she was crying during the movie. *Grease.* Of course.

Where could they have gone to be together? Perhaps the Grain Elevator, for Jack's parents were often out at other people's houses having cocktails or in Atlantic City seeing a show or gambling.

What had I been doing? Watching TV with my grandparents? Or maybe it was one of those weekends that my cousins were over and my grandmother made me stay home to entertain them. Strange that I could not remember. That summer Rachel and Jack blotted out all my other, more ordinary recollections; it seemed that they were always at the center of my imagination. Whenever I read a romance novel, it was Jack and Rachel I substituted for the hero and heroine; they were perfectly cast for those roles. I was always the heroine's faithful, sexless friend, and Trey was the dashing subordinate to the hero who saved his life now and then. So their stories would end, I thought: Jack and Rachel getting married, living in a giant house in a New Jersey suburb, having beautiful children and going to fancy balls. Instead, it was Jack and I who lived that dream, with some minor adjustments. So I was not, after all, the faithful friend but the villainous "other woman" who betrayed the heroine and stole her man. And I had been duly punished for my crime.

Jack was dead. Somehow or other, that still did not make sense to me. Jack could not be dead. Nothing could kill the hero of the story. He was supposed to be invincible. Yet I had seen him, lying on the gurney in the hospital morgue, his head still wrapped in bandages from the surgery they had done in trying to save him. Jack was dead.

I get in the car and drive, all the way to the end of the island, to 117th street in Stone Harbor. On the way back I stop at the convent, Villa Maria, on 111th. It's a giant white building taking up an entire block of the most prized beachfront property on the Jersey Shore. Trey used to surf there — it was popular for surfing. I see the nuns have taken advantage of their location, selling T-shirts and towels with "Nun's Beach" imprinted on them. I notice from the signage that they are having an annual "Nun's Beach Surf Invitational" in September. Good for them, I think, remembering the familiar sight of nuns in full habit walking up and down the beach, carrying their thick-soled shoes in their hands.

I go back to the Pink Poodle and eat a yogurt from the fridge and try to read a book, but the waiting is unbearable. I keep imagining Caroline and Ben on the Ferris Wheel, kissing, or on the roller coaster, her arms around his neck, screaming. Caroline loves roller coasters. I am sure Ben does too. I hate them. Once my parents took my brother and me to Wildwood, because they thought it was something they should do at least once. I hated every minute of it, the crowded boardwalk, the blinking, flashing lights, the hawking gamers shouting "Three balls only one dollar!" the roar of the coasters that zoom right over your head as you walk along the pier. The place was something surreal, a bad dream where you were always lost, could never find your way out. My brother adored it. I wouldn't go on a single ride.

The door creaks open. I jerk awake, realizing I have dozed off in the easy chair. Caroline appears, smiling, her eyes slightly reddened, her hair askew, wind-blown.

"Hey," I say as nonchalantly as I can. "Did you have fun?"

"Yeah, it was a blast," she says, sitting down on the couch.

"So you like Wildwood?"

"It's definitely wild."

"A little different from the Nags Head Raceway, I guess."

"Yeah. Great coasters. They have this one called the Nor'easter, where you kind of hang suspended. It's a trip."

"I'll bet."

She is silent a moment, waiting for me to ask about Ben. But I cannot ask.

"Thanks for letting me go, Mom. I know it was kind of…hard for you."

You have no idea.

I smile at her. "Well, I'm glad you had a good time."

"What did you do?" she asks.

"Nothing much. Went to the beach."

"No Trey today?"

"No…he's working somewhere else today. But the floor people are coming tomorrow to start pulling up the kitchen floor, so he'll probably be around for that."

"Oh, cool. That floor is so gross."

"Yes, I know."

"Well, I guess I'm going to bed. Gotta work in the morning. Ugh. You?"

"Coming."

I wait until she I cannot hear her on the stairs anymore, and then I go up too.

TWENTY

The "floor guy" whose name turns out to be Gus, tells me that Trey Bennett will not be coming to the house today.

"Said he had to go up to Hoboken, some kind of family emergency," he says in his thick Jersey drawl. "Says he's sorry, but he told us what to do. We're just doing demolition today anyway."

Why didn't he call me himself? I wonder. Was he just giving me space after my brush-off the day before? Was he angry with me? I felt instant remorse at not allowing him to come over when he'd asked; now he obviously thinks he is not wanted at all.

I call his cell, but there is no answer. I'm sure he has his phone with him, which means he is just not answering. I leave a terse message, "Hey it's me. Call me when you get a chance. Bye." I hope I sound annoyed enough that he will call me back.

I mope through the day, watching the workmen, trying to get some long-neglected paperwork done. The house bills are due, the realtor contract on the house in Aspen needs to be renewed, and there is a lot of mail from lawyers I have been avoiding. My own lawyer has left messages almost daily, the last few sounding genuinely concerned for my health. I know I cannot avoid the inevitable anymore.

"Hi Mitch, it's me."

"Mariah, did you get my messages? Don't you have voicemail?"

"Yes, I got them."

We talk for a long time about the pending bills that still need to be paid, the parts of Jack's estate that are still in probate, all the unpleasantness I've been trying to wish away.

"Have you thought of selling the house?"

"Which house?"

"The Raleigh house."

That house, that monstrosity that passes for a house, that six bedroom monolith on twelve of the most beautiful acres in North Carolina.

"Do I need to?"

"You should think seriously about it," Mitch says. "The area is exploding. And what do you need a house that size for?"

Well, I had never needed a house that size. But that was the size house you built when you were a noted surgeon in Raleigh. To build anything less was a sign of failure, or incompetence. No one wanted to have their hearts opened up by a surgeon who lived in a three bedroom raised ranch.

"I'll think about it," I say, not wanting to think about anything. But then, I have a strong desire to get rid of everything of Jack's as quickly as I can. What will Caroline say?

"When are you coming home?"

"After Labor Day," I say.

"That's not for two more weeks," he whines.

"There's still a lot to do on this house…"

"For God's sake, Mariah, I know you are grieving, but do you really think it's wise to sink money you don't have into a house that…"

I hang up on him.

Do I need to be reminded of what a terrible fool I am? No, I do not.

I go out and sit on the porch and gaze at the ocean. The sky is gray, overcast. It will rain soon, as it has almost every day since August began. That's okay today, I am in the mood for rain.

Trey calls me back, finally.

"Everything all right?" I ask, hiding my real concern.

"Okay — my mom had some angina pains, I guess. She called me…she never calls me, so I thought for sure she was going to die or something…no, that sounds bad …"

"I know what you meant," I say. "I was surprised you left…so suddenly."

"Yeah, I'm sorry." No further explanation.

"Why didn't you call me?"

"You said you needed to be alone."

Oh, right.

"Trey, I'm sorry I was so abrupt with you, I was just…upset. I wasn't really thinking…"

"Don't worry about it." He sounds a little less strained. I take a breath.

"When are you coming back?"

"Tomorrow, probably. Or the next day. They may have to do an angioplasty. My sister will be coming in from New York soon, so I'll leave then."

"Okay."

"Gus has all the information, so don't worry about the floor."

"I wasn't really thinking of the floor. I miss you, Trey."

There is a moment's pause on the line. "I miss you too."

I hang up, feeling out of sorts. What was that I heard in his voice? A distance, a pulling away. Perhaps I had been all wrong about our relationship; perhaps, he was nervous that I now seemed too clingy, calling him and leaving messages, angry that he was not there at my beck and call. He had kissed me, twice, but did I read too much into that? "It's not a marriage proposal," he had said. He meant, perhaps, that we were two middle-aged people, alone now with no plans for a future, and so if we wanted to kiss once in awhile, what was the harm in that? He had been through massive heartbreak, he did not need any more emotional complications in his life. But there was still harm, I realize now, that I may be 41 years old on the outside, but inside I am still that 16-year-old girl with that same tender, twisted heart.

Caroline returns at 2:30 to the cacophony of floor demolition and promptly heads to the beach to sleep. It is not quite raining yet, though still overcast and humid. I stay in my room staring at the sea, overhung with a gray mist, so that it seems to dissolve into the horizon. The workmen finish for the day at 3:30, and I am alone again, the house creaking and whispering around me. I listen for my grandfather, but I do not hear him. Perhaps he has decided to leave finally, now that I am here, and I have decided, for the moment, not to destroy his Camelot.

"Grandpa, how did Arthur die?"

"Don't you remember?"

"Yes, but I like when you tell it."

My grandfather puffed on his pipe awhile, rocking back and forth in the creaky wicker rocker on the front porch of the Pink Poodle. My ten year old self looked up at him expectantly, knowing he was gathering his thoughts to tell the tale properly.

"Arthur knew the day would come, the last battle. Merlin had foretold it. He knew, all along, that the kingdom of Camelot would last only a little while, that nothing truly good lasts very long. Arthur's evil son Mordred had aligned a hundred thousand men to fight against him. And from the north the Saxons loomed. Camelot was getting smaller and smaller. Soon it would disappear, and he with it. But did he give up? No, Arthur rallied his forces to fight that last battle.

"The night before the battle Arthur had a dream. In it, Sir Gawain, who was dead by the way, came to him with a train of beautiful young women, and warned him not to fight Mordred. He told the king to make a truce with his evil spawn for a month, long enough to send for Lancelot, who had fled to France. With Lancelot at his side, Gawain promised that Arthur would win. So when Arthur awoke he did just that—asked for a truce. Mordred agreed.

"The two met on the field of Camlann with fourteen men accompanying them to seal the bargain. But Arthur had given his men an order that if they saw any sword drawn they were to attack.

"It all went well, at first. The agreement was drawn up, then the wine was brought out and the two of them drank to it, sitting astride their horses on the battle field, which is how things were done back then. Everything looked as though it would work out, after all. But you know, in these stories, just like in real life, nothing ever goes according to plan. In this case, a snake rose up from the heather and bit one of Mordred's men on the heel."

"How did a snake bite through a boot anyway?"

"Ha! You may wonder, but this is a story and some things you just take on faith. The knight drew his sword to strike at the snake, and of course Arthur's men saw the sword flashing in the sunlight, and that was that. All hell broke loose, as they say.

"It was the most dreadful battle ever fought on England's soil. In the end, all of Arthur's knights lay dead except two, Sir Lucan and Sir Bedivere, but they were badly wounded. The king vowed he would kill Mordred for causing him so much sorrow. He asked Lucan for his spear. Lucan tried to talk him out of it, telling him that the prophecy could still come true, if he would wait, wait for Lancelot. God in His great goodness had preserved him through the battle, but if he were to take revenge on Mordred, the wickedness of the day would never end. Arthur would not listen. He took that spear and ran toward Mordred shouting, 'Traitor, now is your death upon you!'"

My grandfather rose from his chair, his imaginary spear in one upraised hand, his pipe in the other. His voice crested with emotion, making the dogs next door bark in alarm.

"Mordred saw him coming, and ran at him with his sword. A spear is longer than a sword, though, and Arthur pierced Mordred through. But Mordred grabbed hold of the spear and pulled it further into his own body, bringing the king closer to him. He raised his sword and smashed Arthur on the top of his head, breaking through his helmet and cutting deep into his skull. Then Mordred fell, screaming, to his death."

My grandfather got quiet then, panting from the exertion of his tale, staring down at the floor as if he could see Mordred there, writhing in the death throes. Then slowly, painfully, he sat down again.

"The two wounded knights lifted the king and carried him to a little chapel that sat beside the mysterious sea, where the mist lay red like blood in the last rays of the setting sun. Then Sir Lucan fell down and died, for the exertion of carrying his king had torn open his already mortal wounds..."

"What's a mortal wound?" I asked.

"A wound that leads to certain death," my grandfather said without missing a beat. He seemed to be in a sort of swoon himself, as if he now inhabited the body of the dying king.

"The king told the last remaining knight, Sir Bedivere, to take his sword Excaliber and throw it into the lake at the top of the mountain, and then to come back and tell him what he saw. Sir Bedivere went to the lake, but he could not throw the sword in, for it was a beautiful sword, and it had forged a kingdom, so he hid the sword and went back to Arthur. Arthur asked him what he saw, and when Bedivere said he saw nothing, Arthur knew he had not obeyed him. He sent him back, but Bedivere did the same thing again. You can imagine how much time was lost, how much Arthur's condition worsened. Then finally, on the third trip to the lake, Bedivere finally did throw the sword into the lake, and he saw a hand come up out of the dark waters, an arm clothed in shining white samite..."

"What's samite?"

"It is a fabric woven with gold and silver thread...where was I? The hand caught the sword and brandished it three times on high, and then vanished with it beneath the dark water. Now, Bedivere went back to the king and told him what he had seen, and the king was satisfied. He told Bedivere to help him down the grassy slope to the sea. Then out of the mist came a barge to meet them, and in it were Nimue, the Lady of the Lake, and the Lady of the Isle of Avalon, and also Queen Morgana le Fay, Arthur's half-sister and once his enemy. The three ladies took the king onto the barge and laid him down with his head resting on the lap of the Lady of the Isle of Avalon. Morgana grieved that he had waited so long in coming, for his wound had caught cold…I suppose that meant it was infected. The barge moved back into the mist, leaving Sir Bedivere all alone on the shores. He cried out to his king in despair, but Arthur called back with words of comfort to him, saying he was only going to Avalon for a little while, to be healed of his wound, and then he would return, when the land of Britain needed him again, and that Camelot would rise again out of the darkness."

Grandfather was quiet for a long time. This story always managed to choke him up, so matter how often he told it.

"What happened to Lancelot and Guinevere," I asked impatiently. "Did they ever get married…I mean, after Arthur was gone…"

"They met again," said my grandfather. "Lancelot returned from France and went to see her after learning of Arthur's death. But Guinevere had become a nun by then, had already taken her vows, and Lancelot, since his king was dead, gave up his sword and joined a monastery to live out his days as a humble monk."

"No!" I said angrily. "That's a terrible end to the story. After all they had suffered, after all the years they had waited to be together! They should have gotten married and been with each other for the rest of their lives! Who wrote this story anyway? It's a stupid story."

My grandfather laughed at me. "But they both loved Arthur, you see," he said gently. "What bound them together was…Arthur. Without him they were both lost. So they turned to God. And that, I think, is the moral of the story. In this world, no love can compare to the love of God."

"They could have loved God and been together still," I said stubbornly.

"I believe they were both happy, in the end," said my grandfather. "I believe they both found peace, and redemption. Many years later Lancelot dreamed that Guinevere was dying, so he traveled to

Almesbury to see her — but she was already dead. He brought her to Glastonbury and buried her there near the high altar. Then he died too, only a few weeks later, and was buried there also. You know that when the monks of Glastonbury dug up two sets of bones centuries later, during the reign of Richard the Lionheart, they assumed that the bones belonged to Arthur and Guinivere. But I believe that it was Lancelot's bones they found…that he had himself buried beside her, and they are together even now, in heaven."

"What about Arthur?"

"Arthur was carried to Avalon and he is still there."

"I thought Avalon and Glastonbury were the same place."

"That is what everyone always assumes, but no one knows for sure."

"Maybe Avalon is heaven."

"Maybe."

I looked around at the view from our porch, the vast, mysterious sea, the hazy blue sky. "I think this is the real Avalon," I said.

"Yes," he said. "I think you are right."

TWENTY-ONE
September 2003

It is Labor Day weekend and the house is still not finished, far from it. I have not decided what I am going to do with it. Betsy has been calling, asking impertinent questions, the steely nerve in her voice beginning to wear me down. Trey is no help. He has found other projects that have taken his attention away from the Pink Poodle, away from me. I can sense his pulling away as tactilely as I feel the steamy drops of afternoon drizzle seep into my skin. I find myself wanting to leave, to drive back to Raleigh; I need the space and the separation and the endless drone of a boring drive to numb my brain. Ironically, it is Caroline that does not want to go. Because of Ben. I have never been so happy for summer to end as I am now.

"He said he would come and visit," she tells me over breakfast on Friday morning. "And we will be coming back next summer, right?"

"I don't know. I'm seriously considering selling the house."

"What, that again? I thought you loved this house!"

I almost laugh at her distress. "You wanted me to get rid of it. You hate this house."

"I don't hate it," she protests. "Not as much as I used to. Anyway, why did you spend all summer working on it if you were just going to sell it anyway? Didn't that realtor lady say that it would just get demolished if you sold it?"

"I thought I could save it," I say bleakly. "But now I realize it is just too much for me."

I pick up my coffee cup with my bad hand. The doctor said I was supposed to use it as much as possible, but it still feels weak and tender. Caroline watches the coffee mug shake in my hand as I put it to my lips.

"I know why you did it," she says bluntly. She has grown up this summer, the features have lengthened, sharpened. But then I think it is Ben that has brought this new look to her face, a terrible, grown-up awareness that I fear with all my heart. "It's because of Trey."

I put the coffee cup down harder than I intended. My wrist throbs. "That's ridiculous," I say without much conviction.

"Mom, just admit it," she says flatly. "You're in love with him."

"I have always loved Trey," I say, "but…that's not the same thing as being in love."

"Come on Mom, get over yourself," she retorts. "You've got it bad for him, and you know it. Look, I'm not mad. I like Trey. He's a great guy. He's good for you. And there's no reason that you should spend the rest of your life alone. I mean, you're not that old."

"Thanks," I say. But what else can I say? I decide to change the subject. "And how about you and Ben?"

She shrugs nonchalantly, but I see the widening of her eyes, the slight slope of her body as she breathes. "I like him a lot," she says, "but he thinks I am too young for him. He just wants to be…friends."

I am more than thrilled to hear this. "Did he tell you that?"

"Yeah…sort of."

"Oh I see," I say. "Well, I have to say I agree with him."

"Yeah, I know," she says glumly.

"Well, what do you want to do this weekend? I know we have a lot of packing to do but we ought to have some fun…"

"Actually Mom, there's a lifeguard party on the beach…and Ben asked me if I could go." She pauses while I try to absorb this. "There's other kids going too. But Ben thought, since it was our last weekend…"

"*Our* last weekend? What happened to just being friends?"

"So, we'll be going as friends! We just want to hang out once more. Didn't you ever go to the lifeguard parties when you were a kid here?"

Oh Lord. Remind me about that, will you.

"Yes," I say with a sigh.

"Ben said he would pay for my ticket…"

"No, I will pay for your ticket," I say. She rolls her eyes at me. "When is this party?"

'Tomorrow night."

"Tomorrow? Why didn't you tell me before?"

"I don't know. I was going to, but you seemed so sad this week…I thought maybe you'd be upset if I left you alone on your last weekend here."

I am touched by her concern for me. "As a matter of fact, I think Trey and I have plans," I lie. "So I guess it's okay if you go to the party."

"Really?" Her face lights up. The sight of her joy makes me sick to my stomach. "Thank you Mom! You're the best!" She actually gets up out of her chair to give me a hug around my neck. I can hardly believe

I said what I said. Am I really letting her go? It's just a party, I tell my panic-stricken self, what can happen?

I must be out of my mind.

After she has gone off to the beach I call Trey. Surprisingly, he answers, and his voice sounds relaxed and easy, as it used to.

"Hey," I say, feeling unaccountably nervous, "I was wondering if…you'd like to get together tomorrow night, maybe grab some dinner? I'm leaving on Monday…"

"You're leaving?" Apparently, he didn't know this. We had not talked about the end of the summer.

"School," I say to him. "And, well, it's time."

"Oh." There is silence on the line. "I'd love to take you out, Mare. But…would you mind coming with me to this lifeguard reunion party? It's tomorrow night."

"Lifeguard reunion?"

"Yeah, they do it every five years, and Morey roped me into it…there's guys coming from way back, before me…anyway, we'd just need to stay an hour or two and then we could go somewhere else…"

"Is that the same party that the current lifeguards are having?"

"Well, yes, I guess so. All lifeguards are invited. They are going to do it on the 30th street beach, if the weather's good. A clambake, and a band…they got permission to build a bonfire too. Don't know how they managed that; Morey must have pulled some strings…"

"Sure," I say. "I'd love to go. Sounds like fun. What time should I be ready?"

"Six? I'll pick you up."

"Sounds like a plan."

I hang up with a queer feeling in my stomach: the feeling that, when she finds out I will be going to the same party as she and Ben, my daughter is going to kill me.

There are tents set up on the beach, something I have never seen before. One for the band, an ironic alt-retro band called the "Dumbunnies," and one for food. A smaller tent, assiduously guarded, houses a makeshift bar, from which I see Trey emerging with two plastic glasses of wine. He looks gorgeous, I think as he walks toward me, tall and sculpted and silvered with the years, yet he moves with the same balletic grace he had as a teen swimming star.

"It's Chardonnay," he says, handing me the glass. "I know you don't like it, but that's the only kind they had."

"I don't mind," I say, for I really don't mind anything tonight. The sky, for once, is as perfectly clear as it ever is in Avalon, and the setting sun is putting on a spectacular show. I am wearing a long white dress not unlike the one I wore to the Lifeguard Ball twenty-five years ago, yet I feel none of the awkwardness I felt then. In fact, I feel loose-limbed and easy, a woman with nothing to prove and no one to impress. My hair has grown long over the summer, almost as long as it was then, and the Avalon sun has brought back much of the natural curl I had ironed out over the years. Trey is wearing a white button down shirt and jeans, a perfect, ageless look for him. We look good together, I think, and I can feel people staring at us, wondering if any of them had been there at the ball twenty-five years before.

But I don't know any of them, at least I don't remember any of the "old guards" Trey introduces to me. Then Dave, "Bowie," Trey's old roommate, appears, red-faced and pot-bellied, with a drink in one hand and a well-preserved Jersey girl on his arm. He gives Trey a big bear hug. He gives me an equally suffocating hug, spilling part of his drink down my back, and introduces us both to Tracy, his wife or girlfriend, I'm not sure which.

"Hey Mariah, Trey told me about Jack, such a shame. Really sorry." Bowie shakes his head sadly. "He was…quite a guy."

"Yes he was," I say.

"Good to see the two of you though. Twenty-five years! Seems like yesterday. I've been putting Trey to work too. He re-sided my house…hey Trey…remember that house we rented on 31st? God, what a dump!"

They spend some time reminiscing about their house, and their roommates, and the general life of the lifeguard they once led together. Tracy looks uncomfortable, so I try to engage her in conversation.

"Do you have kids?"

"Oh no. You?"

"A daughter. She's over there…" I point toward the band tent, where Caroline is dancing with several other kids. She knows I am there but refuses to look my way, preferring to pretend I don't exist. She wasn't happy to learn I was going to her party, but she calmed down when I promised I would stay with the old fogies and leave her alone.

Trey and Dave are soon joined by several other old guards who swap stories and laugh loudly at their own past antics, some too fantastic to be believed.

"Remember the time we went up to the Avalon Hotel and threw all the lounge chairs in the pool?"

"Remember that time we challenged the Stone Harbor Lifeguards to a game of Beer Die at Jack's Place and Bean got so hammered he got up on the roof and stripped naked and sang the Star Spangled Banner?"

"I remember Bean challenging Eric Carter to an oyster eating contest at Jack's Place—he was puking oysters all the next day. Man, that stunk!"

I remember none of these events, as I was too young at the time to go to bars like Jack's Place. The closest I got was the Banjo Room of the Princeton on teen night. This was a world in which I had not lived, and so I listened, longing to share in some of that bad boy camaraderie. Tracy looks merely bored and wanders away, toward the drinks tent. The sky darkens; dusk sets in. The sounds of the band, which has turned toward 70's fare, looms up from the other tent. I move toward it, gravitating as if against my will toward my daughter, telling myself I am not spying. I feel a hand on my arm.

"Hey, where're you going?" Trey looks concerned.

"Just checking up…on Caroline." I see her, all flowing hair and lithe, supple movement, looking far too grown up in high-heeled sandals and a short, too short, yellow dress. "How did it happen?" I ask myself.

"Time," Trey says beside me.

He puts a hand on my shoulder. I feel a soft shiver at his touch, a familiar ache in my stomach. The band segues into a slow song, one with an antique cadence, and the lead singer tells the crowd that this is for all the old guards at the party. The song is "Reunited" by Peaches and Cream. Trey and I look at each other and burst out laughing.

"Would you like to dance?" he asks me.

"Ah, that is something you didn't ask me the last time. Have you taken up dancing?"

"Well, no, but I'll follow if you lead."

"I always lead."

I lead him with my good hand to the dance floor, trying to stay clear of Caroline and Ben. Many of the old guards are on the floor now. Trey takes hold of me, his arm around my waist, his other hand holding mine, close to his chest.

"I'm sorry I never danced with you," he says softly, looking down at me. I see something sad in his eyes.

"I danced that whole night," I said with a laugh. "Me and the girls."

"You always did like to dance."

"Caroline hates it when I dance. It embarrasses her."

"Well, isn't that a parent's job? To embarrass your kids?"

"It's my goal in life."

He pulls me closer to him, I can feel the hardness of his body against me, the blood pulsing up to my face.

"Do you think she can see us?" he says in my ear.

"Oh yes, I'm sure she can see us," I say, giggling a little.

"So, do you think she is totally mortified yet?"

"Probably."

"Good. Then she's going to love this." He kisses me, his mouth swooping in over mine, taking me completely by surprise. I am halted by it, frozen, feeling his mouth, his tongue, his body still hard against mine. And then I am laughing, sputtering with pent up anxiety and giddiness. Trey is laughing too, our mouths still half connected, his arms still tight around me.

"God, do I feel old," he said.

I look around for Caroline, certain she must be watching, howling in horror at her mother's lack of decorum. But when I see her, I realize she has not been watching me at all. She has her arms around Ben, who is holding her much too close. They are swaying provocatively to the music, her head on his shoulder, his mouth against her ear.

I break away from Trey suddenly, the blood draining from my face.

"What's the matter?"

"Look at them!" I say, pointing. "I've got to stop this!"

"No," Trey says firmly, grabbing hold of my arm as I turn away from him. "Leave them alone."

"Leave them alone? Are you crazy? Look at them! I can't let this go on…"

"Mariah, stop!" I pull away and he grabs me by my bad wrist, yanking me backward. The pain takes my breath away, as if the frailly knitted bones had been pulled apart again. I cry out, holding my wrist.

"Oh, I'm sorry…"

I look up at him, confused, angry, the pain coursing up my arm. "Trey, I cannot let her kiss her own brother!" I whisper hoarsely at him.

"He's not her brother."

I stare at him, my whole body hot then cold. "What do you mean?"

He turns from me and walks away, outside of the tent. He is headed toward the shoreline. I follow, still holding my wrist.

"Trey! Trey, answer me!"

He stops finally, when we are far enough away from the party, from the crowd. He turns and looks at me, and I see something terrible in his eyes, like the vision of his own wife and son being blown up in a marketplace bomb. I wonder what could be as bad as that.

"Ben is not Jack's son," he says in a broken whisper, his voice so ragged I hardly recognize it. "He's mine."

The coldness creeps in again, running through me with a violent shiver, and I wonder if I am still standing up or have fallen, my face planted in the sand. But Trey is still before me, his face swimming before my eyes.

He turns away from me, staring out at the endless ocean. "Rachel was with me, not him."

I continue to stare at him, feeling as though I am sinking further and further into the sand. I can no longer breathe.

"No," I say finally. "It can't be."

"It was. Remember when you went to the hospital with Jack? You told me to take her home. That's when it started. There was something about her...something...I can't explain..."

"No," I say again, feeling stupid now, "I would have known."

"Rachel was good at hiding things," he says. "You didn't know about her baby, did you? I didn't know either. She never told me. She let her family believe it was Jack's, apparently. But as soon as I saw him, I knew."

I have Ben's face in my mind now, and I wonder how I had missed it, the similarity. There had been something familiar about him, now it seemed painfully obvious to me. Ben did not look like Jack at all. He looked like Rachel, but there was much of Trey in him too.

"No," I say. I cannot think beyond that word. *No.*

"We would meet under the fishing pier...just to talk. She seemed really into me and...I was flattered. A girl like that. She was just so different from anyone I had ever known..."

"Stop," I say, putting my good hand up. "I get it now. That's why she was so upset. She said she couldn't look at him. But I thought she was talking about Jack...oh God." I turn to the sea, my only refuge. I suppose people from the party are watching us now, wondering what is going on.

Trey goes on. "The night of the ball, I went looking for her, but she wouldn't talk to me, wouldn't look at me. I followed her out to the fishing pier...I never thought she would do what she did..."

"So that's how you got to her first," I say softly, "how you managed to save her."

He nods.

"When were you planning to tell me all this?"

"I don't know. Later. After this. I wanted to have one more night…with you."

I stand for a long time, facing the sea. And then I turn and walk, down the beach, away from him, away from everything. *Keep walking,* I tell myself. *Just keep walking.*

TWENTY-TWO

Sunday it rains, the kind of dreary, relentless rain that is every child's nightmare in Avalon, for they know as soon as they wake up in the morning that it will last the entire day.

I decide to go to church, to the tiny, red-doored Episcopal church called St. Johns By the Sea. I need to sit quietly and let words wash over me, words of love and reassurance. The pianist, a frail old lady, pounds on the keys with gusto and leads the congregation in a rousing hymn-sing, filling the small church with sound. A black preacher from Virginia Beach speaks about Truth. "The Truth shall set you free," he says, "but first it's gonna make you miserable." Amen.

I spend the day packing, closing up the house, making phone calls. I call Betsy and leave a message about putting the house on the market. I know that I can never come back here again. It is no longer a sanctuary for me. Caroline watches me in perplexed silence but does not try to talk me out of this. She knows that this time it is for good.

We leave on Monday. Labor Day. Ben comes to say goodbye, and he hugs Caroline close, but there is no kiss. I look the other way. She gets into the car and puts on her headphones, tuning me out. I take one last look at the Pink Poodle in the rearview mirror as I turn from 6th Street onto Dune Drive. My heart pounds with its brokenness. I cannot look anymore.

I should know better than to go to lifeguard parties.

The drive to Raleigh is endless and boring, throttled with traffic and heat vapors and downpours and truck tire treads littering the highway. We stop a couple of times for gas and food, and I see Caroline's eyes are red with tears, and I am glad that she is so consumed by her own grief she has no time to notice mine.

I have too much time to think, to put all the events of the summer of 1978 in context, to understand what I had missed. It all makes sense now. Rachel had been far more calculating than any of us knew. She had never wanted to marry Jack, had been looking for some excuse to get out of that relationship, and she had found a willing accomplice in Trey, a boy who would have been mesmerized by a girl like her, with her wealth and her beauty and her whimsical, Alice-in-Wonderland allure. I could not help but imagine the details for myself, shutting my eyes against the vision of the two of them. I had blamed all that on Jack, but Jack was innocent. Jack had never known about any of this. Jack had never lied to me.

I mourn for him, the grief welling in my soul like an unborn baby, like so many I had felt move and die in my womb. I want him back, want him here so I can tell him. I pray he is with God, that the God of the Universe would hold him close and whisper words of assurance in his ear. Ben is not his son, so even though he is still too old for Caroline, I did not have to worry about them anymore. But for Jack I mourn, for the years I spent blaming him for whatever was wrong with our relationship, the hidden memories that were not memories at all. I wish I could tell him how sorry I am.

We arrive home late that day to our house in Cary, on the western side of the city…a suburb so populated by northerners that the locals call it the "Centralized Area of Relocated Yankees." I had never realized until now how much Cary had changed, not unlike Avalon…so many beautiful old farm homesteads torn down to make room for more cookie cutter developments and strip malls. Cary had no real flavor; it looked like every other suburban asylum in the country. It was neat and attractive and completely undistinguished, its soul had been eaten away by urban sprawl, as northerners like me had been driven south, away from the long, dismal winters of a forgotten youth. I feel now like the alien I have always been here, but I don't have any other place to go.

Our neighbors are welcoming and extremely kind, as they have been since Jack's death. Fred MacDonald down the street has been faithfully mowing the lawn and cutting back weeds all summer, his wife Helen collecting mail and packages that had failed to be forwarded to my Avalon address. I have them over to dinner to thank them, and they fill us in on all the neighborhood news we had missed, which doesn't turn out to be very much.

Betsy calls me back promptly on Tuesday morning, eager to talk about listing the house. I give her the information and Mitch's number. She says she will take care of everything. I find I do not want to know the details.

I drift through time, not sure where I am or what I am doing, trying to unpack and restock and organize, but I cannot put my heart into any of it. I feel as if I am going to sink into a well-deserved depression, to lose myself in grief, not wanting to fight it anymore. I don't even bother taking the Prozac, for that will just dull the ache, and I need the ache, I need to feel something.

"You should see your doctor," Helen tells me, apprising the situation.

"Yes, I should, probably," I say. It is sunny and warm. We are sitting on Helen's back porch, watching the birds in her bird feeders. She had a dozen or so feeders, and she and Fred love to sit on the deck and watch them, singing with joy at the first sign of a bunting or oriole or the elusive green-tailed towhee.

"We had bluebirds this year," Helen tells me. "First time ever! But they're gone now. I even saw a common redpoll this year—quite uncommon for this area."

I find it somewhat therapeutic to visit Helen; her lively chatter, so similar to the birds she loved, distracts me from my own thoughts. The future looms before me like a formless shadow, a wasteland. Jack was my one connection to this world, and he is gone. Avalon was the only other place where I had felt grounded and safe, but that is gone too. Once the Pink Poodle is sold, the last cord will have been severed.

I call Mrs. Rosen. I have a question to ask her.

"I'm just curious," I say, trying to sound nonchalant, "but what name did Rachel put on the birth certificate for the father?"

"I don't remember," she says quietly. "it was not a name I knew. I assumed she made it up."

"Oh," I say. Then I ask something else, "I know this sounds strange to ask, but what is Ben's full name? Is it Benjamin?"

"No," she says, "Ben is actually his middle name. Bennett. Jonathan Bennett is his name. Rachel wanted to call him Ben. I thought it was odd—we have some Benjamins in our family, but no Bennetts. But Rachel liked to be a little different, as you well know."

Bennett.

"Thank you, Mrs. Rosen," I say.

"Call me Amanda," she says.

"Thank you...Amanda," I say awkwardly. I doubt her own husband calls her by her first name.

I do not tell her about Ben's true parentage. I had meant to, but could not bring myself to do it. That was Rachel's choice, I could not betray her now.

Friends come to see me, their faces pitying and solemn, as if they were attending a funeral. They tell me I look wonderful. They like my new hairstyle. They are all hopeful that I have gotten over it, finally, that I have moved on, that they no longer need to feel strained or wary in my presence, afraid of saying the wrong thing. I suppose this is normal, but it riles me. I stop answering the phone. If they come to the house I stand in the front door and talk through the screen without opening it — it sends the message that I do not want company. I want, seriously, to be alone, to wallow in my own misery without anyone disturbing me.

"Mom, we need yogurt," Caroline says to me on Saturday two weeks after coming home. "And milk. And bread. When are you going grocery shopping?" Caroline has launched into school, her friends, and the cross-country team without missing a beat. Ben is, apparently, forgotten. But after two weeks she is beginning to get annoyed with my continued moping.

"Oh, I'll go today," I tell her. I am watching the news. A weather flash has come on the TV — a hurricane brewing in the Atlantic.

"Can I borrow the car?" she asks.

"Where are you going?"

"To the mall. With Nicole and Anna."

"There's a hurricane coming," I say out loud, not even listening to her answer. "Category 4."

"Well, at least you won't have to worry about the house at OB now," she says, from the laundry room. "Where are my skinny jeans? Did you wash them?"

I don't hear her. I am watching the storm tracking models. At least one of those models shows Hurricane Isabel heading northward, toward the Jersey Shore.

This information is like an electric shock to my system. I switch channels, hoping for better news. The storm is huge, as big as the state of Colorado, and moving slowly, picking up a lot of ocean moisture. This is a rare storm, achieving Category 5 status for almost 3 straight days, an unheard of phenomenon. The weather forecasters are pumped with energy, excitedly proclaiming that this is the biggest storm they have seen in at least five years. Though it is now a Category 4, it will most likely go back to a 5 because of its slow movement and the particular atmospheric conditions in which it lies.

As a homeowner on the Outer Banks, I had become a sort of expert on hurricanes. Locals paid very little attention to the news until landfall was imminent, but I was not a local, and the giant storms were a source of mystery and wonder to me. Since I've been here we've averaged about four storms a season, though only a few have been really memorable: Diane, Gloria, Charley, Emily, Bertha, Fran, Bonnie and Floyd, and then there was Hugo, the only one to skip the coast and ravage the inland part of the state. I talked about them as if they were my wayward children...*you remember what Floyd did to our beach front? How Bonnie pulled up our landscaping?* Jack always thought I was a little mad about the storms, but I was born in a storm, I had wind in my blood. I could sense the bad ones and this one, still building in the mid-Atlantic, was going to be the worst yet.

I call Betsy to ask about storm preparation. She doesn't know what I am talking about.

"The hurricane," I say impatiently.

"I didn't know there was one," she says. "I haven't watched the news in awhile."

"Hurricane Isabel, it could possibly hit the Jersey Shore in less than a week," I say, trying to keep my voice calm.

"Oh. Well, I will check into it and get back to you."

I get nowhere with the Avalon Highway Department, which is equally clueless. So I do the one thing I promised myself I would never do. I call Trey.

He doesn't answer. I get his voicemail instead, and I leave a message: "Trey, it's me. I'm watching the news and there's a hurricane headed for the coast and some of the stations are saying it may hit New Jersey. I don't know what to do. Call me." I hang up.

I always knew what to do when a storm raced toward the Outer Banks. That house had been built to sustain hurricane winds of 100 mph and a storm surge of 20 feet; it had concrete pilings and multi-sided walls to channel the wind. It had aluminum shutters that sealed the windows and outward-opening exterior doors, which would not be blown in during high winds. It had a metal harness-reinforced roof, because we had learned that most of the time a house was destroyed when the wind got under the roof and lifted it off its foundations. That house was a fortress.

Next to that, the Pink Poodle seems as fragile as the house made of sticks by the second little pig. It had survived the storm of '62, barely, but that storm could not compare to a real hurricane, the huffing and puffing of that monstrous wind which could pull fully grown trees right out of the ground with roots intact. Once in OB an improperly secured motorboat had tumbled onto our deck, which was on the second floor. I had seen what that wind can do.

Trey did not call until late that night.

"Sorry I didn't call earlier," he says. "I've been drafted into the Emergency Coordination Commission for Avalon. We get to decide if there's going to be an evacuation."

"Is there?"

"Not yet. What can I do?"

He sounds so…normal. I'm not sure how to handle this, what to say to him. But my fear overrides my lingering anger.

"I'm sorry to bother you…but the realtor was clueless and I didn't know who else to call…"

"The house needs to be boarded up," he says without waiting for me to mention it. "I'll take care of it."

"No, Trey, I can't ask you to do that…"

"You didn't ask. I'll take care of it. Don't worry."

I hang up, feeling numb. When Caroline gets home from school I tell her.

"I'm going back."

"Where?"

"To Avalon."

"What?" She looks at me like I just confessed to murder. "What for?"

"The storm may hit the shore, even if it's not a direct hit, it could be bad. I need to take care of the house."

"Mom, this is crazy…the house is for sale! You said yourself it would just be torn down anyway. You have insurance…"

"It's not about the insurance," I snap at her.

"Then what is it about?"

How could I explain to her that I could not let this house go down without a fight? I could not sit idly by five hundred miles away while Isabel ravaged the only place I had ever truly thought of as home. I had to fight for it, as my father and grandfather had fought. Even if there was no chance of winning.

I make hasty arrangements for Caroline to stay with friends *(I can stay by myself, Mom!),* and I call what people I know who might be interested in the fact that I am going back to Avalon. One of them is Mitch, who tells me I am foolish, that the storm is much more likely to hit North Carolina.

"But there's nothing I can do about that," I say. As if that were answer enough.

I call Helen and Fred. They are equally dubious of my journey.

"Mariah, I don't think you should go by yourself," Helen says, clearly worried by my agitated state.

"I'll be fine," I say.

"Is there really anything you can do? I mean, don't you have that caretaker fellow boarding up the house? What else is there to be done?"

I don't know the answer to that. It just seems important that I be there, in the house. I feel it in my very marrow — this is what my grandfather wanted. Maybe it was he who was propelling me north again, refusing to accept my decision to rid myself of the Pink Poodle forever.

I load the Explorer and head out on Tuesday morning. It is still brilliantly sunny in Cary, no hint of a coming storm. The computer models show the storm tracking farther south than they originally predicted, but already Maryland, Virginia and New Jersey have issued hurricane warnings. A hurricane was a feckless creature, given to twists and turns, it's path unknowable even to those who spent their lives studying them. I had learned to never trust weather forecasters or computer models any more than I could trust the storms themselves.

I drive all day. Traffic is light. I usually love to drive alone, listening to books on tape, making phone calls to people I never have time to talk to when I am home. But this trip I listen to the weather forecast, which does not change much from hour to hour, and I cannot concentrate on anything else. My mind goes to dark memory, to the eye of this storm, to the gray terror of a hurricane in full fury. Pictures of past storms, news footage, old movies, play endlessly in my brain. The pictures of Avalon after the '62 storm that line the walls of the post office and museum — the empty pilings, the houses collapsed and leaning, crumbled like houses of cards. The sheer nothingness of those pictures…where once there stood homes there was often nothing left at all — not even scraps of wood. How could whole neighborhoods disappear so completely? A storm by the sea, there was no deadlier combination.

I arrive in the early evening, unsettled at seeing the house again and startled by the changes I had made…the new deck, the reinforced porch, the roof that no longer looked pitted and frayed. I shut off the car and stumble up the steps to see piles of lumber sheeting sitting on the porch, more piles around the house. Trey has already been here.

The house is dark and stuffy. I turn on a light, surprised at the new things I see which I had already forgotten, the pillows and rugs, the lampshades, the curtains, the fresh coat of paint, the bright new kitchen floor. How cheerful it looks, how welcoming. Was this only the house beckoning to me again, hoping this time I will stay?

"No," I say aloud. I cannot stay. I just want to sleep now, so I turn out the light and go upstairs.

Trey calls at midnight, waking me out of a restless dream.

"What is it?" I snap into the phone, fearful.

"Sorry," he says. "I called to see if you were okay. I saw your car."

"I was asleep."

"I'm sorry…it's late, I guess. Go back to sleep. I'll be there in the morning to put up the sheeting."

I know I will not fall asleep easily, and suddenly I do not want to be here alone anymore.

"Can you come tonight?"

There is a silence on the line.

"Yes."

I am waiting for him at the bottom of the stairs when he knocks. I open the door. He is wearing a T-shirt that says "Avalon Beach Patrol" and torn jeans, heavy boots. He looks very tired. I want to put my arms around him, but then I remember, and I stay where I am.

"Thanks for coming," I say. "You look exhausted. You can sleep in Caroline's room."

"I'll sleep on the couch."

"It's as old as the hills."

"So am I. We'll get along fine."

He goes there, sits heavily on the couch then leans over and puts his head down. His eyes are closed, he is asleep before he can even put his feet up. I do that for him, pulling off his boots. I watch him sleeping, wondering if this is how he looked in Afghanistan, when he was at war, when sleep happened at random moments, a rare gift of peace. I wonder if he dreams of her, his wife, and his child, and wakes up to realize they are gone. Often I dream of Jack. He is so alive in my dreams, and they are so real that the moment of waking is like going through the initial shock of finding out all over again, the stark realization happening as if for the first time. That is the worst part about sleeping, about dreaming. The dreams don't last long enough.

I take an Ambien and go to bed and dream of storms, and Jack on a white horse, like King Arthur, fighting a losing battle, the last battle. Trey is not in the dream. I call for him but he never comes, arrives when it is too late, when the battle is already lost.

TWENTY-THREE

September 17, 2003

The piercing wail of Avalon's fire siren breaks the lulling silence of the morning and Trey sits up, almost to his feet before he even realizes he is awake. I am sitting in the easy chair opposite the couch, watching him, a cup of coffee in my hand. It is 7 o'clock, but I have been up for over an hour. The house awakened me with soft whispers; the wind had kicked up, brushing against the old shutters and thrumming the windows. The sky is still clear, but the air feels different, charged. According to the New Jersey Office of Emergency Management, a hurricane watch was in effect for the entire coast of New Jersey. The storm itself would hit the coast around North Carolina and head north, creating a possible storm surge on the Jersey shore of 8 to 12 feet. The storm surge was the real danger to the Pink Poodle, which sat on the precipice of the inlet, mere steps from the sea wall. I had always feared that sound, the sound of the waves thrashing the rocks outside our window. It was the sound of power untested and unknown, relentless and unstoppable. An 8-foot storm surge would easily overcome that wall. Combined with high winds…

I tried not to think about it, going downstairs and making coffee while Trey slept on. I wonder when was the last time he slept. I did not want to wake him, though I was anxious for him get started on helping me board up the house.

But the wail of the siren does the work for me.

"Hey," I say, just so he knows I am there. He looks up, blinks.

"Hey," he says, his voice still raspy with exhaustion. "That damned siren."

"Does it mean they're evacuating?"

"No. It's a signal to turn on the radio."

"I've had it on already. It's an official watch, which will become a warning by tomorrow."

He nodded. "You need supplies…"

"I brought everything. Water, food, flashlights, batteries…I'm an old hat at hurricanes, you know. Want some coffee?"

"Yes, please."

He gets up and follows me into the kitchen. He takes the coffee cup and sits heavily at the table.

"We spent yesterday sandbagging the dune walks. It's like sticking your finger in a hole in the bottom of a boat to stop it sinking. The beach is so narrow here. Not like Wildwood. Even a little storm surge can be brutal. We're going to lose a lot of beach this week." He seems to be talking more or less to himself.

"I have doughnuts," I say. "Sugar and caffeine is what you need. Then you can take a shower, and we'll get to work."

I do not want to talk today. I do not want to have the conversation we need to have, the one I know is coming, so I avoid it with busyness.

Trey does as he is told, eats and drinks his coffee and goes upstairs to take a shower. He tells me he has a change of clothes in his truck, so I go out to the drive and root through his stuff — it seems as though he has been living in his truck — until I find a duffle bag that seems to have clean clothes in it, along with flashlights and energy bars. I bring it into the house and up the stairs, leaving it in Caroline's room. Then I go back downstairs and drink more coffee and listen to the radio and wait.

We spend most of the day doing the windows, me holding nails and boards while Trey crawls up and down the ladder, hammering relentlessly. I glance at the big house next door and see it has aluminum shudders that roll down over the windows, just like the OB house.

When we are done I make sandwiches, and we sit on the porch in the rising humidity, eating and staring out at the ocean, which has already begun to make overtures of the symphony to come. The spray of the breaking waves is visible over the sea wall in front of us.

"You can feel it," I say. "The sea coming up. It seems so calm on the outside, but underneath…you can feel it rising."

Trey nods. "When I was a lifeguard we had to go out in the mornings and test the current. It became like a person, almost…like it had hundreds of moods, and you never knew what it was going to be like. The sea is a woman, I think."

I laugh at that.

"You're right. The Ancient Greeks called them the Nereids. They were the moods of the sea, as you call them, the tides, the currents, the waves, the foamy brine that washes up on the shore. They were beautiful and deadly, powerful and mercurial, calling up storms to sink ships at a whim. They rode around on dolphins with their mother, Amphitrite, who was the wife of Poseidon. Sort of like mermaids or sirens…mischievous and willful, calling to sailors with their songs so that they become distracted and run their ships aground."

"You would know that," Trey says with a wry smile.

I shrug. "I like stories. Especially old stories. Ancient ones."

"Yeah I know. King Arthur."

"Yes. I like the…grandness of them. The larger than life aspect. The tragedy, I guess. Maybe because I was always trying to escape my own boring life."

"But you did escape," he says. "You went to a first-rate university, the first in your family I'm guessing. You married a prince and lived in fairy tale palace…happily ever after."

"Sure," I say ruefully. "It was all I ever wanted. That was the problem. After Jack died I thought I should try to get a job. But then I realized that I had absolutely no marketable skills. I had no resume. I didn't even have a college degree. What sort of job could I possibly get?"

"There's got to be some wayward group of volunteers that need organizing."

"Ha ha."

"You could come and work for me," he says quietly. I look at him, wondering if he is serious. He shrugs. "I could use your eye for design. And your organizational skills. Business is picking up, surprisingly. I'm not going to be able to handle it all myself."

I don't know what to say to this. He talks as though he thinks I will stay here. "It's nice of you to offer…really." I look away, to the far distant horizon. "I just don't know…Jack lived a life of purpose. He saved people. Like you did. Your life has had…significance. While I was arranging place cards at charity balls, you were changing history."

"Was I?" he says, a note a weariness in his voice. "You at least ran *to* something. I was just…running away. I wanted to escape. But you can't really escape, can you? I often wonder if what happened in Kabul…was not a punishment for what happened in Avalon."

"Do you believe that?" I say softly, gazing at him.

"Sometimes. Aren't the things that happen to us…the bad things…some kind of divine justice? A way of paying for our sins?"

"No." I turn to him. "Your wife and son died because of evil people who did an evil thing. Not because of anything you did."

To my surprise, he smiles, as if there is some great weight lifted from his shoulders.

"Arya would have said something like that," he says.

Just then the fire siren blows again, shattering our little, fragile peace. It goes on for a solid minute, the piercing whine that used to send us diving for cover as kids. I always hated that sound. An announcement is made on the radio shortly after, reiterating the hurricane warning in effect. As if we needed reminding.

"I need to go check in at the station, see if there is anything new," he says, putting his coke down and standing up. "The house is buttoned up as well as can be. Now it's just a waiting game. Are you sure you want to stay?"

"Yes. I'm staying. You know I have to."

"The smart thing is to go inland and wait it out."

"The captain is supposed to go down with the ship," I say flippantly, hoping it would sound like a joke. But somehow it doesn't. "I'll be fine. Like I said, I've done plenty of hurricanes. I'm a veteran."

"Yes, I guess you are," he says, gazing at me. "Has there ever been a hurricane named Mariah?"

I laugh. "Strangely, no. There was a snow storm named Mariah, in the Sierra Nevadas back in the 50's. And there was a racehorse named Mariah's Storm, though. About 10 years ago. She suffered a broken leg but recovered fully and even went back to racing. They made a movie about it."

Trey grins. "You're amazing. Thanks for lunch." He heads down the steps.

"Will you come back?"

He turns and looks at me, surprised. "Do you really want me to?"

I hesitate, uncertain of even why I had even asked. I had momentarily forgotten that I was still mad at him, or that there was something between us that could not be repaired. I only saw him, this man who had once been a god of this beach, now weathered and wind-torn and desperately in need of grace.

"Sure, if you…have time."

The corner of his mouth twitches slightly, a gesture I have come to recognize in him. "I'll see you."

I watch him get into his truck and pull out of the driveway and disappear around the corner to Dune Drive. I look up at the blue sky, the high wisps of clouds, thinking how incongruous it was that a giant storm lurked just off the horizon, and that tomorrow this peaceful shore would be a very different place.

"Grandpa," I whisper softly into the air, "I'm here."

TWENTY-FOUR

I spend the afternoon bringing in chairs and flowerpots and anything else that could become a missile in a bad wind. Then I make calls: to Helen, to Caroline, to my father who is grateful that I am at the house, and my mother who thinks I'm an idiot. *You should have stayed in North Carolina with your daughter. That's where the storm is! Why would you drive all the way to New Jersey by yourself?*

She's probably right. But Caroline is oblivious to the storm. School will be cancelled tomorrow, and she and her friends are all together at her friend Monique's house, making plans for a slumber party to end all slumber parties. I envy her fearlessness, as I always have.

Trey calls later in the afternoon to tell me there is a meeting at the community center for all residents to go over emergency evacuation plans, in case of a flood. So much of Avalon's dunes have been eroded or destroyed that there is precious little standing between the ocean and the million dollar homes along the beach. I don't feel like going but I do anyway, mainly because I want to see Trey. I'm pathetic.

The community center sits across from the 30th street boardwalk. It has a large gym, which is used mainly for basketball camp and for family movie nights on Tuesdays if it's raining on the beach. Anxious people are milling about, many gathered around a long table filled with pamphlets and bulletins and flyers put out by the OEM: "What to do in the case of a hurricane." I cannot help but feel superior to these clueless amateurs and berate myself for feeling that way.

I see Trey surrounded by a cluster of residents asking nervous questions of him. He is wearing an OEM windbreaker over his T-shirt; apparently he had been recruited as an official. He sees me and smiles, and I blush when the people around him turn to look at me. He disengages from the group and comes over to me.

"Are you in charge now?" I ask him. "That didn't take long."

"Stan is doing the briefing. I'm just supposed to help Morey keep the surfers out of the water. So many crazy surfers think they've died and gone to heaven."

"How are you going to do that?"

"We've got some guys who will be patrolling the beach in trackers throughout the storm."

"Sounds kind of dangerous."

"We've done it before. It's not a big deal."

He stays with me during the briefing, which is pretty standard stuff. Stan encourages everyone who can to leave the island. "We aren't evacuating, but there is always the chance of flooding, in which case help will be slow in coming." He is basically saying: *if you get stranded, don't call us*. It is a fair warning. Many people do decide to leave, booking hotels or staying with friends. Trey looks hopefully at me again, but I shake my head.

"I would feel better if I knew you were safe," he says.

I am surprised at the concern in his voice.

"You're the one who's going to be riding around the beach in a tracker," I say, trying to sound cool about it all. "How about some dinner? I'm starved."

We decide to walk to the Rock 'n Chair, the only restaurant that is still open. Most of the rest of the town is there also, which does not amount to many patrons. The dry, air-conditioned air feels refreshing after the sticky humidity outside. The hostess takes us to a table, chatting with Trey about the coming storm. She acts as though it were going to be a great party. She has that clueless invincibility of the truly young.

We order burgers and beer and sit looking at each other in the dim light, wondering what there is left to say. I can think of only one thing.

"You need to tell him."

He doesn't look at me. "He knows, Mariah."

"He knows?"

"Yeah. After you left, I went up to see Rachel."

I stare at him. "You saw her?"

He nods. "You told me she was at that place, Maple Grove? She's there. She's sick. Really sick. Cancer. But she won't do anything about it. Some holistic diet or something. She told me that Ben had gone in search of his real father without her knowing. He found his birth certificate with the name and confronted her about it. So she told him the truth. That's why he came here. To find me."

This information astounds me. "But he never said…"

"No, I guess he didn't want to spook me or something."

"Mrs. Rosen said Rachel used a fake name on the birth certificate."

"I wondered about that. So I went up to Trenton to the Office of Records. She used my name, my *real* name: Taylor Bennett.

"Taylor? Your name is Taylor?" I say incredulously.

"Yeah. Trey is a nickname. I never told anyone that—would you want anyone to know your name was Taylor? My father always said my mother named me after Elizabeth Taylor, her favorite movie star. She named my sister after Rita Hayworth. Or Rita Moreno, I can't remember. At least she didn't name me Elizabeth."

I smile. "How did Rachel know?"

"I told her. She asked me once, about my name. No one ever did that. It's bizarre when you think about it—she put the truth on that birth certificate but everyone thought it was a lie. But she knew that no one in her family would recognize the name."

I take a minute to absorb all this. Finally I look at him.

"So…she has cancer? Is it bad?" I ask.

He sighed. "I don't know how bad. She wouldn't tell me. She looked good though. Like she hadn't aged at all. Time seems to have stopped for her. But it was like…another world, another life. I didn't know whether to be angry or grateful. She had lied to me, lied to all of us, but it didn't seem to matter anymore. She said she was sorry she never told me about Ben. God, Mariah, how different my life would have been, if I had only known."

"I'm sorry, Trey," I say, overwhelmed with his sadness.

We sit in silence.

"What are you going to do?"

"About Ben? I don't know. How do I call up a kid who barely knows me…a kid who is 24 years old, and tell him I'm his father? It's way too Darth Vader."

"You could challenge him to a light saber fight," I say helpfully.

The burgers arrive, thick and juicy and we both eat as if we have not eaten in days.

"I haven't had a hamburger in ten years," I say. "Jack was very into fitness, healthy eating. Lots of fiber. I've eaten Boca burgers for so long I forgot how wonderful real ground beef is. This is delicious."

"I haven't exactly been on a meat diet the last twenty years either," he says. "Though I wouldn't call it healthy."

"I'm sorry. I keep forgetting about that."

"I'm beginning to…forget. This summer helped. It's like all that happened in some other life. When I try to remember what they looked like…it's hard to remember even now."

"I know," I say. "I have the same problem. I thought I would never forget his face, his voice…now there are days when I don't think of him at all. How can that be?"

"Maybe it's a way of surviving. Of not just stopping and laying down and waiting to die."

"Yes, that's it, I guess."

We look at each other.

"Come on," Trey says when we're finished. "There's still light left. Let's go down to the beach, one last time."

He reaches across the table and takes my hand, pulling me out of the booth. He doesn't let go of my hand, and I don't protest. The past seems to have dissolved in the space between us; there are no more secrets now. The truth, as the preacher had said, *will* set us free.

Trey pays the bill and we walk back to the 30th Street beach, feeling the gathering wind in our faces. Even the clouds looks tossed about, spreading across the sky in a hectic array. On the boardwalk the initial effects of the storm surge can already be felt, the wind carrying the sea spray across the dunes and into our faces. The arcade and the ice cream parlor are boarded up, and someone has spray-painted "Blow Izzy blow" on the plywood. It is in our nature to dare the wind, I guess. We are all mighty warriors before the storm hits.

The 30th street beach is dotted with surfers getting in their last good turns before the patrols come out. We can hear their hooting and hollering as we skirt the sandbags and hop across the dunes, a move that is normally quite illegal, for the dunes are sacrosanct in Avalon, and walking on them is punishable by a heavy fine.

The party atmosphere intensifies as we get down to the beach, with several of the surfers shouting at Trey in their high, surfer-dude calls, beckoning him out on the waves. I look up at him and see the veiled longing in his eyes.

"Go on," I say, nudging. "You may never get a chance like this again."

"I'm supposed to be keeping people out of the water," he says.

"That's for tomorrow. Go on."

He doesn't move, but soon a group of young men approach him, taunting. "C'mon, old man, show us how it's done!" He finally obliges them, pulling off his OEM jacket and T-shirt, and stripping off his pants, revealing a pair of old beach patrol swim shorts. They cheer as he takes the board they offer and follow him like lemmings down to the shoreline, toward waves the likes of which I have never seen in Avalon before: not overly high but astoundingly strong, as if the nereids themselves were hurling themselves en masse at the shore.

A group of them go out together, Trey in their midst, paddling hard over the huge swells, and I see that he has not forgotten much of his surfer skill. He looks like one of them, his body lean and wiry from years of near starvation and rigorous physical activity, browned from the hot Avalon sun. I see his scars for the first time: one whole side of his body is puckered and reddened with burn scars. I stare at those scars until I don't see them anymore; I watch Trey Bennett surf for the first time in twenty-five years, his tall frame rising up from the board as a jaw-dropping wave comes nearly over the top of him, pushing him forward, up out of the sea, with unimaginable force. He dives and dips, the board like a living thing under him, while surfers around him crumble to the power of the surging waves. He rides onto the beach to thundering cheers, and for moment he is that 19-year old boy I remember, his long body moving with the churning ocean like synchronized dancers under the dusky sky. He leaves the boys after exacting a promise that they will be off the beach by dark, then returns to me, dripping but smiling, his whole body exuding a peerless joy.

"I see you've been keeping in practice," I say, handing him his clothes.

"I've been doing some lessons," he says with a shrug. "Helping Morey on my days off. It's been...fun. Weird, too, being back with Morey. He hasn't changed a bit. Guy's got more energy than ten of these kids. Still yells like a demon too."

On the ride back to the Pink Poodle the wind sounds ominous, like the distant rumble of an oncoming train. I know at its worst it will be a high, keening sound, a shrill persistent wail that chills to the marrow. I shudder at memories of winds past.

"Thank you," I say to him as I get out of the truck. I don't invite him in. I need some space. Being near him makes it hard to think. "For...everything."

He smiles. "Get some sleep, could be a long day tomorrow."

"Yes. I will." I turn away and move up the stairs to the porch.

"Mariah."

I turn and look back at him. He's gotten out of the truck and is standing on the drive, looking up at me.

"I need to tell you something. All this has been kind of crazy...Ben, Rachel...this storm. I don't know where you are with all that...I know there's probably a lot of stuff you are still...upset about. But I'm just going to say this, okay? I love you. I want you to stay

243

here. With me. Forever. Or for whatever time we have. You don't have to say anything. Just…think about it."

I stare at him, speechless. He turns and gets back in his truck and pulls away, leaving me on the sagging porch of a shambling house by a raging sea.

TWENTY-FIVE
September 18, 2003

A noise like knocking wakes me the next morning. At first I think
it is simply the screen door on the back porch banging open as it
always did in windy weather. I sit up in bed, my eyes straining to stay
open. I cannot remember falling asleep, or dreaming…only listening to
the wind and the waves, growing in their power through the dark night.
Today is Thursday, September 18. The day that Isabel will come.

The knocking comes again, louder, more persistent. Not a
slamming screen door. Trey? I think. I pull on sweat pants and a baggy
sweatshirt and tumble down the stairs to open the door.

It's Ben.

Ben?

He smiles awkwardly at me. He is wearing jeans and a Rutgers
sweatshirt under a windbreaker. He's got a large backpack slung over
one shoulder.

"Hi, Mrs. Pendergrast. Sorry to surprise you…"

"Good Lord, Ben. What are you doing here?"

I had assumed it was early in the morning. With the windows boarded up I have no idea what time of day it is, nor can I tell anything from the sky behind him, which is thick with clouds, already misty with rain.

"I called Caroline," he was saying, "and she told me you were here alone, so I thought I would come down and see how you were doing. Classes were cancelled today anyway."

"What time is it?"

"About 10."

"10? No…" I put a hand to my hair self-consciously. "Come in. I'm sorry. I didn't sleep much last night…" In truth I had taken an extra Ambien to block out the wind. "You came to see how I was doing?" I say, as if that part of his speech had finally entered my consciousness. The room is as dark as a cave so I start turning on lights.

"I think Caroline was worried about you."

"Oh." I stand still a moment, staring at him blankly. "I need to get dressed, I think. Do you know how to make coffee?"

"Sure."

"Good."

I take a quick shower and put on makeup and actual clothes and return to the kitchen with a bit more presence of mind.

"Ben," I say, "it was nice of you to come all the way down here. But I'm fine. Don't feel as though you need to babysit me."

"To tell you the truth, Mrs. Pendergrast, I knew it was going to be a boring day on campus, and I've always wanted to see a hurricane up close — you know, on the ocean."

"Oh, so you came for the drama? I feel better."

"I hope I made this okay for you."

He hands me a cup of the black stuff, which smells extremely strong. I reach into the refrigerator for some cream.

"Better make use of the appliances before the power goes," I say. "Did you eat breakfast?"

"Oh, I picked up some bagels on my way. And cream cheese."

"Bless you."

We sit down at the table to eat. The room seems to darken even further.

"It's weird, isn't it? The darkness," he says.

"Caroline didn't tell me she talked to you," I say, ignoring his comment. He flushes a little.

"Maybe she wasn't sure if you'd approve."

"Well, I'm not sure I do, but since you were so gallant as to drive all the way down here into the tail of the storm, and bring food, I will forgive you."

"Thanks. I appreciate it."

"Do you want me to call Trey and tell him you're here?"

He hesitates. The wind howls as if in answer to my question. I can feel the boarded windows shake and rattle, as if the house itself is crying out.

"It's okay Ben," I say. "I know about Trey."

He looks surprised. "But how…?"

"It's a really long story, and I'm going to tell you all about it. But first we need to get ready for this storm."

We check all the windows and doors then gather up the supplies and the flashlights and settle ourselves in the cupola room, my grandfather's room, which I discern to be the safest place in the house because of the added strength of the cupola walls. I am really only buying time, working out what I am going to tell him, for there are some things I do not think he needs to know. I am startled by how much of Trey I see in him, in his movement and mannerism, the way he brushes back his hair even, the slight dimple in his left cheek when he smiles. In fact, I feel as though he is becoming Trey for me, the boy I knew twenty-five years ago, before war and death took pieces of his soul.

We settle into the wing chairs with our flashlights and blankets and food supplies and, while the wind rattles the bones of the Pink Poodle, I tell him about that summer of 1978, about Trey and Jack and Rachel and me. But the story changes as I tell it, becoming more a story of Trey and Rachel, of the secret things I had missed the first time around, and then the story becomes something else altogether: a story of a love that could not survive beyond the shore of Avalon, like the stories my grandfather had woven for me for so many years in that house. And the house moans with the telling, with the revelation of a story that had been so long untold. I can feel it shivering around me, battered by the strengthening wind, assailed by a sheeting, horizontal rain that could have been driven straight through the walls. When I am finished, we both are quiet, listening to the house cry out in its long forgotten grief.

"Wow," he says when I am done. "This is so weird."

I laugh. "Weird is a good word," I say. Then I add: "Ben, it's none of my business, of course, but I am going to ask anyway: why haven't you told him?"

Ben shrugs. "I almost did. A few times. But I figured, since he didn't want me then, why would he want me now?"

"Ben, he never knew about you."

Ben looks at me, surprised. "He didn't?"

"Your mom never told him."

"Oh. Wow." Ben is silent awhile, absorbing it all. I look at my watch.

"Hey, it's past noon. If you want to see that hurricane, you'd better get out there."

He seems to come out of his reverie. "Oh yeah. Cool. I brought a video camera." He gets up and retrieves the camera from his backpack. I see it has a waterproof casing on it. "I'll be back in a few minutes."

He goes out, battling the wind for control of the door. I wait, listening to the battery-operated clock on the wall tick the minutes. He is back in five minutes, soaked and flush with excitement.

"Wow. Awesome waves out there."

"How's the seawall holding up?"

"Oh, you're fine so far. I got some cool video."

He could care less if a wave overtook the house, so long as he got it on video. I laugh. "Let me get you a towel."

We go back to our perches and watch the footage he's gotten on the little screen of the camcorder. It's impressive.

"You have a future as an extreme storm videographer," I say.

"Kind of wish I'd gone down to the Outer Banks," he says. "That would have been amazing."

"Do you have some kind of death wish?"

He laughs. "Just like the adrenaline rush. I'm kind of a junky."

"What other adrenaline-inducing activities do you do?"

"Growing up in Vermont, it was mostly mountain climbing, rapelling, skiing. I did a little aerial ski jumping too."

"Sky-diving?"

"No, but I've always wanted to."

"Naturally." I swallow hard. "I'm going to make us some lunch, while you tell me about…your life."

I make peanut butter and jelly sandwiches while he talks about his life, split between the rustic commune and the rich suburban neighborhoods of North Jersey. He seemed the sort to have been comfortable in either place, not really noticing the differences.

"The commune was a fun place to grow up," he says with perfect candor. "For a kid it's like being at permanent summer camp. I didn't have to go to school. The adults there educated us kids. Lots of them were teachers or professionals who had retired or wanted to escape the real world. My mom taught poetry. She even got some of her poems published."

"Really?"

"Yeah. But she didn't tell the commune board because you aren't allowed to make money outside of the commune."

"Did she ever…get married?" I ask cautiously.

"Nah. Marriage wasn't really a thing there anyway. Guys at Maple came and went, not many of them stayed very long. None of them interested her. Ken—he was one of the elders there—used to say the only sort of people the community attracted were losers and loners. Still, there were good people there. Everyone took care of each other. We had our moments, though. Once a friend of mine and I went to visit some kids at another commune about ten miles away…we stayed out too long and we didn't know how to get back cause it was dark, so we borrowed one of the commune's vans, but neither one of us knew how to drive! My friend drove it right into a tree. The elders were really mad about that. We had to pay for the van ourselves. Five hundred dollars. That's a lot of labor credits, let me tell you. But it all turned out okay."

"Why did you leave?"

"Well, as I got older, the life became a little …confining. I mean, did I want to spend my life making hammocks and maple syrup? It's a small world, the commune. I guess if you've been out in the big world and are done with it, it can seem like nirvana. Maybe I'll go back someday, I don't know."

"But you're going to be a lawyer."

"Yeah, maybe. My grandfather offered to pay my way. He's anxious for me to follow in the family tradition. But I'm not sure I really want to be a lawyer, to tell you the truth."

"Is that why you took a year off? To go on your adventures?"

"Yeah, it was awesome. I was afraid a lot, but I felt really like I was doing something significant, you know? I mean, does the world really need another lawyer?"

"You're asking me?" I say with a laugh. "Definitely not." I am silent a moment, looking at him. "You are so much like him."

"Yeah? I guess…him joining the Berets, going off to Afghanistan. That's some adrenaline rush."

"Sometime he will tell you all about it." I had not told Ben about Trey's wife and son. That was not my story to tell.

"I hope so."

"Let me call him," I say urgently. "At least let me tell him you're here. So he can come over when he's done. I'm sure there can't be any more people to chase off the beach by now."

"OK." He doesn't hesitate; he seems ready. But when I call there is no answer. I leave a message.

"Cell service is still working, anyway," I say as I push the end button. "Hopefully he'll get the message."

I find I don't mind the storm so much, with Ben leaping in and out of the Pink Poodle while I hold the door to keep it from breaking inward with the force of the wind. The rain is propelled horizontally by the wind, so that it feels like tiny daggers slicing through our faces when we open the door. The waves catapult over the seawall like mad specters, dousing the road to our driveway, which is already flooded. I see it creeping toward my front porch, rising steadily. Avalon has floods even in the mildest of thunderstorms, for the storm sewers can never quite handle the excess. The tires of my car are almost completely under water. I can only hope that the water will not rise above the house's pilings.

I decide I don't really like standing so near the storm, so while Ben takes his video I go up to my aerie and gaze out through the tiny dormer window, which we had not covered. The inlet bridge has virtually disappeared, washed out by the ocean. The grasses and trees along the shoreline are bent over, flattened by the wind, which has reached its high-pitched whine, almost a whistle, constant and piercing, obliterating all other sound. The Nereids, lashing out with spitting fury, churning the waters to white foam. But the house creaks and whines with effort, but it feels solid, unbendable, despite the shingles and bits of gingerbread molding flying like shrapnel upward, into the sky, whirling in circles as if undecided about which way to go, now that they are finally free.

Oh Grandpa, I wish you could see this.

I hear the door slam again and return to the front hall with a towel for Ben. The power has long since gone out. But the house, I know, is safe. We are both safe.

I call Trey again and again, though the cell service is intermittent. I suppose he is too busy, or has not been getting my messages. I try to peak through the boards of the sliding door to the deck, hoping to see him riding his tracker up the beach to check on us. I notice the deck has not moved an inch. Just like he promised.

As dusk settles so does the storm. Ben and I stand on the porch at 6 pm, gazing at the water still rising on the road, slipping toward the house. It will rise for several more hours, I know, until the storm sewers can catch up, until the tide settles down. We can see people out now, dancing on the beach, wading in the high waters, laughing, as if enormously relieved. I want to join them.

The land lines are out, but I manage to get through to Trey's cell phone again at 8. But it is not Trey's voice, or his message, that I hear. It is an older, gruffer voice, weary and strained.

"Hello?"

"Hello…I was calling Trey…"

"Who is this?"

I am confused by the question.

"This is Mariah Pendergrast," I begin.

"Oh, hold on." There is some muffled talking. I feel a cold chill creep up my spine. The voice comes back. "I'm sorry, Ma'am. Are you able to drive?"

"Drive? Where? Is Trey all right?"

"He's…he's at the hospital."

TWENTY-SIX

"Are you Mariah?"

I am staring into the crevassed face of Morey Woods, Avalon Beach Patrol Captain. He's a big man, bigger than I remembered, though still in fighting trim after thirty odd years on the beach. I nod. I have just gotten off the elevator of the trauma floor, where Morey directed me to go. The pace here seems unnaturally slow for a trauma unit.

"What happened?" I ask, my own voice breathless and shrill. Ben is beside me, holding my elbow. Thank God Ben is with me.

"He was out for a rescue, tore his leg up on the outflow pipe at 21st Street…he's in surgery now. I've been trying to answer his calls, seeing as how I don't know how to get a hold of his kin. You know his mom's number?"

I shake my head, the movement making me dizzy. "She's in Hoboken, but I don't know…she's changed her last name…"

"Have to wait until he wakes up then."

"How is he?"

"Lost a lot of blood," Morey says darkly. "Don't really know."

"Maybe you should sit down," Ben says softly in my ear. He leads me to one of the padded folding chairs that sit along the wall.

"Heard there was a surfer killed in Wildwood," Morey is saying to Ben. "We could have used you out there today. Too many stupid kids."

"Yeah, I just came to take some video. It was pretty cool."

"What happened?" I ask, annoyed that they are talking over my head. "Can you tell me what happened?"

Morey sits down next to me, Ben on the other side.

"He and I went out to check the beaches on the trackers, we did that every hour or so…I sent the two others south and we went north. Only four of us on patrol…couldn't get anyone else to come and help. So it was around three, I can't remember, the wind was kicking its worst then…we were just driving down by the 21st street outflow pipe when Trey said he thought he saw something. I couldn't see anything with the waves the way they were. But he saw a board that was bouncing around in the waves near the shore. No way, I thought. If there was a kid out there he'd be dead. But Trey thought that he might be holding onto that pipe. I couldn't see anything. I got on the radio to call for help. But Trey grabbed the rope which we keep tied to the tracker, attached it to his vest and went in."

"Alone?" I say, barely able to speak. Why would he do such a thing? But even as I ask myself the question, I know the answer.

"I yelled at him to wait for backup, but he didn't listen. Said that kid, if he was out there, didn't have time to wait. He dove under and I didn't see him for a long time. Too long. Then I saw him, working his way down the pipe, trying to hang onto it for stability. Then I saw that stupid kid too, bobbing up out of the water. I drove the tracker closer to the shoreline to give Trey more rope. I didn't think he could make it back though. I'd have to call in the chopper to get them both out of there, but it would have been damn tough getting a chopper in that wind.

"My other guys arrived about twenty minutes later. We just stood there and waited until Trey gave us a signal that he had the kid. Finally, we felt three tugs on the rope. That's the signal. The three of us grabbed the rope and hauled. We pulled them in, the both of them. But Trey's leg was all cut up and bleeding. He said he'd gotten it caught on that damned pipe—it's all rusted and broken in a few places, I keep telling them to replace it but no one listens to me. I had a tourniquet in the tracker so we bound him up and brought him in here…the streets were all flooded too…it took a while, so I hope they can get it in time. He may lose the leg."

Lose the leg.

"How's the kid?" Ben asks.

"The kid? Oh, shook up, feeling really bad. Swallowed a lot of seawater. But he'll be okay."

We are all silent. I can feel Ben looking at me. I turn to him.

"Call Caroline for me, and tell her."

"Sure." He seems glad for something to do.

"I need to get back to the beach. You okay here?" Morey asked him. I nod mutely. "Here's his phone. And here's my number. Call me when you hear something." He gets up and leaves.

There is nothing I can do but wait and pray.

I remember praying for Jack, as I sat in the hospital waiting room while the doctors worked to save his life. But that prayer had come to nothing. Was God listening? Can He hear me now?

*The Lord is my shepherd, I shall not want…*how does the rest of it go? I search my faded memory…something about leading me by still waters, restoring my soul…*though I walk through the valley of the shadow of death, I fear no evil, for You are with me…*

When I was little I had a picture of Jesus in my room, the one with the eyes that would follow you wherever you went. I talked to it all the time, that Jesus with the beautiful, gentle, all-seeing eyes. Over the years His face, His presence, has slipped from my memory. I can only hope that I have not slipped from His.

Save him, I say now. Save him. Don't let him die. I don't care about the leg. He has lost so much, he will hardly miss it. But I need to talk to him again. I need to tell him that I love him, that I forgive him...I need to ask him to forgive me too. Just let me talk to him one more time...I never had the chance with Jack.

Ben returns.

"Hey, she didn't answer so I left a message," he says. "Probably having trouble with service down there too. You ok?"

"Sure, you?"

Suddenly a surgeon appears in the doorway of the waiting room. He pulls his mask down. His bearing and demeanor remind me vividly of Jack's father.

"Are you here for Trey Bennett?" he asks me. "Is his family here?"

"Yes," I say. "We're his family." I look at Ben, who nods silently.

"Well, he's out of surgery. We got all the metal out of the wound. He needed a transfusion. I think we were able to save the leg, though only time will tell."

Save the leg? Time will tell? What does that mean? But I don't ask, because I don't think I really want to know.

"Can we see him?" I ask.

"He'll be out for a few hours. If you want to wait, I'll have the nurse come and get you."

So, we wait.

"Funny," Ben says after awhile, "I had already started to think of him as my dad. Now this happens."

I don't know what to tell him. I cannot think, cannot process, cannot imagine losing Trey so soon after I had found him again, so soon after losing Jack. But I cannot even imagine what Ben must be feeling.

"When I was a kid, I used to imagine what he looked like," Ben says. "I thought maybe he was the poet type, the loner…like the guys who came through the commune. I actually thought that one of them might be my dad, cause in that place, well, you never knew. Everyone was everyone's father and mother there. There wasn't anything we didn't share."

"You had a very strange childhood, didn't you?"

"Yeah, you could say that." He laughs a little. "Probably made me a little more warped than the average guy."

"Welcome to the club," I say.

Caroline finally calls back. I let Ben talk to her, to tell her the truth about everything. Then I get on the phone.

"Mom, I'm so sorry." I can tell she's been crying. I am unexpectedly touched.

"It's all right," I say. "Everything will be all right." And for some insane reason, I believe it. I tell her I will call back when I knew something more.

My mother calls, wanting to know how it went with the storm.

"Since when do you get hurricanes way up there? Are they following you around, Mariah? You were born in an unlucky wind, you know."

How could I forget?

"The house is fine," I tell her.

"Too bad," she says. "Was hoping we could finally cash in on all that insurance we pay." I'm the one who pays the insurance, but I don't mention this to her.

"So, do you think you'll ever come back?" Ben asks me when I am off the phone again.

I don't know how to answer this. "Do you?"

He smiles. "I like it here."

"And you like Caroline."

"Yeah. I do." I see him blush. "I suppose I shouldn't tell you that."

"No, you shouldn't."

"Mrs. Pendergrast, don't you think that sometimes things are just meant to be? I mean, I came to find Trey, or least find out about him. But then meeting Caroline and you…it can't be a coincidence, can it?"

"No," I say after a moment. "I don't believe in coincidence either."

Hours pass. We doze. Ben gets some chips from a vending machine. I pray and pray and pray.

The nurse finally comes, and I realize it is the same nurse who took care of my broken wrist a month ago. She actually smiles at me this time.

"Well, you two must like it here," she says, clearly remembering. "He's awake if you want to see him."

We follow her down the hallway and through a set of double doors to the recovery area. Trey is lying on a gurney while machines beep incessantly all around him. His eyes are closed, his skin looks rather gray despite his tan. There is an enormous bandage around his leg, which lies exposed from the rest of the sheet that covers him. I have an urgent desire to pull the sheet over the bandage.

He opens his eyes and looks at us, smiles at our stricken expressions.

"Hey," he says. His voice is still raspy from the anesthesia.

"Hey," I say back to him. "You had us pretty worried."

"Oh…sorry. I was going to call…"

"Sure you were."

He smiles. Then his eyes narrow as he notices Ben beside me.
"Ben?"

Ben steps into the small light surrounding his bed, his hands in his
pockets. "Hey…Trey."

"What are you doing here?"

"Well, I just came to keep Mrs. P company in the storm. Took
some video too."

"Oh." Trey looks at me, a stirring in his eyes. I smile.

"I'll let the two of you talk," I say. "I'll be outside."

I go out and wait in the doorway, spying on them through the glass
window. There is no movement for a long time. Then I see Trey raise
his hand and Ben clasps it, and I feel a well in my throat that becomes
a sob and tears start streaming down my face.

After a long time Ben comes out to stand beside me. "He wants to
talk to you," he says. His eyes look wet, glassy, like he'd been crying.

I go in, moving slowly, contained by some unnamed fear. Trey is
not looking at me, he stares blankly toward the opposite wall, and I
cannot read his eyes.

"Trey?"

He turns and smiles bleakly. "Hey. I feel a little weird. Don't mind
me if I say something that doesn't make sense."

I nod, my eyes already filling again, though I don't know if it is
from sorrow or joy or fear or love or some strange concoction of them
all.

"I'm glad you're okay," I say finally.

He closes his eyes. "Every day I think…maybe I could have saved
him. He was right beside me, I was holding his little hand in mine, he
was begging me to buy him something…I don't remember what.
There was almost nothing worth buying…Why was he taken and not
me? It never seemed right. In five years of lifeguarding I rescued

maybe a dozen people. In my job in the Near East I rescued hundreds. Why couldn't I rescue the one who was the most important?"

I put my hand on his brow, which is slick with sweat. His skin feels hot and cold at the same time.

"We will die with our 'if onlys.' But, Trey, we both came here because we lost something. It doesn't make any sense and it wasn't fair. But look what we found. You found a son you didn't know you had. And I found...you. We can heal here, Trey. We just need more time."

"But...you're leaving. You're selling the house."

I stare at him, swallowing. "No, I'm not selling the house."

He looks at me.

"I love you, Trey. I have loved you since I was 10 years old. I don't think I ever stopped loving you. Avalon is where we belong, where we were meant to be, I think. I'm not going anywhere."

He smiles, relief in his eyes, though the pain lingers there, a permanent resident. We are not unscathed. We are the walking wounded in this war, but at least we are walking. Well, I am anyway. I bend down and kiss his lips, which are hot like his skin.

"I'm apparently not going anywhere either," he says softly. We both snort with laughter. I kiss him again. It's the first time I feel right in doing this.

"Will you marry me, Mariah?"

"Why don't you ask me again when you're off the drugs?"

"I may not have the nerve when I'm off the drugs."

His eyes close. The nurse re-appears, hovering over him, checking the machines. "He's probably going to sleep for awhile," she says curtly. "We'll let you know when he's been moved to his room."

Feeling dismissed, I leave the room and meet Ben in the hallway. I smile at him.

"Quite a day," he says with a shy smile.

"Yes," I say. "Quite a day."

EPILOGUE

September 2004

The dirt road seems to go on forever, through gnarled trees and heavy brush, so that I think I have probably lost my way. But a sign nailed to a tree comfortingly tells me, "Almost there." Before long the forest gives way to a golden meadow, with a big, dilapidated white house standing in its center. It looks deserted, but as I trudge up the front steps, desperate for a drink of water, I see that the front door is open, leaving only a frayed screen door between the porch and the darkness inside.

An elderly but hardy-looking woman greets me, opening the door so I can step in.

"You must be Mariah."

"Yes. Thanks for letting me come."

"It's not the usual thing."

She hands me a ceramic cup of water, as if she is used to giving water out to everyone who comes through the door of this house, which is a sort of welcome center. I take it gratefully, thanking her, but she does not acknowledge my gratitude. She hands me a map.

"You need to go up the lane a ways...it's the third complex on the right. But she'll probably be out in the garden today. That's where she spends most of her time now."

"Thank you," I say again.

"You can stay for two hours. I will expect to see you back here by 3 o'clock."

That is not a request. I check my watch to make sure I am on the right time.

The woman does not seem interested in making small talk, so I thank her again and leave the house, following the handwritten map up the lane. I pass two housing units, rambling affairs that looked not unlike ancient resort condos in the Catskills. There is no grass in the yards, only fields and wild brush. Landscaping is obviously frowned upon here. Beyond the buildings there are large gardens, open fields and more woods, the famed maple groves. I can make out the bobbing heads of the people of the commune working their land together under a hot, late September sun.

I walk until I come to the unit I am looking for, Tantalus. All the units are named for various Greek gods. I can only wonder why. The door is open; I enter into a large main living area. It reminds me of summer camp: mismatched couches, plain, serviceable furniture, an ancient wood-burning stove. Rugs on the bare plank floor are tattered and faded. The paneled walls are lined with homemade art, some of it quite pretty, some of it horrendous. Like a giant refrigerator door of children's masterpieces left up a little too long.

Two women are cleaning. They are probably in their twenties with scrubbed, wholesome faces. They look up and stare at me as if I were a new species of human.

"Hello," I say, seeing the confusion on their faces. "I'm...looking for someone."

The younger one answers. "Who?"

"Rachel Rosen."

"Rachel?" She looks puzzled, then her expression clears. "You must mean Rose."

"Rose?"

"Everyone changes their name here. She's out in the garden. I'll take you to her. I'm Star, by the way."

Star puts down her broom and starts to head out the back door. I follow quickly, afraid of being left behind. The other woman returns to her work, ignoring us both.

"Rose is one of the head gardeners," she informs me. "That's her job here. Everyone has a job. I'm hoping to move up to cooking eventually. I love to cook. But I don't have enough time in yet."

Star is very talkative, which surprises me. I sense she is fairly new to the community and still in the throes of passion for it.

"Look! Those are Rose's rose bushes. Isn't that funny? She grows roses. Sells them to fancy catalog places too."

"Is that how the community raises funds?"

"Roses? Not really. Maple syrup and hammocks. We make rope hammocks for those fancy yuppie catalog companies. If it weren't for those capitalist pigs who buy that stuff, we wouldn't survive, that's for sure!"

This makes me laugh, though I don't think Star intended it to be funny. She is dead serious.

"Well, the rose business is sort of new. Rose really has a knack for them. She's created some new varieties too."

The garden is bushy and overgrown, like almost everything else. Organic farming is not necessarily neat and tidy.

"There she is. Rose!" She waves and walks faster down a row of smaller bushes. I follow, catching a glimpse of a small woman in an enormous striped man's shirt and baggy pants, huge wide-brimmed hat, clunky boots. This is Rachel? I can hardly believe my eyes.

But it is. Her blond hair is shot with silver, held in a braid down her back. She is surrounded by roses of every variety, gorgeous, succulent blooms that seem to frame her like a portrait. She looks up and I see her face, still pale and smooth, thanks to her penchant for hats. She may dress like a migrant worker, she may wear her hair like an aging hippie, but the face is still that of a fairy princess. She straightens when she sees me but says nothing.

Star smiles at the two of us during the awkward silence that follows.

"Here's your friend, Rose...Well, I better get back to work. See ya." Star trudges off. I stare at Rachel, taking her in, trying to find some words to fill in the silence of the lost years.

"So...it's Rose now," I say.

"And still Mariah, like the wind," she says finally. "It's good to see you again."

"It's good to see you," I say breathlessly. "You look...the same."

"You don't." I'm not sure if this is a compliment or not. Her tone is straight forward, like the woman in the white house. Perhaps it is something ingrained in the commune, this unvarnished honesty. There is no need for niceties.

"This is a beautiful place," I say. "Your garden, the roses..."

"Yes, the roses are beautiful right now," she says, lifting a bloom to her nose to take in the scent.

"You like it here?"

"Well enough."

She goes back to her work, deadheading the rose bushes. I wait, wondering what to do. Then she says, "I was sorry to hear about Jack."

"Thanks," I say. It seems strange to be talking to her about Jack in this way.

"I should have sent something. A card or something. You must think I'm a terrible person."

"No, actually. I thought you just hated me."

She looks at me, puzzled. "What for?"

"For…Jack."

She shakes her head, lopping off another dead rose head. "Mariah, you must know that wasn't your doing."

I stare at her, blinking. "What do you mean?"

"I knew you were in love with him. I knew you'd be better for him than I could have been. I told him so."

I open my mouth. "You…told him?"

"Yes. He came to see me, at the hospital. I told him he should marry you. That you loved him and no one else would ever love him like you did. I wanted that for him. And for you. You were a good friend to me. Better than I deserved."

I think I might faint. I cannot speak at all. Rachel notices that I am swaying slightly.

"It's hot here. Why don't we go inside for a bit."

She walks me back to her house, and though it is quite stuffy, at least we are out of the sun. She leads me to a small kitchenette and gets me a glass of water from the tap. The water is tepid and not quite clear, but I drink it anyway.

"Weird hot spell we're having," she says. "Usually it's quite cool this time of year." She looks at me. "We had a lot of secrets, didn't we? Too many. Are you feeling better?"

I nod. I need to change the subject, steady myself. I sit on a hard hand-hewn stool at the counter.

"I have to admit I would never have imagined you living in a place like this," I say.

"Me neither. Communal living was not my thing. Eating in a buffet line every night? Sharing a bathroom with eight other people? Not to mention the plumbing was from the dark ages. They had me doing laundry and cleaning…I had never done those things in my life! I was so bad I was sure they would kick me out. If you can't meet the work standards here, they just expel you. That's why this sort of thing couldn't work on a large scale. In order for communes to work, you have to be very selective about who you let in. I learned that the hard way."

"But you stayed."

"Yes."

"You didn't find it…confining?"

She smiles. "Freedom is not about walls. Didn't you tell me that?"

I smile a little. "I guess I did." I'm surprised she would remember that.

"I thought about leaving, quite often. But I had nowhere to go. I had burned all my bridges. I couldn't continue to be a burden to my parents. And I had a small child to take care of. So I learned to work. It was hard. I did menial jobs. I got my hands dirty. I broke my nails. Some days I even forgot to comb my hair, I was so tired.

"But a weird thing happened. I started to get better. I started eating like a normal person. I slept all night without nightmares. I stopped calling my shrink every other day. I stopped thinking about my issues and started just…living. All the big decisions of my life were taken away—where I should live, what I should wear, who I should be with — so all I had to do was get up in the morning, do my work, take care of Ben, and go to bed. I began to feel…useful. Like I could do something worthwhile. I started to work in the garden and found out that I enjoyed it. Growing things. My mother came to visit and brought me a rose bush. That's how the rose thing started. I sent away for bare roots from a catalog with the extra money we get each month…I found out that I was good at something. I had a purpose, finally. I think that was what I had been missing all along."

I smile through half-lidded eyes, heavy with tears.

"We don't have tissues, too wasteful," she says with a smile. "But here's an organic paper towel. It feels like sandpaper, I know."

She hands me a scrap of harsh paper, and I use it to dab gingerly at my eyes.

"I suppose you know about the cancer," she says off-handedly.

"Yes…how are you anyway? I should have asked sooner."

"Good days and bad days. Today is a good day. It's very liberating, actually."

"Liberating?" I say, shocked.

She smiles, her eyes lifting to the ceiling, as if she is remembering something she hadn't thought of in a very long while. "You know, when I threw myself off the pier, I really did want to die. Now I will die. I don't really want to. But I don't want to do a lot of tests and hospitals and medicines that will make me feel sicker. I just want to enjoy what I have. What God has given me."

"God?"

"God is good."

I have never heard her talk of God before.

"I've been reading the bible," she goes on. "Funny how you can live your whole life without ever reading the manual. I began to see things differently. I was brought up Jewish…well, sort of Jewish. Not religious at all. So I didn't know much about Jesus. But reading the

271

Gospels I realized…it's really true. The price has already been paid. That no matter what I have done, I am…forgiven. I need that. We all do, don't we?"

Looking into her eyes, I see that this is true, that she believes it.

"How is the Pink Poodle?" she asks.

"Oh…coming along. Trey is practically rebuilding it."

"So you and he are…"

"Yes." I look down at the paper towel crumbled in my hands.

"That's good. I'm happy for you. For him too. And I'm glad you still have the house. Your grandfather would be so happy. I still remember him vividly. What a great soul he had. Remember the *Idylls of the King*? I was going to write my thesis on it. I still reread it from time to time. I had always cast myself in the role of Guinevere, poor misunderstood Guinevere, who didn't know what she wanted. I would have joined a convent too, except they don't take Jewish girls. This was the next best thing. I joined a church choir, if you can believe it. There's a little church down the road I go to every week. I love the hymns, the way harmonies are formed, the shape of the sounds…it's so beautiful." She stops to glance around at her surroundings. "I miss beauty," she says. "There is very little that is beautiful here. It's all very utilitarian. Our clothes, our food, our furniture, our lives. Beauty is frowned upon as frivolous. I guess that's why I love the roses. They bring some beauty to this place. And I enjoy that little church, with its frivolous stained glass windows and frivolous organ and beautiful, frivolous harp. Even the velvet cushions on the pews seem luxurious to me."

She opens a cupboard and takes out a tin of nuts. "We're very organic here. Want some?"

"Thanks." I take a handful, though I doubt I could swallow even one. She refills my glass of water.

"So how's Trey?" she asks. "I heard there was an accident."

"How did you know?"

"I saw the news on the Internet. Are you surprised we have Internet here? We have a very nice website, you should check it out. Trey was quite the hero, as usual."

Her directness again unnerves me, but I nod. "They saved his leg, though it still causes him a lot of trouble. He can't surf or run anymore. But he can still swim. He's…healing."

"That's good."

"How do you feel about him?" I ask. I need to know this.

"I feel…sad," she says. "I hurt him badly, perhaps worse than Jack. I can never undo that. But I'm glad he and Ben know each other now. Ben is so like him. Wants to go off doing missionary work in Africa…saving the world."

"You're not upset he gave up law school?"

"Heavens no! Trying to live up to other people's expectations is what nearly killed me. Ben has a heart for people. If he had become a lawyer he would have been one of those working in the city *pro bono* helping people who couldn't afford lawyers. Probably would have starved to death."

How like Trey, indeed.

"I think my Ben and your Caroline will get married one day," she says. "How about that for poetic justice! Your child and mine. He emailed me a picture, she's a lovely girl. Does she want to go to Africa, too?"

I cannot imagine Caroline living any place with big bugs and bad plumbing, but I just shrug my shoulders. "Well, she still has college. But I guess, if she wants to be with him, she will have to learn to love it."

Rachel nods, her eyes closing slightly, her head bowing. "Invite me to the wedding. If I'm still here, I will come."

"That would be wonderful," I say. "Rachel…if you ever want to come to Avalon…"

"No," she says abruptly. "I cannot go back to Avalon." She glances outside. "I still have a lot of work to do before the sun goes down." She gets up, gathering her gardening gloves. I take hold of her arm impulsively. She looks at me, but before she can pull away I give her a hug. She feels light and bony under the layers of clothes. After a moment she hugs me back, and I feel her strength, bought with years of backbreaking work.

"You can always come back," I whisper in her ear. She pulls away gently.

"I did love that house. It was the only place, besides here, I felt truly…loved." She turns away from me and I realize she might cry and doesn't want me to see. I look at my watch.

"I'd better go too. I don't want the commune police coming after me."

"We don't have police. But the community elders are much scarier." She smiles. "Maybe you can come back sometime."

"Maybe," I nod, though we both know I never will.

She walks me to the door and stands as I head down the path. I don't look back.

We had known each other so briefly in that one small, sweet summer in Avalon, and yet that moment had altered the course of our lives forever. I could not help but be amazed at how so much of life hinged on such seemingly inconsequential things. Was it only happenstance that Rachel and Jack came to Avalon that summer, or was it the plan of some Designer whose purpose we cannot fathom without the heartbreak of years?

I walk down the dusty road alone, past a bank of old cars that make up the community motor pool, past a pile of rusty bikes heaped next to a dilapidated barn, past people coming in and out of the vast gardens with their bushels of vegetables, nodding uncertainly at me. As I make the long trek back to my car, parked on the edge of the commune property, I remember words from Tennyson's poem that Rachel was fond of reciting. The words did not make sense to me then. Now, perhaps, they do, for Guinevere's lament has become ours as well:

Ah, my God,
What might I not have made of thy fair world,
Had I but loved thy highest creature here?
It was my duty to have loved the highest:
It surely was my profit had I known:
It would have been my pleasure had I seen.

THE END

Gina Miani lives in Buffalo, New York with
her husband Steve and three daughters.
She still visits Avalon, where much of this novel was written.

Acknowledgements:
Avalon, on the Seven Mile Beach, by Robert L. Penrose
Pier Memories, compiled by Dave Coskey
Hurricanes and the Middle Atlantic States by Rick Schwartz
America's Painted Ladies by Elizabeth Pomada and Michael Larsen
The Avalon Museum
To all those who shared their memories of the
Avalon Pier on websites and blogs.
To the little pink house on the inlet, which is no longer pink,
and to its builders and owners for saving it. I am grateful.
To Michele Steinhauser and Mary Akers,
wonderful friends and fellow writers,
who gave me the courage to share this story
and helped me to get it right.

Miani, Gina.
Avalon

CPSIA information can be obtained at www.ICGtesting.com
Printed in the USA
LVOW08s0007010415

432821LV00012B/330/P

9 781479 376803